ANNE NEVILL

QUEEN OF ENGLAND

Front cover: By permission of The British Library (Loan 90, Page 154).

Anne Nevill 1456-1485

Queen of England

Eleanor Mennim

Sessions of York
The Ebor Press
York, England

ISBN 1 85072 228 5

Printed in 11 on 12 point Plantin typeface
from Author's disk by Sessions of York
The Ebor Press
York, England

CONTENTS

Lesser characters other than relatives used in the story who were actual people historically

Mrs Raven the midwife at Warwick.

Father Birtby, the priest at Sutton.

Thomas Gower – the father – owner of the manor at Stittenham, and Constable of Sheriff Hutton Castle

Sit Thomas Gower, son of the above, a retainer of Richard III.

Lady Alice, wife of Thomas Gower of Stittenham.

Sir Edward Hardgill of Lilling, retainer of Richard III.

Sir John Conyers, member of the household of Richard, particularly at Middleham.

Mistress Gower, teacher to the Nevill children.

Lady Elizabeth Darcy, lady mistress of the Woodville nursery.

John Roos, Anne's chaplain.

Ankarette Twyntine, nurse/midwife to Isabel Duchess of Clarence.

Father Beverley, priest at Middleham.

Fictional characters used authentically:

        Ella, the nursery maid.

        Merryman, the clown (dwarf).

        Thomas and Ben, the grooms.

        Mrs Green the wet-nurse at Warwick.

        Mrs Shepherd, the wet-nurse at Middleham.

        Mr Warwickson, the dancing master.

ILLUSTRATIONS

ACKNOWLEDGEMENTS

THANKS ARE DUE to owners of illustrations who gave consent to include them in my book. I am most grateful to His Grace The Duke of Buccleuch & Queensberry KT for the picture of Anne Nevill in her coronation robes.

To Shropshire County Council for the painting by A. E. Everitt of Ludlow Castle.

To English Heritage for plans of Middleham and Scarborough Castles, and the painting of Barnard Castle by Terry Ball.

To Reverend Brian Rogers, Rector of Fotheringhay for the photograph of Fotheringhay Parish Church.

To Edward Whiteley ARIBA, for his drawing of St George's Chapel, Windsor.

To my husband, Michael (AMM), for arranging or drawing all the other illustrations, and also for his professional advise on the mediaeval buildings described, and for editing the manuscript. Moreover for his encouragement in the research and writing of 'Anne Nevill'.

To the librarians of York Reference Library for advise and tolerance.

And especially to Mrs Susan Beyer who (not for the first time) undertook the re-typing of the finished product with her usual unruffled efficiency and good humour.

Lastly, I owe Mr Sissons of Sessions of York a debt for much wise advise and guidance in the production of my book.

PREFACE

IT IS DIFFICULT now at the end of the twentieth century to appreciate the moral bondage of women in earlier years, which continued to varied extent in England right up to the First World War. Women possessed nothing of their own, except in the rare cases where there was no male heir in the family and a daughter or niece inherited wealth or title in her own right. Officially she had no say in decisions affecting her personal life since she did not even own herself. She was a chattel, usually of her father, and it was he who owned her and quite legally could deal more or less as he pleased with her.

A girl normally had two particular attributes. She could bear children and, therefore, was of value in the marriage market for that purpose. But her value was greatly enhanced if she also brought to a marriage wealth, or potential wealth in the future. A marriage was a legal agreement between two families for their most marketable commodity, and the fathers of both prospective bride and bridegroom had no interest in whether the young people liked, let alone loved each other; indeed whether they even knew each other before betrothal. It was not unheard of for the couple to meet for the first time at the marriage ceremony. Usually a girl recognised that the arrangement of her marriage was entirely a matter for her father, and it was not her business to question his decision, however much she loathed her prospective husband, be he old or young, kindly and elegant or with disgusting habits and repulsive features. Her duty was to marry him, go to bed with him and produce a string of heirs for him, in return for which her own family would benefit with a share of the inheritance. She had now become the property of her husband.

The importance of sons was not only in the retention of the family title, wealth and land, which in themselves were synonymous with power. It was also to head the army of fighting men which

1

every great family owned, and also to replace men killed in the perpetual warring which particularly took place in the mid-fifteenth century, or of those executed after battle, often for treason as they indulged in a change to what they perceived as the winning side at the time. Daughters who for one reason or another were unmarriageable - because of lack of appropriate attraction, including that of a dowry - had in noble families only one alternative, which was to become a Religious for life, often the lot of the younger daughters or those with mental or physical defects. A peasant girl was still marriage fodder, but in addition had practical uses about the homestead and the family croft. The lives of the highborn girls seem to have been essentially empty until (usually) their own marriage, frequently in childhood, and the commencement of the fearful business of continual child-bearing, often to die at an extremely early age when a confinement or infection thereby killed them. There was no choice, and yet one feels that these young wives took great pride in their titles and their demesnes.

Sometimes the wives were tough, intelligent or manipulative and retained control over their own lives, as indeed did many of their female descendants in England right up to the First World War when our grandmothers - often covertly - ruled their husbands and their households with a firm hand. Some of these fifteenth century women figure in this account and two such ladies influenced Anne Nevill[17], in particular Queen Margaret of Anjou[13] (wife of Henry VI) was notable for her strength of character and, in many ways, Anne Beauchamp[12] (Anne Nevill's mother) coped well with her marriage to the ruthless Kingmaker. The latter's younger daughter, Anne, was fond of her own second husband, but otherwise seems to have drawn the short straw, and her life was full of tragedy though she became Queen of England. She was typical of her class; born into the enormously powerful family of the Earls of Warwick, augmented by the riches of the Beauchamps and Despenser families inherited by her mother; married at fourteen, widowed within a year, remarried but unable to produce more than one son, who soon succumbed; she was less than thirty when she herself died after the dubious honour of occupying the throne of England for two years as queen consort of her cousin Richard[22].

How did this girl handle her sorrows and anxieties? The tale recounted here attempts to provide an answer and follows historical fact. Placed in its contemporary social and domestic background, the characters are all taken from actual people, except for Ella the nurserymaid, Merryman the clown, Ben and Thomas the children's grooms, and the wet-nurses, Mrs Green and Mrs Shepherd. The conversations and intimate details such as Anne's own feelings are drawn from supposition within the context of the fifteenth century in an attempt to bring alive the history of the period, particularly as it affected women, just preceding as it did the characterful queen-consorts of the Tudor period, together with the "Virgin Queen".

Anne Nevill's life almost exactly spanned the years of the War of the Roses and was greatly influenced by it. There was no national army in England unless the king cared to hire (and was able to pay for) the "private" armies gathered from the retainers of the nobility. Part of the serf's due to his local landowner in return for a strip of arable and probably a croft with or without housing thereon, was his undertaking to fight for his master when called upon to do so.

Training for warfare was often minimal for the rank and file, although after certain large battles or in fear of future ones, various injunctions were issued by the king - notably Edward III[1] - for every male to practise archery with bow and arrow (of his own manufacture) after Sunday Mass each week. Besides their own tenants, landlords could also recruit enthusiasts eager for the windfalls (if not payment) of battle as they marched the country. Thus, at big international contests such as Agincourt, the king (Henry V)[2] headed a vast concourse of fighting men, gathered and equipped and, to some extent, trained and lead by nobility who backed his cause, although the king's own contingents contained the best of the disciplined soldiers.

When civil strife occurred, the ordinary rustic labourers and their women and children were at the mercy of any army who attacked them or raided their homes, unless they could be brought within the protection of the castle precincts of their lord. Castles in England were still mainly defensive in the mid-fifteenth century, but since the end of the fourteenth century, new building tended to be, at least in part, more domestic with relatively comfortable living quarters for the lord and his family, and his main retainers and officers. Windows were larger, some rooms smaller and more

3

intimate, and fireplaces with hoods but no external chimney stacks until about 1450, and garderobes were placed strategically and in suitable numbers. But the main features of the highly defensive Norman castle were only in part superseded, and often the keep and the several surrounding "curtain" walls continued to be used for their original purpose of protection, although "softened" by further domestic buildings erected against them, and finally even pleasure gardens (largely containing culinary herbs) laid out to entrance the ladies.

Just as the local civil strife did not envelope the whole country at the same moment, so parts of England would remain completely free of fighting for much of the time during the War of the Roses, the main centres of conflict being allied to the great castles of the more eminent nobles - Ludlow belonged to the Duke of York[6], Warwick to the powerful family of Warwick[11] and Beauchamp[12]; Sheriff Hutton and Middleham to the Nevills; Penrith, Richmond and Carlisle to varying royal dukes. With each castle was a large estate of land in thrall to the master, for whose household its tenants provided food, servants for his castles, and fighting men, when and where needed. The feudal system, though running out of time, was still the basis of village life, although the small landowners - "gentlemen" and "yoemen" - were gradually creating their own wealth. As is richly illustrated in the following pages, wealth and land were synonymous with power, and the civil War of the Roses in the fifteenth century was a struggle for dominance, and ultimately for the throne of England which had been sadly neglected either by royal absence (Henry V)[2] or incompetence by his son (Henry VI)[8].

As to the title of that war, the emblem of the Rose was little used until the final stages, at the time of the Battle of Bosworth in 1485, although there are good examples to the contrary, such as the Rose Window in York Minster, erected in honour of the marriage of Henry VII and Elizabeth of York in 1486 when the symbol began to come into increased use. More frequent was the employment of the heraldic device of each leader - the White Boar of Richard III[22] (and when Duke of Gloucester); the Falcon and Fetterlock of the Duke of York[6]; the Sun in Splendour of Edward IV[18]; the Bear and Ragged Staff of the Warwicks[11]; or the Portcullis of the Beauforts[10] and Tudors[15].

4

Most of the contenders in this war were descended from one of the sons of Edward III[1], notably from the third son, Lionel Duke of Clarence; from the fourth son, John Duke of Lancaster by two of his wives; from his fifth son, Edmund Langley Duke of York; and from his sixth son, Thomas of Woodstock, Duke of Gloucester, whose line gave rise to the Stafford family, Dukes of Buckingham. Because of the use of marriage as a means of preferment and acquisition of wealth, the family trees of these families are particularly complicated to the point where some of the subjects appear twice, and relationships similarly become confused. As far as possible the accompanying tree has been simplified. However, Richard Plantagenet, Duke of York[6] is a case in point: he was a descendant, through his mother, of Lionel Duke of Clarence, third son of Edward III[1], and through his father of Edmund of Langley Duke of York, fifth son of Edward III, and so could appear twice on the tree. All the Mediaeval and Tudor monarchs to follow Edward III were descended from one of his sons. Henry IV, son of John of Gaunt Duke of Lancaster, was the first Lancastrian king, and thereby absorbed the huge wealth of the Dukes of Lancaster into the crown through his father's marriage to Blanche, the daughter of one of them. Henry IV was succeeded by his son Henry V[2] and then by his grandson Henry VI[8], both Lancastrians. Henry VII[15] also was descended through his mother, a Beaufort, from John of Gaunt and was, therefore, a Lancastrian, while Edward IV[18] and Richard III[22] were sons of Richard Plantagenet[6] Duke of York and a Nevill mother, and thus were Yorkists.

There is the added complication of frequent change of sides by some nobility in the struggle, though sometimes this resulted in execution for treason, as in the case of George Duke of Clarence[21]. However, Princess Elizabeth[24], daughter of Edward IV[18] and consort of Henry VII[15], was very firmly a Yorkist, and by marriage she brought together the Houses of York and Lancaster to form the House of Tudor and the conclusion of the Mediaeval period of English history and the War of the Roses.

The War of the Roses was a civil war and is often considered to have commenced with the First Battle of St. Albans in 1455 and ended with the Battle of Bosworth in 1485, followed by the union of the embattled Red and White Roses in the marriage of Henry VII and Elizabeth of York in January 1486. Finally, the triumph of the king at the Battle of Stoke, in which the rising of Lambert Simnel was defeated in June 1487, brought long-term peace and firm government to England. Its causes and characteristics were of much more ancient provenance, but the war had been precipitated by the weakness of Henry VI[8] which opened the way for power-hungry contenders for the throne. Anne Nevill's life was deeply, if innocently entrenched in the plotting which underset the conflict. Her destiny was to be swung between the causes of York and Lancaster by her ambivalent father, but in the end to be married to a young man[22] who remained a fervent Yorkist, and England's last Yorkist king. His lasting motto (unlike many of his contemporaries) was "Loyaltie me Lie" - "Loyalty binds me."

As the War of the Roses was commencing in 1455, another conflict, more widespread and long-term, was concluding in Europe. This was the Hundred Years War in which England and France struggled for power and where the fighting took place exclusively on the continent.

It is difficult now to accept how much of France was under English rule in the Middle Ages, although the boundaries of the two sovereignties altered as the fighting determined. Back in the twelfth century almost the whole of the western half of France was held by England under Henry II, from the mouth of the Somme in the north, right down to the Pyrenees, including all of Normandy, Brittany and Maine, and south of the Loire, Anjou, Poitou, Gienne and Gascony. Flanders (including the valuable ports of Calais and Boulogne), Paris and Champagne, Burgundy and the county of Toulouse in the east and south, remained French or belonged to the Holy Roman Empire. By 1360, in triumph Edward III had claimed Calais and the area around Crecy, just south of it. The whole peninsular of Brittany and Normandy were now within the French kingdom, but the large area between the Loire and the Pyrenees called Aquitaine remained under English rule.

By the height of Henry VI's[8] reign in the second half of the Hundred Years War, and largely due to the victory at Agincourt in 1415 by Henry V[2] , English territory extended from a few miles north of the important port of Calais down to the mouth of the

Loire, without a break, and included all Normandy, Brittany and Paris, and a much narrower strip of land than previously remained to England around Bordeaux and down to the Pyrenees. Burgundy in the east was by this time independent of France and at daggers drawn with it. It was lured into friendship with the English by the shrewd dynastic marriage of Margaret of York, sister of Edward IV[18] with Charles Duke of Burgundy against Louis XI of France.

Access to and from the Continent with all parts of England was thus simplified and could conveniently be achieved, using the area of the Loire as well as Flanders. Ports all along the southern coast of England were employed for the crossing, from Kent to Devon and even Pembroke. So also were East Anglia and Ravenspur useful in this respect. On the French side of the channel, Calais was by far the most valuable component in the chain of access, not only for its geographical position, but for its ease of docking and short sea voyage from England. Calais is repeatedly mentioned in this story, and indeed the Earl of Warwick[11], Anne Nevill's father was for several years the King's Captain of Calais. She herself used it on several occasions. The port was held on to with tenacity by the English until in the next century it slipped through the grasp of Queen Mary Tudor, completely separating the kingdoms of England and France, and continuing ever since as a French property.

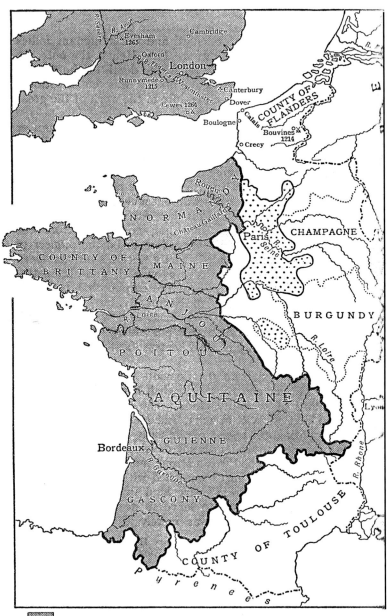

The possessions of Henry II – 1154-1189

Lands directly ruled by King of France

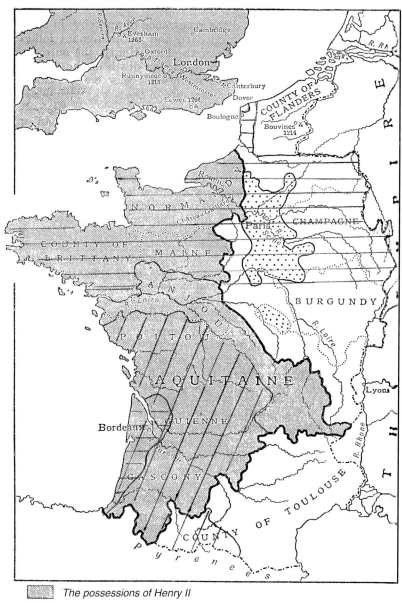

The possessions of Henry II

Land under English rule 1360

Remaining land under English rule 1430

CHAPTER 1

THE MIDWIFE AND HER ASSISTANTS were scurrying to and fro, preparing the Great Chamber for the confinement of Countess Anne Beauchamp[12], wife of the Earl of Warwick[11]. The castle was alive with anticipation for the arrival of a baby son to carry on the name of Nevill, and an heir to the Warwick estates. The arras on the walls of the Chamber were shaken so that clouds of dust flew across the room before slowly subsiding onto the flagged floor where newly-gathered rushes and sweetly scented sprigs of thyme and rosemary had been spread. Candles of wax, very costly, but suitable for the occasion, were scattered around the room. Sheets of huckerback (or coarse linen) were placed over the feather mattress on the great bed with its deeply embroidered testers and drapes. The bolster and plenty of feather pillows were in place, and two yards of linen tied round the Warwick Arms at the head of the bed, which the mother-to-be could pull on with all the strength left to her as labour proceeded. A horn mug with the finest chaste silver rim was filled with wine and another with some concoction of herbs and poppy seeds were at hand to administer to the patient in due course when she flagged in her efforts to fulfil her duty.

The blaze in the massive fireplace was poked into life in spite of the warm June weather and further logs were stacked nearby. Infront of the hearth was a low stool and table, and on the table a large polished copper bowl, a supply of linen squares and a bar of the best Castile soap of Bristol. A towel of fustian and some wraps and swaddling bands for the baby completed the equipment except for that specifically for the delivery, including a strong length of best flax twine with which to tie off the cord. There were more shifts and lengths of linen in the oak chest at the foot of the bed, under which was the truckle bed for the use of the midwife if the labour was prolonged, and for the weeks after the delivery.

Anne Beauchamp was dressed for the occasion in a night-gown of grey velvet, decorated with a white fur collar. She was perhaps the richest woman in England and had no qualms about discarding a soiled garment to be replaced by similar rich apparel. The thick stone walls of the castle shielded the room from the hot sunshine outside and she was glad of the comfort of her gown as her pains began. This was her second confinement - the first had produced a little daughter, Isabella, five years before. This time it surely must be a boy. Her own father had had repeated misfortune in his offspring - by his first wife, three daughters and by his second, a son, Henry who became Earl and then Duke of Warwick at his father's demise in 1439, and herself Anne Beauchamp. Henry had married Cecily Nevill (sister of the Kingmaker) and had died in 1446, leaving a daughter, Anne, who subsequently died aged five in 1449. The title passed to his sister, another Anne Beauchamp[12] who now became Countess of Warwick in her own right. Her husband, Richard Nevill[11], Earl of Salisbury, to whom she was married when she was nine years old and the Earl only six, in 1434, was granted by King Henry VI the prestigious title of Earl of Warwick in 1450, including possession of Warwick Castle. In addition, she also inherited the wide estates and immense wealth of the Beauchamps, much of it from her mother who was a Despenser. Now the failure to produce sons must be righted, thought Anne in this year of 1456, as she held firmly onto the tiny golden cameo of the Agnes Dei which was her mother's and which she knew would help her through her own labour. Another similar Agnus Dei hung over the Great Bed, and still another, set with precious stones, was at hand for the midwife, Mistress Raven, to draw down over Anne's body to speed the baby's approach into the world. Each cameo showed meticulously fine engraving of the Trinity on one side and of the Nativity on the other. Anne felt very safe in the presence of these jewels, and as the weary hours wore on, she grasped hers more tightly as every pain wracked her frame.

Many hours later the people of the little town of Warwick, which was adjacent to the castle, were still keeping an eye on the castle turrets expecting to see the standard of the Bear and the Ragged Staff being hoisted to salute their new heir. But no such sign arose, and word gradually passed round that the baby was another girl. In the Great Chamber the midwife gently lifted the little child

Beauchamp Tree
showing dates of Earldoms of Warwick

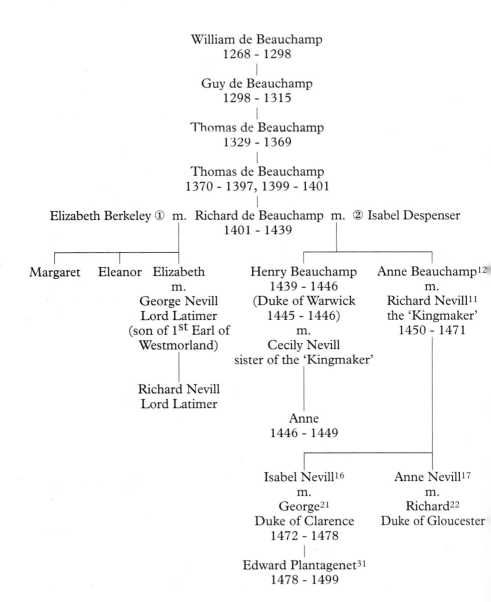

William de Beauchamp
1268 - 1298
|
Guy de Beauchamp
1298 - 1315
|
Thomas de Beauchamp
1329 - 1369
|
Thomas de Beauchamp
1370 - 1397, 1399 - 1401
|
Elizabeth Berkeley ① m. Richard de Beauchamp m. ② Isabel Despenser
1401 - 1439

Margaret Eleanor Elizabeth   Henry Beauchamp   Anne Beauchamp[12]
                   m.   1439 - 1446   m.
              George Nevill   (Duke of Warwick   Richard Nevill[11]
              Lord Latimer   1445 - 1446)   the 'Kingmaker'
            (son of 1st Earl of   m.   1450 - 1471
              Westmorland)   Cecily Nevill
                              sister of the 'Kingmaker'

              Richard Nevill
              Lord Latimer   Anne
                                           1446 - 1449

                              Isabel Nevill[16]   Anne Nevill[17]
                                    m.   m.
                                 George[21]   Richard[22]
                              Duke of Clarence   Duke of Gloucester
                                1472 - 1478
                                    |
                              Edward Plantagenet[31]
                                1478 - 1499

12

from the bed and handed her to the nurse who took her to the fireside, and from a copper can, poured warm water into the bowl on the table, and softly washed the baby, dabbed her dry with the towel and anointed her tiny body with precious oil which sent an exotic perfume up into the room. Then she wrapped her in a fine linen cloth and swaddled her in fustian to straighten her legs, whilst the midwife saw to the mother, gave her a drink of wine and water and left her to await a visit from the Earl.

Next day he still had not come. He was occupied in coming to terms with the arrival of another daughter when he so much needed a son to grow up beside him, to lead his forces into battle, to become one of the King's favourites. He did not care about this child, and yet it was true that daughters could be juggled in the marriage market, auctioned to the highest bidder, sold ever upwards in the social scale, which for a Nevill could only mean royalty - a Prince of the Blood. Just as he himself had been married when he was a little boy to Anne Beauchamp, thus making sure of the enormous possessions of her family, so he would be able to trade in this girl and her sister for great riches and status. He wondered if he could arrange for her to marry Edward, Prince of Wales[14], the three year old only son of King Henry VI[8] who was himself but a poor weak-brained creature with nothing much in his head but religious mania, and further, was a Lancastrian. But Henry had fortunately married a strong wife, Magaret of Anjou[13], so perhaps the Prince would take after her; but then again, who could judge at this time whether to back Lancaster or York? And as far as the market for girls was concerned, three of his own aunts became duchesses by that very ploy; of Norfolk, Buckingham and York, thereby bringing into the Nevill grasp, all manner of power. Perhaps in due course, one of the sons of his aunt Cecily of York[5] would prove the most rewarding match.

At that moment there was a rustle at the door with the appearance of a page to announce the arrival of that lady. Cecily had travelled over from her favourite York castle of Fotheringhay to inspect her new great-niece and to commiserate with her nephew, the Earl, over the gender of the child. She herself had been much more fortunate over this problem and, although losing three sons in babyhood, still was the mother of four lusty boys as well as several girls, three of whom were destined to become duchesses (of

Burgundy, Exeter and Suffolk). Cecily herself, unlike her domineering nephew, Warwick, was a quietly religious person in a gentle unobtrusive manner, and would be a comfort to her weary and disappointed niece-in-law. That the baby had not yet been baptised horrified her. Suppose the little girl should take ill and die before she had been sanctified by a priest - not a moment to be lost. Cecily was all too familiar with the hazards of life, especially in the new-born, and that this new baby of the Warwick line must be baptised before the devil claimed her for his own. A messenger was sent to the priest immediately, and orders for warm water for the font, and the midwife to be ready to take the baby to the chapel that very day.

And so it was that the tiny scrap that was Anne Nevill, took her place in the hierarchy of the House of Warwick, and immediately became a pawn in the marriage stakes for her ambitious father who, as he reminded himself of her potential thereby, recollected that he had not yet actually seen his new daughter and noisily set off in the direction of her nursery, next to the Great Chamber, humming hopefully to himself.

"And so, Madame," he bellowed at his wife who was lying back limply on her pillows, weak and exhausted, "You have thought fit to present me with another girl child. Perhaps next time you will do better and produce a son, and then another and another, until eventually you achieve a king."

The poor Countess could only murmur an acknowledgement of the Earl's presence - "As you please, my lord," she whispered as he turned his attention to the heavily carved oak rocking cradle to inspect its contents.

"Has a wet-nurse without blemish of character been found?" he demanded. The midwife curtseyed, for she knew a pouch with forty shillings was prepared for her by the Receiver General (the accountant) of the castle, if all went well.

"Yes, my lord. Mistress Green recently gave birth to her ninth child and is experienced in the handling of bairns."

The Earl nodded approval, cast an eye briefly around the Great Chamber to see that all was appropriately in order for his Countess and strode out of the room. His place was shortly taken by a little girl in an embroidered cap over her long fair hair, and wearing a long linen shift and petticoat. She glanced anxiously around the room, holding her nursemaid, Ella, tightly by the hand; and then seeing the coast was clear, she pulled Ella towards the cradle to look at her baby sister. The countess feebly opened her eyes when she heard the child exclaim in awe over the baby's diminutive size.

"Is that you, Isabel[16]?" was all she said. Isabel bobbed a little curtsey as she had been taught by her dominie.

"Yes, Madame," she replied in a small voice. And the visit was over. On the way back to her own nursery, she screwed up her face so much in thought that when she was safely alone with Ella, she needed no encouragement to ask the question which she had not dared to ask her mother.

"What will the baby be called, Ella?"

" 'Anne', after your mother; 'Anne Nevill of Sheriff Hutton' ", went on the nursemaid; "That sounds nice, doesn't it?" And as she saw that Isabel was still not satisfied, she added "You were called after your grandmother, Isabel Despenser, 'Isabel of Warwick', so that seems fair, doesn't it?" And that set Isabel thinking for quite a long time. At length, she said "If Madame had a little boy, what would he be called?"

"Perhaps he would be called 'Richard' after my lord, your father."

Silence once more, then with a distant look in her eyes, Isabel said "I think I would like to marry a Richard."

Anne, the baby, grew and thrived and her mother, Anne the Countess, returned gradually to health after a long lying-in and a diet of slops. The wet-nurse, Mistress Green, played her part well and with ever a kind word for Isabel, who loved to come and watch the baby feeding. Mistress Green lived in the castle so that she was at the beck and call of her tiny employer day and night, for which she was handsomely rewarded, out of the proceeds of which she could afford to pay her neighbour to act as wet-nurse to her own baby. She loved the two Warwick children very much but missed her own children badly and sometimes had to wipe away a tear when she thought of them. Anne was a quiet baby and caused little trouble almost as if she realised that she had already committed the most heinous of sins, that of being a girl, and must do nothing further to attract odium. She saw little of her mother, but her nursemaid provided affection and cuddles, especially after Mistress Green returned to her own family when Anne was in her second year. Isabel usually played near the baby, talking to her in her little-girl squeaky voice and also providing the answers in their "conversations". Their father they hardly ever saw face-to-face, but he came and went from the castle as events dictated, and when the children heard the clop of horses' hooves on the cobbles of the courtyard, they ran to the window to peer out, and sometimes were in time to see the Earl riding away, surrounded by his servants, each on a fine horse, through the gatehouse to the east of the bailey and along the High Street.

Warwick Castle was a town in its own right. The private residence to the south had a string of state rooms which made up a very fine terrace overlooking the River Avon in a manner of regal grandeur. This part of the castle had only been rebuilt around the ancient Great Hall and chapel a hundred years before by great great grandfather Thomas Beauchamp. Far below was the watergate and to the north was the huge courtyard formed from the outer bailey of the Conqueror's Norman castle. The courtyard was surrounded by high stone walls and to the north-east was the rebuilt gatehouse incorporating living quarters for some of the vast numbers of retainers who spent their time in the service of the Earl. Further dwellings followed the walls round to the great man-made mound on the north-west, on which the timber shell-keep of the eleventh century castle had been built, later replaced in stone but now decayed and mainly derelict.

As they grew up sometimes the little Nevill girls would walk to the grass-covered mound with their nursemaid, Ella, and roll their balls down the steep slope. The curtain wall of the castle ran over the mound, but they could soon climb up it by the original path, and then turn to survey the whole area of their present castle, secure within its containing defences, across to the gatehouse with its barbican, and south-east to their own regal apartments. If Ella was seen dozing in the Summer heat, Isabel would beckon and the two children would lie down and roll and slither ecstatically down the mound to the level ground at the bottom, heedless of their grand dresses and unsuitable furbelows, their little embroidered caps and their frilly pantaloons. Ella would awake to their shrieks of delight,

Warwick Castle: Barbican

hurry to control their exuberance and box their ears before bustling them back to their nursery.

Other days they would beg to walk to the gatehouse, which fascinated them with its long forbidding barbican. They longed and yet dreaded to walk through its prison-like walls, a tunnel partly roofed, dank and claustrophobic, and yet they knew that Ladies only passed through on horseback, pillion or side-saddle, or on a travelling litter. They looked up at the line of the two portcullises drawn aloft into the towers above, and sometimes they were lucky enough to arrive there in time to see them being lowered into the gateways. Then the fearful dark passage with the "murder holes" in its cciling, through the barbican and over the draw-bridge above the deep dry ditch which surrounded the encircling walls of the castle, to the outer world, which was quite shut off from them and they from it.

To north and south of the gatehouse were its vast flanking towers, built by that same Thomas de Beauchamp, which were definitely out of bounds to the Nevill children, thereby filling them with awe and curiosity, tinged with fear. Sometimes they were excited to spy the guards on the rampart walking high above them round the towers, and just occasionally to see the pennant being raised on the central turret of each.

Thomas de Beauchamp, 11th Earl of Warwick, had built the two corner towers a hundred years ago during the French wars. Both towers reached the zenith of defensive warfare and served as warning beacons across the unbroken landscape to any army contemplating assault on the castle. Guy's Tower, named after Thomas' father, was to the north-east corner of the outer walls. It was twelve-sided, 128 feet high and with five stories in all, the first four with a central stone-vaulted room with two small side-chambers off each. The fifth floor had a hexagonal guardroom, and above it the battlemented roof from where there was a view across the countryside to east and north. Anne longed to go up the tower to have a look down on the courtyard and the road from the town to the drawbridge over the ditch, but she was never allowed to go up the steep stone staircase, however much she cried. The Caesar Tower occupied the south-east corner of the curtain wall, and was even taller than Guy's tower, built on solid rock rising from the bank of the river Avon and completely inaccessible from without the castle. This tower was 147 feet high, with a bulbous quatrefoil shape beautifully rounded off, so that Anne, when she saw it from the river bridge, felt as if it must be smooth and warm to the touch, almost good enough to lick like her sweetmeats. It was, like all the castle, built in the fine yellow sandstone quarried in the area, and had long narrow windows like big vertical arrow slits, but headed with the gothic pointed arch of the period. There were only three storeys in this tower, surmounted by a platform which had a crenellated and machiolated parapet, and topped with a smaller hexagonal guardhouse with its own battlements and arrow slits.

Anne thought it was "tres jolie", and so it was, but for a long time she did not understand that beneath the tower, carved into the rock was a rat-infested dungeon of ghastly cold and filth and darkness, where the dregs of human suffering existed like ghostly remains of their mortal selves. This tower, however, had been the pride and joy of Thomas Beauchamp, the greatest and almost the last mediaeval fortification to be built in England. It was also a monument to the Earls of Warwick, the mighty Beauchamps - and to himself - and so he named it the Caesar Tower since it had no equal, but was above all others.

Now there was only one other small addition which Earl Thomas planned for the castle, and this was over on the south-west perimeter between the mound and the family living quarters on the south, to provide a small gateway and guardhouse tower to give access to the river bank. This little tower was Anne's favourite, perhaps because it was of miniature proportions, like herself. She pretended it was her own little house, although she was not supposed to explore the upper guardroom. However, it was a great treat for Ella to take her and Isabel down along the river bank to pick the wild flowers, to throw maslin to the ducks swimming in and out of the rushes, sometimes even to see the swans flying along the river, just skimming the surface as they kept watch on their nests. Ella taught the children to make sweet posies of the wonderfully scented flowers, pot pourri for their rooms, necklaces by weaving the stems of the flowers into others, and garlands for their heads. Coming home through the little gateway, the sandstone of the castle glowed golden in the western sunlight, until the old stones were almost orange - "So beautiful!" sighed these grandchildren of the mighty Kingmaker, returning to their own small world protected so far from the upheavals of civil war. Colour in all its natural variations was one aspect of their lives which at present impressed them most.

Isabel and Anne led solitary lives though they themselves did not recognise this yet as they had known no other. The children of the very highest officials who lived in the castle were allowed to come to play with them now and then, and to join them for some of their lessons such as when the girls learned the elements of embroidery - which they hated because their poor fingers so frequently were pricked. Both boys and girls joined them for singing, which they loved, and all joined in with gusto if not with great expertise when their singing master visited with his lute player. Most of all they loved the dancing class, and Mr Warwickson, the dancing master was a great favourite, so that when he bade them point their toes or lift their chins, stand up straight or curtsey or bow, they did their best to oblige. One day Mr Warwickson brought the castle dwarf with him. "Merryman" he said "is his name and merryman he is by character!" And to their delight, Merryman joined in the ballads and sarabandes, adding an enthusiastic party spirit to the otherwise rather dour lives these children lived. They loved Merryman. "Why is he so tiny?" they wanted to know. He was only about the same height as Isabel when she was seven, but his little fat arms and legs were much shorter than her long thin limbs, though his muscular body was much larger. His huge head set on his thick neck added a bizarre element, turned to fun and laughter by his strange adult clothes or especially when he wore his jester's suit so that the bells on his cap rang as he danced in his lively and peculiar way.

Warwick Castle was run by an enormous staff which continued to function in the absence of the Earl. At the head was the Chancellor, Steward of the Household and the Treasurer. At a more lowly level there were the Ushers, the Butler and the Master Cook and their staffs. For the more military pursuits, there was the Sergeant at Arms, the Heralds and grooms and many others, such as stable boys, blacksmiths, bakers, carpenters, tailors and leather workers. For the Earls' manors and baronies there were a host of other posts such as bailiffs and stewards, who regularly called at the castle for instructions, as well as tenants coming to pay their dues, and those accused at the manor courts and subsequently fined.

As the household travelled from castle to castle, it took its own priest, its minstrels and any number of personal servants with it. The Warwick children only came into contact with the more domestic of these who cared for their personal welfare, the laundry maid, the nursery staff, their teachers and even their gardeners. Very soon they came to know their own personal grooms, especially when riding pillion to another residence such as a visit to their great-aunt, Duchess Cecily[5] at Fotheringhay, but Grande Madame was often away following the Duke on his duties, even if in France.

Great-aunt Cecily was a favourite with Isabel and Anne. They admired her elegance, even when they were small.

"I think Madame is so pretty" sighed Isabel who was very conscious of her own lack of front teeth, and her present gaukiness. "Her Grace was called 'The Rose of Raby' when she was young" Ella told her, forbearing to add that nowadays, behind her back at Fotheringhay, Great Aunt Cecily was known more prosaically as 'Proud Cis'.

Born Cecily Nevill at Raby Castle, County Durham, the youngest of twenty-three children of the Earl of Westmoreland[3], the fourteenth child of his marriage to Joan Beaufort, she had grown up in a noble family which had high ambitions of attaining royal status, which was about the only social advancement they still had to achieve. Four of Cecily's brothers married heiresses and became respectively Lords Fauconberg, Latimer, Abergavenny and Salisbury. Another became a bishop. Two of her sisters became duchesses, of Buckingham and Norfolk, but she herself outdid them all by becoming Duchess of York, when at the age of fourteen in 1429 she was married to the fifteen year old Duke of York[6]. Richard Plantagenet was a Prince of the Blood Royal, each of whom had a claim in decreasing degrees to the throne of England through their descent from Edward III. Cecily's husband, Richard, was the grandson of the fourth son of Edward III, Edmund of Langley, and by 1450 he was beginning to perceive the possibility of attaining the Crown. He was one of the greatest landowners in England after the king, with land in the West Marches including his favourite residence at Ludlow Castle, the earldoms of Ulster, Rutland and Cambridge as well as properties of the Dukedom of York.

Nevill Tree

John Lord Nevill
of Raby
'The Builder'
(d. 1388)

m.

Margaret Stafford ①   Ralph³   ② Joan Beaufort
                            1st Earl of
                            Westmorland
                            (1354 - 1425)

Edward
Lord Abergavenny

Cecily⁵
m.
Richard
Duke of York⁶
k. 1461

Edward IV
etc.

Robert²⁷
Bishop of Salisbury
then Durham

Eleanor   5 others
m.
① Richard
Lord Despenser
② HenryPercy
Earl of Northumberland
d. 1455

George
Lord Latimer

Anne
m.
① Humphrey⁷
Duke of Buckingham
k. 1460

William
Lord Fauconberg
d. 1463

Catherine
m.
① John
2nd Duke of Norfolk
④ John Woodville
ex. 1469

Richard⁴
Earl of Salisbury
ex. 1460

Margaret³³
m.
John
Earl of Oxford
d. 1513

Catherine
m.
William
Lord Hastings
ex. 1483

Eleanor
m.
Thomas
Lord Stanley
d. 1503

Alice
m.
Henry
Lord Fitzhugh
d. 1472

Cecily
m.
Henry
Earl of Warwick

Joan
m.
William
Earl of Arundel

George²⁸
Archbishop of York
d. 1476

John
d. inf.
at Sawston

George Nevill³²
Duke of Bedford
d. Sheriff Hutton
1483

5 daughters

John
Marquis Montagu
k. 1471

Thomas
k. 1460

Ralph
3rd Earl of Westmorland
(1456 - 1523)

John
Lord Nevill (d. 1461)

Ralph
2nd Earl of
Westmorland
(1408 - 1484)

John
(d. 1420)

8 others

Anne¹⁷
Duchess of
Gloucester

Richard¹¹
Earl of Salisbury
& Warwick
The 'Kingmaker'
k. 1471

Isabel¹⁶
Duchess of
Clarence

22

"His Grace" announced Isabel one day, in an effort to impress upon her ignorant younger sister the importance and wealth of their Aunt Cecily, "is master of all these lands and one day perhaps he will be king!"

Only that day the children had heard the sound of horses and men gathering in the courtyard below and had flown to the window in expectation of seeing their father resplendent on horseback, with his followers also mounted, trotting off on some exploit, through the barbican to the High Street. They soon realised that the scene differed from the usual gay atmosphere and seemed more purposeful. The men on horses were dressed differently from usual and were holding pennants with their father's emblem of the Bear and Ragged Staff. Some carried pikes or long bows and had knives tucked in their belts, and on their heads they wore helmets, some with visors, and on their legs protective metal plates. The most important officers including the Earl, wore plate mail. There were also hundreds of men from the town and the country roundabout, gentlemen from the manors, yeomen who owned their holdings, labourers straight from the fields, some quite young boys who had hardly started to shave. These foot soldiers were dressed much more informally, but mostly had, somewhere on their person the badge of the Bear and Ragged Staff.

"What are they all doing?" The children wanted to know. So Ella tried to explain that they were setting off to the Welsh Marches and on the way would gather more and more fighting men and meet up with their Uncle York[6] and his eldest son, Edward Earl of March[18]. They planned to capture the wicked King Henry VI and his queen, Margaret of Anjou.

"There's your grandfather, the Earl of Salisbury[4]." Ella pointed out a tall figure with the Nevill crest - the Dun Cow - on his horse's rich caparison. Isabel and Anne stayed with their faces glued to the window, thrilled with the excitement below, until the huge army of men and horses had disappeared through the gatehouse, to the neighing of the horses and shouts of the men. Before the last man had passed through the gate, already they could see the column clip-clopping along the High Street and hear the shouts and cheers of the townsmen. It certainly seemed to be a very important day, so the children thought.

After that they did not see their father for several weeks, and when they asked Ella where he was, she answered evasively as if she did not want to talk about it. Then, when the Autumn days were becoming cool and fires were beginning to be lit in the nursery, she told them that there had been a great battle near their Uncle York's castle at Ludlow, not far from the Welsh border. The fighting had broken out around the crossing of the River Teme at Ludford at the bottom of the steep Broad Street which led up to the Butter Market in the High Street. The battle became a rout of the Yorkist forces and destruction of much of the town. Many of the soldiers of the Duke of York's army fled and the Duke and his eldest son, Edward, Earl of March, escaped through Mortimer's Tower which constituted a back exit from Ludlow Castle high above the river high over Dinham bridge to the north from where there was a direct route to Wigmore Castle and Wales. The Duke travelled secretly to Ireland, and his son was taken in charge of his grandfather and cousin, the Earls of Salisbury and Warwick to Calais, of which Warwick had been Captain for the last four years. The Duchess of York - Aunt Cecily - and her younger children were captured whilst still at Ludlow Castle and sent to one of the Duke of Buckingham's[7] manors to be under the custody of his wife, Anne - who of course was Aunt Cecily's elder sister.

Ludlow was less than two day's journey from Warwick - a man on a strong horse could travel it in one - and so news quickly transferred from the York family castle there to Warwick, and it was inevitable that Isabel and Anne, though so young, would hear rumours of the battle at Ludford, followed gradually by details such as the removal of Aunt Cecily and her family to the control of her sister, her Grace the Duchess of Buckingham. Most of this news washed right over Anne's young head, but Isabel was more aware of the implications, especially when she heard that the Duke of York had escaped to Ireland, though the word used was less pejorative, and sometimes she thought her great uncle by marriage, Richard Duke of York, had merely been raised to a more august position. It became obvious to her though, as she listened to gossip between the servants at Warwick, that many of them had lost sons and husbands at Ludford, that it had been a major and very bloody battle, one of a string of encounters occurring since St. Albans the year before she was born.

Ludlow Castle – A. E. Everitt   SHROP. C.C.

Gradually through most of their lives, the Warwick children were aware of the bitter struggles for the Crown of England, but as far as the rank and file of the armies were concerned they were taught by common consent that the peasant soldier was a commodity belonging to his lord to whom he owed service in the lord's private army in return for land and living. Usually the fighting man was expendable and his physical wounds were his own affair, and that of his family whose duty it was to rally around to take over the care of his strips of cultivation and any livestock he might own, sending up to the lord's demesne as usual a percentage of their produce as part of the deal. As far as their own relatives and noble acquaintances were concerned, death or wounding in battle was an unfortunate result which inevitably sometimes occurred, and although Isabel - and later Anne as she grew up - was sorry indeed to hear of this mishap, she followed the example of those around them of accepting such as the possible outcome of internecine warfare. Only when the heir to an estate of lordly significance was killed, especially when there was no younger brother to succeed to the title, was the calamity recognised for its full impact, and the girls learned to grasp the horror for the family involved. Thus they grew up to hold very pragmatic and philosophical views of the casualties of war and found it hard to feel personal sadness for the victims. This was perhaps the only way they could deal in their minds with the repeated tragedies in their short lives. To have dwelt on the deaths and mutilations in a personal way would have been insupportable to two young children, as it was unbearable to visualise the scenes of battle, the sights and sounds and smell, the blood and mess.

CHAPTER 2

LIFE AT WARWICK CASTLE carried on in its usual routine as far as the Nevill children were concerned, but before long there seemed to be more bustling and hurrying in building and bailey, and when they asked Ella what was happening, she said they were packing up to move to Middleham, their grandfather's great fortified castle at the entrance to Wensleydale in Yorkshire, which he had inherited from his father, the Earl of Westmorland, and so on right back to their great great grandfather, John the Builder. Before him, John's grandfather, Ralph Nevill, whose mother, Mary of Middleham, was a lady of considerable character, had inherited it. The castle had been built first by Mary's grandfather, Robert Fitzrandulph in 1170 to supersede an even older castle built by the Conqueror, but Great Grandfather Westmorland had added to and modernised the later castle so that it was both defensive and (like Warwick Castle) a gracious home in which the lord could live with his family, though still it was primarily a fortress. Ella warned the children that the courtyard was not so light and open as that at Warwick because a large rectangle of it was occupied by the huge keep containing the Great Hall and the principal chambers, kitchen and chapel. She said the curtain walls, built by four Greats Grandfather Ralph Nevill to restrain the invading Scots, had been heightened by Great Grandfather Westmorland[3] and were lofty and forbidding. Only the domestic apartments built onto the inside of the curtain walls were of smaller scale and more friendly, and the children's room in the west range would delight them as it was situated beside a corner tower and was quite self-contained, with their own spiral staircase in the D-shaped south-west tower. There was a connecting wooden bridge, roofed against the winter weather, nearby across the courtyard from the south range to give access to the State Rooms in the Keep. Not far away from the "nursee" was the room where their mother lived when in residence, in the south range although when their father came, she moved into the Keep

27

to be with him. The nursee was lovely and warm as it was over the big bakehouse and it also had its own fireplace to make it snug. They would have their own garderobe, not used by anyone else, built in the thickness of the walls. The other apartments round the curtain walls were for guests, or lodging for staff, but approached by separate staircases, and with their own garderobe and fireplaces.

Middleham Castle turned out to be square and strong and uncompromising. Its stone was the brown millstone grit or Dunstone from the edge of the Pennines, its weather that of the North, its invaders potentially those from Scotland. Its temper was that of the Fells. It lacked the open courtyard that Warwick boasted, its severe keep dividing the space within the curtain walls into dark narrow areas which reflected little of the northern sun, which rose late and set early because of the surrounding hills, which though not steep increased that isolation of enclosure. Middleham Castle was masculine and mighty and echoed the severity of the northern way of life and its fears. Later in her life, Anne would compare it to the femininity and charm of her favourite home at Sheriff Hutton, a younger, sunnier, joyful creation less than a hundred years old. Middleham seemed to her a weary old man who still had fight in him, but was used to the harder life of the soil.

When they first arrived at Middleham, Isabel and Anne were very weary after having spent nearly a week on the journey from Warwick. Most of it they rode pillion in front of their grooms, Anne in a sort of sling suspended from his shoulders so that she could not slip down. Both children slept fitfully for much of the way, but at one point they were so tired that a travelling litter was rigged up for them between the two horses so that they could safely be left to sleep. When at long last they knew, by the echoing of the horses hooves on the cobbles of the marketplace, that they had arrived in a township, they peeped out of their covers.

"Nearly there!" called the groom.

"Nearly there, Ladies!" said the horseman leading the litter.

"Thank the Lord!" said Ella fervently, quickly echoed by Isabel. At the head of the street they could see above them the dark awesome towers of Middleham Castle which, as the sun came up from the dark clouds riding high over the Pennines as if to welcome them, the stonework changed to a soft yellow ochre. Through the outer bailey they rumbled, the children now sitting forward in their excitement, all thoughts of sleep suddenly vanishing. At the Northern Gatehouse, well lit by rush torches, they stopped whilst the leading guard of their cavalcade commanded the gates to be opened for the Ladies Nevill. Up went the portcullis with the clanking that became so familiar to the children, and so they entered one of the Earl of Salisbury's[4] great fortresses in Yorkshire, and the train of horsemen and servants and baggage mules came to a halt. Without more ado, servants came forward to carry the weary children up to their apartment with the big bed which they would share, and after hot milk and frumenty, they were quickly asleep, while Ella, lounging in her big oak chair near the fireside, let her head drop lower and lower onto her chest until she too was fast asleep.

Next morning they were all awakened early by the world around them, the country sounds of clucking and mooing and baa-ing, and the clip-clopping of horses, the grinding of the millstone in the bakery below them, the shouts of the guards, and the ringing of bells for Mass. Soon they were up, dressing, peeping out of the windows, urging Ella to take them around their new home, for walks around the castle, around the outer bailey, the town, the hills, until both Ella and they themselves were quite exhausted by all the new possibilities.

From the high gothic windows of their apartment next to the south-west tower of the curtain wall, the children were elated to find that once they had clambered up onto the stone cill, they had breathtaking views over large expanses of the beautiful valley of Wensleydale, golden in its Autumn foliage, whilst up on the hills which surrounded them were the browning grasslands and the intermittent yellows and beiges and greys of the stone outcrops, mirrored on the lower reaches by the little stone huts of the shepherds and the stone circles used as pens at lambing time. On a hill to the south-west, not so far away, was the mound where the first castle, a wooden keep, had been built by the Conqueror, though now only the remains of the motte and bailey were left as lumps in the grass. If they directed their gaze to the foreground, they saw the green meadows by the moat round their own castle, where the cattle were grazing, and if they were lucky and sharp in recognition, they might see a peewit scouring the skies for food, or flocks of wild duck flying home from the ponds around the river. Sometimes they saw a fox furtively tracking a hen which had strayed from its stackyard, or with its latest quarry in its mouth being taken to feed its cubs. They soon learned the different country sounds - of birds and animals, as well as those cries from the villagers at the different seasons - at harvest, at Christmas, at the markets, at haymaking and threshing, and the church bells at festivals calling the people to Mass. But they also were surrounded within the castle by the teeming life of its inhabitants, its fighting men, its craftsmen, the butcher, the baker and even the candlemaker, and the most important of all, the blacksmith with his busy forge in the stableyard in the east bailey towards the town. Most exciting was the clanking of the chains of the drawbridge and the resounding thud at the lowering of the portcullis in the gatehouse to the north-east of the mantill wall.

Once installed in their new quarters, the initial excitement abated, and the children discovered that all their own nursery servants had come with them from Warwick. They recognised numbers of the officials and guards, although many of them were Yorkshiremen from Middleham or Sheriff Hutton near York, or from Raby near Durham, which belonged to Nevill cousins. The Constable of the castle soon came to visit them and turned out to be a Nevill uncle, Sir John, a much more jocular gentleman than most of their relations. Quickly Middleham became home for them and the routine of everyday was resumed, as at Warwick, which disappointed them. What was different was the large number of "courtiers", young men living there for a while to learn the knightly pursuits of court life, manners, horsemanship and hunting, wrestling and archery. Some of the faces they saw down below in the Inner Courtyard or on horseback without the castle walls, were quite young, mere boys. Some evenings there was jousting to watch, accompanied by the cheers of onlookers; other times it was feasting and merriment, the sound of which drifted across the courtyard to the south-west tower, keeping the children awake till the small hours. Next day the young gentlemen slouched along to their duties looking rather the worse for wear. One day Isabel spied the figure she knew only too well for its small stature, large head and short limbs. She watched the shambling gait and knew it was their dear friend, Merryman.

"Oh Ella, Ella," she cried in excitement, "Just look who is here! Please, please can he come up to see us?" Ella quickly came to the window.

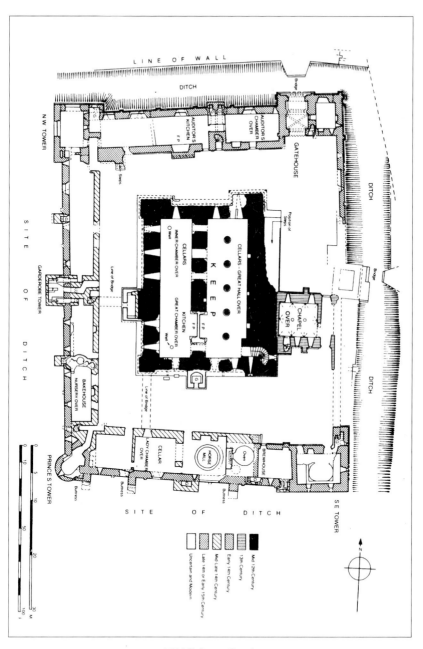

Middleham Castle   ENGLISH HERITAGE

31

"It's Merryman" she said, and sent the page down with a message. That afternoon they were learning to sew, wearing their new horn thimbles, sitting by the west window to catch every vestige of light before the sun set. Isabel was working at her name on a sampler, Anne practising the stitches and hating every minute of it as she constantly pricked her poor fingers. Suddenly they heard footsteps ascending from the courtyard, the door opened and there, to their joy, was the little dwarf, grinning from ear to ear.

"Good day, little ladies," he greeted them, bowing deeply as he doffed his cap. "And how do you like Yorkshire?" And without waiting for a reply, his lumbering body was turning cartwheels across the room until he reached the trussing chest, which contained their clothes, at the far end. Onto this he leaped in one bound, before jumping off again and cart wheeling back to the astonished children, where he pretended to collapse. In reality he continued to lie on the rushes in front of them, winking and grimacing until they were breathless with laughter.

"Please dear Merryman" cried Isabel. "Will you dance with us?" Up he jumped in a trice, throwing his cap to the other end of the chamber and taking Isabel's outstretched hand in his right hand, and Anne's in his left, and singing a ditty in suitable rhythm, solemnly stepped in a mock sarabande, one foot then the other, down the nursee whilst Ella clapped in time.

After that, Merryman came to see them as often as was seemly and as often as his presence was not required elsewhere in the vast concourse at Middleham. He livened them up and made them laugh and Ella thought laughter was good for small children as long as it was balanced by serious times. Besides, she enjoyed the fun also. It was during one of his visits that they heard the clip-clopping of a large group of horses arriving at the castle. A page arrived to say the Countess had driven from the south to see the children and would like them to come to her apartment at midday. Merryman disappeared as if by magic, and Ella bustled the children into their velvet gowns. They had to wash their hands and have their hair braided and tied in loops in the way Madam like to see them, and finally don clean linen caps with embroidered frills. They felt excited and a little nervous, but when Ella took them across the courtyard to their mother's chamber, they found she was just as they remembered her at Warwick - a small beautiful lady in lovely apparel and with jewels sparkling on her chemise and her fingers. They curtsied to her as they had practised and she inclined her head at the two small figures before her and enquired how they liked their chamber at Middleham, and whether they had been taken out to see the horses in the stables - the famous horses from Jervaulx. They answered Madam as well as they could and then Ella took them back across the courtyard to the nursee. It was rather a formal interview, but after that, they saw the Countess quite often over the next few weeks, and although they were in awe of her, replying to her became easier and she was not the frightening figure that their father was. Countess Anne had had plenty of sadness in her life to be able to sympathise with the anxieties of small children, and these two began to feel that their mother, whom they hardly knew, was quite a kind lady after all. She, in turn, felt some warmth for them even though she actually saw very little of them. She had seldom more than pecked a kiss on their cheeks, and had never sat them on her knee. This would have been demeaning and indulgent, and was for Ella (if anyone) to do, if necessary.

Much more to their liking was the day when Ella announced that she had a surprise for them, but first they must dress in special clothes, with green velvet jackets to keep them warm, wide skirts that were no impediment, and little tricorn hats over their veils, and lastly thick kid gauntlets and stout boots in green Portugese leather. When they were ready, she took them down their private staircase to the courtyard and there, waiting patiently, with every now and then a gentle padding of a foot, stood two young Jervaulx ponies, white with long manes and tails tied in coloured ribbons and with splendid new leather saddles. A groom held the reins of each and bowed as the children emerged with anticipation written on their faces. Isabel immediately ran to the pony nearest to her with great excitement.

"For us?" She exclaimed.

"Yes, little lady," said Thomas, the groom, in his rough country accent. "But first you must learn how to sit on the saddle and then we can gradually see how you go." And he lifted her onto the ornate backcloth of the sturdy little animal and fitted her feet into the special stirrups he had fetched that morning from the castle blacksmith in the stableyard.

"Me too!" cried Anne, and she also was lifted by the other groom, Ben, onto her pony, which had a specially-shaped saddle with pommels for her to hold. Then they slowly walked round the courtyard, to the curiosity of the retainers going about their daily business.

"Can we ride again tomorrow?" They chorused, when at last Thomas said they had done enough for their first day.

"Of course," Ella assured them. "Every day, if you are good children and have done your lessons well."

And so riding became a daily joy, and as they gained strength and control, they were taken by Thomas and Ben out of the castle into the pasture land round abouts, and before long, they were allowed to canter, and then to dispense with their leading reins, and very soon became proficient, though never allowed out on their own. One day Thomas and Ben led them through the main street of Middleham, in order to begin to accustom the ponies to noise and bustle. The children were somewhat in awe of all the people, the mules and donkeys, and the dogs which roamed around the streets, but most of all the children who stared at them. They passed the market cross and the church and became used to inclining their heads when the townsfolk bowed or curtsied as they passed, and on a wet day when they rode through the square, the mud from the cobbles and the mire in the High Street splashed the gay hangings of the ponies' tack.

The peasants' houses filled them with curiosity. Some little more than one-roomed hovels, they looked dark and smoky inside, like witches' caves, and none of them had glass in the windows, usually just a curtain of thick huckerback or canvas. The yeomen's demesnes were larger, lighter and more appetising, but everywhere was muddy and the local children were surprisingly grubby to the Nevill girls' way of thinking. Isabel and Anne had virtually never before had a glimpse at the houses or conditions of their father's retainers' and tenants' homes and they did not think much of what they saw now. It opened a whole new world to them, and they were relieved to return to the warmth and security of their nursee and their Ella.

"How dirty they all are," said Isabel, and Anne screwed up her nose to show how they smelt.

"Pooh!" she said. "Pooh, pooh, pooh!" And tossed her head until her tricorn hat and veil nearly slid over her face. "Why don't they live in nice houses?"

"They're poor tenants," explained Ella. "Their forefathers were serfs, and even now they all depend on your father, my lord the Earl, for their livelihood, and in return have to till his fields. They have to look after the sheep and cattle which my lord owns, and in wartime they have to fight for him in battles."

After that, the children took more interest in the view of the Dales from their nursee windows and saw the cows being driven to the pastures by the river, and up on the hills of Uvedale the many tiny dots which were the hundreds of sheep grazing until they were shepherded down to their stone pens at lambing time, or to market for sale. Sometimes the lambs were sent to Coverham Abbey where the monks herded many hundreds of sheep. The baa-ing of the flocks echoed round the valley at this time, and the track to Coverham was one mass of woolly bodies, whilst the sheepdogs scudded round the frightened groups, barking sharply as they busily

Peasants' Cottages   W. S. GILLY, 1842

35

scurried to and fro, to keep their charges in tight groups, delighting the Warwick children as they looked on from their high windows.

The evenings were now closing in and in the nursee the log fires not only made it very cosy but also provided light. Candles were lit early, so that sewing could continue, and this winter a spinning wheel was introduced to their apartment so that they could learn to card and spin the rough wool from the Coverham sheep. Strong bundles of teasels were brought in to comb out the tangles of fleece into straight lengths of twine, and then the girls, especially Isabel, learnt to feed several strands into her little spinning wheel whilst working the revolutions with her foot. They began to associate the stages of these processes with the woollen cloth which was used for their hosen and jackets, and Ella explained the way it was woven on great looms which almost filled the living rooms of most of the cottages at Middleham. Flax they had to wait to see being made into linen until they visited Sheriff Hutton where it was grown as great areas of blue mist, and for silk perhaps they would one day see the weavers in Spitalfields or Canterbury.

Day after day passed without change of routine, only punctuated as the weather dictated when they could not ride or walk on the rising slopes above the town or along the gushing river, Ure. Normally lessons in riding, singing, dancing and embroidery filled their days, with daily instruction from the chaplain on the Faith of Rome and the monastic rule, the latter in the eventuality of their becoming nuns, should marriage fail them. In contrast with the many children working throughout the castle, the Nevill children followed a different, but just as strict routine, so that when it was broken by visitors arriving at the castle, whatever their reasons, they brought interest to the children, and to the rest of the inhabitants gossip, news from the outer world, reports of market prices at York or Durham or any of the lesser marts. Tenants came to pay their dues, or complain of their neighbours. Others came to deliver corn or honey or beef. Men or women who had been convicted by the manor court came to pay their fines or protest their innocence, pedlars with their goods, the miller with sacks of flour, or any sort of official from one of the many other Nevill estates, all with their problems. Middleham was not just a home, or even a fortress guarding the way through the Pennines, but a court which was at the centre of the Nevill empire, doubling with Sheriff Hutton which oversaw the more southerly parts of Yorkshire. In addition, itinerant friars called for alms, vagrants begged a meal of maslin and skim-milk cheese, travellers requested a night's lodging, and normally were given one which would set them on for another thirty or forty miles of their journey.

Messengers from the Earl occasionally arrived to confirm that he and Lord Salisbury were still in Calais with young Edward of March, and less often a word from Ireland from the Duke of York, though that was usually second hand via Duchess Cecily. Never a day passed without the sound of horses arriving or departing, or the creaking of the heavily-constructed farm carts or the

The Bear and Ragged Staff – Emblem of The Earl of Warwick

more carefully made baggage wagons with their beautifully spoked wheels, and the braying of donkeys as their burdens were unloaded. There were bales of fabric for the tailor, lengths of fine Flanders cloth, sable for tippets, Bruges lace for trimming, bobbins of silk thread of all colours, leather for jackets and hosen, boots and gauntlets, all to be made up by the craftsmen at the castle. Sometimes Isabel thought the courtyard looked like a market place, but it was annoying not to be able to see either entrance gate from their apartment, blocked as the view was by the keep in the centre of the inner bailey.

In late November a lone horseman covered with mud and obviously at the end of a long journey, galloped wearily up to the castle gate. The porter, armed with his heavy mace, stepped out of his lodge in the gatehouse to question his credentials. When the horseman produced his password and his badge of the Bear and Ragged Staff, and said he had come from the south with a letter for the Countess from the Earl, he was quickly admitted to the courtyard where a groom took charge of his sweating horse, and a page escorted the rider up to the chamber in the keep. There the Countess heard his story and news from France, and since my lord demanded her presence in Calais for Christmas, immediately set in motion plans for her journey. Her women packed up her clothing and items for the journey including bedding in a large oak trussing-chest, and next day, riding astride a strong but beautiful chestnut horse, she set off, accompanied by her ladies, her chaplain and a small but well-armed retinue. She would just about achieve the distance by Christmas, given good fortune, favourable weather, and a series of restful lodgings en route. She came to the nursee to bid her daughters farewell, and left New Year presents for them with Ella.

It was a little sad to see their mother depart from the courtyard at Middleham, but the Nevill children were so used to their own unchanging days, and happy with their dear Ella, that once they heard the horses clatter away over the bridge and across the market place, Countess Anne passed temporarily out of their orbit, and life continued undisturbed in its usual way. There was no question of tears at parting.

Although the daily bustle of this busy castle provided never-ending interest, Christmas this year of 1459 was relatively quiet and uneventful. The number of individuals living there, even though only temporarily, reached less than two hundred, compared with the thousand or so when it was at high pitch. It involved some neighbours, including Scropes from Bolton and Masham, Lord FitzHugh from nearby Ravensworth, and Lord Dacre with his young son, Humphrey. Lord John Nevill, brother of the 2nd Earl of Westmorland, who had been called to Parliament after the Yorkist collapse earlier in the year, was there with his three-year-old son, Ralph, who was glad to be brought up to the nursee to see his cousins, especially Anne who was almost exactly the same age as himself. But most of the Nevill clan were dispersed this year and since the Countess of Warwick was by now supposed to be in Calais, there were no visiting Beauchamps at Middleham. There were, however, two of Aunt Cecily's children just come up for the festivities, young though they were.

Isabel and Anne spent a good deal of time peeping out of the narrow windows over the courtyard as Christmas drew near, watching the arrival of visitors and their baggage trains, the general hubbub and jostling of their retainers. None of them realised that two small faces were peering at them from the southern range high above them, and Isabel and Anne would have blushed scarlet if anyone had recognised them. They were too young to be let loose amongst the crowd or to join in the festivities, and it was understood without comment as being improper. But they were fascinated by all the comings and goings including the many wagons of supplies far outnumbering the usual quota from the local farmland, and the continuous sound of the castle mill working overtime to produce extra meal required for the large assembly. Superimposed on all this excitement was a most glorious smell of new bread sailing out from the ovens beneath the nursee, incidentally sending up warmth to the tower rooms above throughout the day and night. Casks of wine were carried up from the cellars under the keep, adding to the merriment which continued far into the small hours, with feasting and debauchery, and the seductive aromas of roasting meats of all sorts to satisfy the large gathering.

In contrast, the chapel on the east side of the keep was given over to Christmas Masses and the monastic services chanted in condensed form by the chaplain and his acolytes, to the flicker of candles lit along the summit of the rood screen, lighting up the wall paintings of the Trinity, the Judgement and the Saints. The floor had been spread with fresh rushes from the banks of the Ure, and strewn with sweet herbs tossed over them to blend with the scent of the incense lavishly used by the priest. Lengths of ivy and branches of holly were trailed along the cills, softening the usual austere appearance of the 14th century building. Ella took the children to one of the first Masses of the day, before the majority of the company were stirring, and with them they took the presents from their mother, a rosary each, cut from a series of tiny jewels set in rosewood and strung on a length of twined flax. The beads felt smooth and friendly as they fingered them along throughout the Mass, finishing with their Hail Marys, and accompanied with much crossing of their small flat chests just as they saw others doing.

As they left the chapel to walk through the Great Hall on their way to the connecting bridge to their own apartments, a boy bowed to them. He was dark, round shouldered and not particularly attractive, but there was a purposeful glint in his eyes as he smiled at them. He seemed the same age as Isabel, but was much smaller. His older brother was, in contrast, tall, athletic-looking and fair. He too bowed to the girls so as not to be outdone by his brother.

39

Isabel bobbed an offhand curtsey, and Anne followed suit and then they hurried nervously on with Ella to their own accommodation.

"Who were those boys?" they wanted to know as soon as they were hidden by the jambs of the entrance door into their tower.

"The small dark one is your great aunt Cecily's youngest son, Richard[22] of York; the tall one is his brother, George[21]. They are just here for the festive season, arrived from her Grace, the Duchess of Buckingham's care."

That gave Isabel food for thought as she tried to work out the relationship to themselves. Aunt Cecily[5] of York was the youngest sister of their grandfather Salisbury[4], so George and Richard were their father's cousins, now aged ten and seven. "Marriage" to these two little girls seemed still just a sort of fairy story with as yet minimal reality, and yet they knew that in truth they would each be married by their father to a high-born young man at any time in the future - the Earl himself was only nine when he was betrothed by his own father into the Beauchamp family for dynastic reasons - an exciting prospect at this stage before they realised the implications. This was a world where girls of aristocratic background were mere chattels who could be bought and sold by their fathers or husbands at will. In this case marriage would very likely in time bring them into royal status;

"With a crown" said Isabel;

"Sitting on a throne" said Anne, and their eyes grew large and round as they considered the possibilities. Through their spy hole windows in their corner tower they saw many handsome young men, talking, dancing, jousting and even riding away to battle. It was all very thrilling to contemplate and would, they had no doubt, happen one day, perhaps very soon. That was their future - or if it failed to materialise, they would become nuns, and from their present view-point, that was more than acceptable - Isabel could see herself in the long white robes of a novice at the Priory of Marrick in Swaledale from where the prioress sometimes rode over wearing her beautiful silk veil to visit them.

Anne put her thumb in her mouth in thought and sighed contentedly. She was thinking how lovely she would look in a nun's habit, but Isabel was now imagining the jewels and coronet and gowns she would have when she became a duchess.

CHAPTER 3

AFTER THE FESTIVITIES OF CHRISTMAS, Middleham grew much quieter, particularly at night, and also much more dull, thought the Nevill children. The social life of the local aristocracy which had as usual been lavishly spent at the castle, now dispersed, and the Fitzhughs and the Scropes and the Dacres and all the rest, departed. Although Isabel and Anne had been able to enjoy the jollity only secondhand, now in comparison the great stone bastions of Middleham became shadowy and threatening, and the passages and stairways of the ghostly old castle were so cold after the fun of Christmas.

The ponds and water butts were frozen over, and the cattle troughs had to be freed of ice before the herds which had been preserved from the big Autumn killing and salting exercise, could drink their fill. The snow deepened as the month progressed, and although very beautiful in the sunshine, the continual cold and difficulty in getting about soon depressed the most phlegmatic of characters as their cheerfulness was worn down. For the young people, the joy of winter sport was counteracted as fingers and toes were attacked by chilblains, and noses were reddened and sore. The deep red sunsets foreshadowing further snow storms only gave passing wonder before the reality of deepening drifts served to make for irritation with the daily battle with the cold, and January did nothing to help this mood. Mists rose from the pastures to meet the lowering clouds descending from the hills, combining to darken the castle with the usual February gloom. From mid-afternoon it was too dark to read or sew without candles, and the constant flickering made concentrated use of weary eyes an unpleasant chore. Dejection and boredom descended on the nursee until the dancing lessons were switched to late afternoon to take up some of the time when they could not see well. They became proficient in

41

playing miming games, learning songs and poems by heart as Ella repeated them, composing verse themselves, and developed a strong bent for story-telling, an art which they copied from anyone who called on them and could be persuaded to join in. Stories about the castle were the most popular, about the earliest Normans to come to Uvedale such as Gilbert de Nevill who was an Admiral of the Conqueror's fleet; Robert Fitz Randolph who built the first stone castle at Middleham; Mary of Middleham through whom Middleham came into the Nevill family, and about Robert Fitz Maldred of Raby and his forebears right back to Algiva, daughter of Ethelred. Often the stories launched into myth and a good deal of imagination, and even fairyland, but it passed the dark days until Spring, when they were wakened by the doves cooing on the ledges of their tower, the hopeful twittering of nesting birds waking to the early signs of life, and the cocks crowing in the outer bailey.

Then suddenly, or so it seemed, Ella announced that they were all going to move down to their father's other big northern castle, Sheriff Hutton, near York, "for a change", and so that Middleham Castle could receive its spring clean, its floors scoured and its drainage thoroughly rinsed through to be made sweet again. Almost the whole staff would move with them, leaving only those needed for the cleaning, and to carry on with everyday management of the estate.

Isabel and Anne immediately brightened up in anticipation of a change from the dreariness of winter in Uvedale, and the excitement of riding all the long way down to Sheriff Hutton. The castle now came alive with preparations for the exodus, and the main groups of servants and baggage wagons set off in a few days, followed by the officials and soldiery needed to run and guard the Earl's household. After they had had at least a week's start, it was time for the children's train and all the gentlewomen who looked after them and their mother the Countess, should she join them later.

"You will have to ride pillion" said Ella. "It's too far for those ponies, and anyhow much too far for you to ride all the way. We shall call in for refreshments and a rest at Masham and also stay the night at Sir John Conyers' demesne near Ripon to shorten the journey for the next day. If fortune favours us, we may just be able to manage the rest of the journey in one day, but it is a long way, so," she continued gloomily, "we may have to find somewhere else for the following night as we shall be very tired."

And so the cortege set off, each little girl perched up infront on her groom, and Ella sitting astride her own fine horse, her voluminous linen veil billowing out behind her like a windmill, and her prodigious riding skirt hiding her legs right down to the ankles and half of the horse's rump as well. At first they walked the horses along the muddy track beside the River Ure which wound and bubbled and seemed unable to make up its mind which direction to take. Then gradually the party began to canter until they reached Masham where the grey stone houses were so closely built around the large town-square that they provided protection to the inhabitants and any stock they brought within its pale when threat of raids raised its fearful head. The buildings huddled so close to each other spelt warmth and comfort, as their occupants gradually emerged to see who this grand party was that had arrived in their midst. There were several inns in the square, some of them nothing more than filthy hovels, so they stopped at the first and largest, "The Bear", where the host was ready with mulled apple juice straight from his crab-mill, and pottage made from chopped meat, herbs and pulses served in special wooden bowls. Then followed honey toasts with chopped pine nuts on top, which they ate sitting on forms drawn up to trestle tables, from where they could see the sloping market place.

Soon they were up on their horses again, clip-clopping down the cobbled square and the lane down to the bridge over the Ure, and making for Ripon through open bounding country until the stubby central tower of Ripon Cathedral, with its elegant spire to match the two on the west front, came into view. Instead of taking the hill down into the town, they turned off eastwards for the last few miles to Hutton Conyers where Sir John's impressive but unmodernised Norman castle met their gaze. Sir John was remaining at Middleham over the spring, but the constable of the castle greeted them at the outer gate built in the first of the concentric banks and ditches which the Norman Conyers had dug to protect the outer bailey, and now the children could see near to the huge man-made mount surmounted by the shell keep on each side of which were outer platforms. Two later courts had been added to north and east within the bailey, and now held a variety of buildings to house the trades which were needed to run the household and its guards. Within the keep there was a central prison, but although the children badgered Ella to show them this horror, of course she knew better than to risk her job.

The Nevill party alighted at the bottom of the motte, handing over their horses to the stable boys who came forward, and other servants took charge of their travelling chests to carry them into the guest room in the keep - Sir John was taking no chances over the Kingmaker's heiresses with members of the Percy family only five miles away at Topcliffe. Once again their chamber provided far-reaching views over the landscape through their windows which were of the narrow Norman style; the Pennine Fells were easy to pick out to the west, the bare Wolds to the south-east, and Black Hambledon lowering along to the east.

Hutton Conyers was a small castle, but because of its age, breathed the usual ghostly atmosphere which Isabel and Anne enjoyed for the thrilling tingle it shot through their spines. It was the sort of old castle which oozed stories of battles, courageous knights, exciting escapades, beautiful duchesses (like Aunt Cecily), and romance. It was fun to stay in - as long as Ella did not leave them on their own. But she was content to settle herself by the fireside, and to rest after the long ride, and be waited upon by the young country girl who brought them their supper of thick vegetable pottage and pandemaine (bread). The warmth of the fire combined with all the fresh air they had had that day soon made them sleepy, until the lake scenes on the wall tapestries became blurred, the skaters on the lake merged into each other, the sledges became one with the ice, the trees with the windmills, and very shortly children and nursemaid were deeply asleep.

Next day they were up early, and soon off on the last leg of their journey. They crossed the River Swale at Topcliffe, and thought how sedate it was compared to the Ure. They eyed the Percy's Norman castle near the township with awe as though expecting their traditional enemy to pounce out at them, and hurried on to Brafferton, and then through the Nevill manor property of Raskelf. The woodland grew much thicker here, punctuated by grassy launds through which deer bounded hurriedly away as the riders approached.

"Let's count the animals we see," called Isabel." "Look, look!" as the rabbits scurried hither and thither and the movement of bushes indicated the whereabouts of other occupants of the undergrowth. Very soon she had reached one hundred, and became distracted by the groups of pigs munching beechnuts under the trees. A fox stealthily hurried along the edge of an assarted area, a stolen hen clucking in its mouth and strewing feathers behind them as they made for a thick covert.

"This is the Forest of Galtres," said Ella, "the beginning of the King's hunting ground," she explained as they crossed the River Kyle near Easingwold, and made for the northern edge of the Forest. "This is where the Saxon Kings hunted long before the Conqueror came, when the Royal Forest was much bigger than it is now."

"Why was it bigger?" asked Isabel.

"Because the sides of it to east and west were gradually taken over for good crop lands and pasture, and since King Henry II's time it has only reached from the River Kyle to the River Foss. Before that it stretched all the way from the River Swale which we crossed today, to the River Derwent to the east. Then there were more homesteads and settlements still within the Forest; now there are far fewer, mostly on the edge of it near the rivers. But right in the middle, there on a ridge of land above the bogs and wetlands, the peasants have built the township of Sutton-on-the-Forest where your great grandmother, Joan Beaufort helped to beautify and enlarge the Church of All Saints."

"Can we go and see it soon?" clamoured the children.

"Of course you shall." Ella promised.

"Will our ponies be there for us at Sheriff Hutton?" they asked.

"Oh yes, little Ladies" answered Ben "and some lovely rides for you to explore."

"In the Forest?" asked Anne for whom "Forest" sounded exciting, as if wolves might jump out at her.

"Yes, sometimes," he said, "or go over the Gowers' land at Stittenham, to Hinderskelfe, or to Hovingham or - oh so many lovely places, as soon as you learn to ride so far."

They had now passed through the old market place at Easingwold, surrounded snugly by its timber-framed houses overlooked by the solid stone church on the hill behind the tanning pits, and were now riding with their backs to the setting sun, under the ancient castle at Crayke on its crag. To their right the land swept gradually down to the flat plain of the Forest of Galtres. Here and there shone a glint of sunlight like a jewel as the ponds in the marshy areas reflected the clear northern light. There was no hint of habitation or of the assarts hidden amongst the woods except near their track, and especially as they approached Stillington where they first saw the River Foss which they crossed on a crude wooden bridge that creaked ominously. They paused to watch the water wheel of the mill grating as though its load was too much for it and it would soon give up and die. Marton, its church already ancient, at the top of the next hill, soon appeared, and then down past the inn at Farlington before they waded through the waters of a tributary of the Foss. Finally up the last hill, and past the track off to Cornborough on their right, along the ridge of the northern escarpment of the Forest. From the yard of the windmill on the summit, which was busily working its sails, they glimpsed another view of the cathedral of Saint Peter at York as the setting sun shone on the white stone of the new west tower. The miller's wife, who was bringing in her washing, bobbed a curtsey as soon as she saw the Bear and Ragged Staff emblem on the horses' livery, and waved to the children as they set off on the last mile of their journey.

Still riding along the narrow spine of the hill, they could see far to the east the moorland above Helmsley and very soon now they realised that the battlements of the four corner towers of Sheriff Hutton Castle were becoming visible above the curve of the hill infront of them. As they drew nearer, the towers seemed to grow, until they were all joined by the inner curtain wall which connected them. The upper part of the towers were relieved of their severity by large gothic windows, but there were very few of them, and in the curtain wall windows were small. Around the whole complex appeared an outer surrounding wall containing the middle and outer courts. The children and their companions passed an increasing number of wagons now as they neared the township, some making for the mill they had just seen on the hill, others bringing in loads of carrots and swedes from the common fields. Now that it was almost dark, men, women and children were also returning home from the fields carrying culters used on their ploughs, or slings and baskets for transferring stones to the balks of their strips from the centres which were shortly to be ploughed and sown.

Sheriff Hutton Castle in c.1852 showing
the South-Western Tower on the right THOMAS GILL

The ridge of the hill along which they had been travelling now gave way to a gentle slope down to the township, and the immense size of the castle became evident. Their road divided, the left arm making its way to the centre of the town, to the church at its eastern end, and to the common grazing land which constituted the Green, and was surrounded by timber-framed cottages and the Castle Inn, with every now and then a house of superior quality using at least some building stone, which belonged to a yeoman. It was in this direction that lay the old Norman castle of Bertram de Bulmer and his descendants, and from where John Nevill decided to build his new castle once he had received the king's permission "to crenallate" in 1382 - which Ella explained, meant building a castle for defence of the king's realm.

"Can we go there one day to see the old castle?" immediately asked the children.

"Of course, as soon as you can ride your ponies." replied the ever-patient Ella. "That will be a very exciting visit, better than the mound at Middleham which is difficult to imagine in its early days. But today we will go straight to our apartments in the new castle because we're all tired, and anyhow it's now much too dark to see it from here."

Their way now led straight to the outer gate of the base court, near the village pound, through a smaller middle court and up to the great gateway on the east of the castle which reminded them of the entrance into the inner court at Middleham - no wonder, as like this one, it had been added by their grandfather, Salisbury[4]. Through the first great oak door they trotted, the keeper on duty bowing when he saw who was coming, though he had already received warning of their approach from their outriders and from a sentinel on the roof. Soon they were through the arch of the portcullis and within the inner court, surrounded by the numerous guest houses and the various domestic buildings which formed the inner structure of the curtain wall.

"Our chambers are at the top of the south west tower" announced Ella as the grooms lifted the tired little girls down. "Just a short way and then we'll be there," but in fact both children were so weary that the waiting pages picked them up in their arms with the greatest of ease and carried them up all three flights of steps to their nursery, where there was a fire burning brightly in the large fireplace, and the frightening shadows were dissuaded from becoming awesome by the large number of tallow candles casting their light on the tapestries around the cheerful room. A gentlewoman followed them with a bowl of hot milk and frumenty each, and after that they were soon tucked up in their big double bed and sound asleep.

Sheriff Hutton Castle turned out to be very like the one at Bolton, Wensleydale, which was not surprising as Lord Henry Scrope had built his new domain there at the same time as John Nevill was engaged on erecting his new castle here. Both castles owed much to the need to be partly defensive, or at any rate self-sufficient in time of siege. Although to some extent fortified, the castles were also designed to have some elegance and comfort, thus notably different from the great stone keeps of old. The big difference between the two, and indeed of Middleham as well, was the position of each. Whilst Bolton and Middleham were backed by high moorland hills and were situated low in the valley of the Ure in Wensleydale which they guarded, to keep watch over the east-west passage of troops and goods, Sheriff Hutton high on its craggy hill surveyed the flat land of the Forest of Galtres to the west and south. All three castles were approached from the High Street of their supporting township. Middleham Castle seemed strong and masculine to the children (could they have expressed it in that way) - they thought it was like "a warrior". Sheriff Hutton was feminine - "like a beautiful lady" - and although it was ready to defend itself if the need arose, it was not belligerent, perhaps because it had no keep. Bolton, to the children's way of thinking, came halfway between the two in terms of awe. At Bolton and Middleham, the sun, shaded by the hills, rose late, and sank early behind the Pennines in the afternoon. But Sheriff Hutton on its friendly green hill received all the sunshine offered. It was light and welcoming, and never caused the children to have nightmares as did the dark corners of Middleham.

When the Warwick children woke up on their first morning at Hutton, their immediate pleasure and excitement were the large gothic windows of their apartments. From both the south and west aspects there was a quite startling view, both of great distances. The hill on which the castle was built was so precipitous that the ground, especially that to the south, seemed miles away below them across a waterway, and then it melted into the distance for many leagues over pasture and common fields, woodland and grazing, until the outline of the bare Wolds could be made out rising above the trees. If they looked out of the west-facing window, in the foreground were one or two barns and yeomen's houses, and ploughed land awaiting Spring sowing. Amongst the fields was the track to Strensall and thence to York, winding muddily along until it disappeared from view as it plunged over the edge of Bracken Hill down to the flatlands of the Forest of Galtres. Once again they had a spectacular view of the cathedral at York which dominated the picture with its magnificence eight miles away.

"And I suppose you want to go and see that too, do you?" teased Ella. The view from their tower here was even more dazzling than that from their nursee at Middleham, but like that aspect, shielded them from the village, and from the castle stables and barns which here were to the north and east. However, the road from the forest, with its frequent travellers and wagons, herds of pigs and cows, flocks of sheep even, gave them endless interest to invent stories about their journeys.

Next day they were awakened by the persistent crowing of all the cocks in the district, or so it seemed, as if they had joined a choir for the sole purpose of waking everyone up. The inhabitants of the castle were mainly already about their business, as were the peasants who were off to their fields and to milk their cows. Isabel and Anne soon had their breakfast of white bread soaked in hot milk and were fidgeting to be taken down the stairs to see the courtyard and explore the castle, but first they were to receive a visit from Sir Thomas Gower who was Constable of the Castle. He was responsible for everything that went on within the pale, and wished to make the acquaintance of these young Warwick girls who were to be in his care. He was a kindly man and immediately became a friend. He also was a local man whose home was at Stittenham, a hamlet of only fourteen houses situated on a small hill resembling a country loaf, about two miles east of Sheriff Hutton but within the jurisdiction of the Priory of Malton. He greeted the children with a slight bow and an avuncular smile which reassured them, and having children of his own, recognised the state of excitement confronting him.

"Take them around the Castle, Mistress Ella, so they become familiar with it, and then they can ask all the question they wish next time I see them." He bowed again and left.

First Ella took them to the Chapel of the Holy Trinity and Saint Mary which lay at the east end of the courtyard, and there they lit three candles, one for each of their parents and a third one for their grandfather, Salisbury, to grant them God-speed as they went about their business to safeguard the king.

When they emerged into the light they looked round with interest, and their eyes quickly followed the four corner turrets up and up, until their necks quite ached. Then they looked round the inner court itself, noticing its general similarity to the inner court at Middleham, which also was lined with living quarters and housed the Great Hall, but in this case the hall was built along the south wall of the court and not in a keep. It was lit by narrow windows both inwards across the courtyard, and as it was situated over the edge of the steep southern slope of the hill, and therefore safe from attack from that quarter, also looking outwards to the Wolds. Under the hall were the cellars and kitchen as at Middleham, and in one wall were the ovens, and nearby the well. There also was the bakehouse, this time, sadly, not directly under their chamber.

"I like this courtyard better than Middleham" said Anne, "it's lighter and more friendly, and you can see who is coming through the gateway." Which was perfectly true, as at that moment a wagon piled high with furze and logs was being hauled through by two oxen, with a peasant tugging at the halter.

"Firewood from the Forest of Galtres" said Ella. "The man with the wagon is from Sutton-on-the-Forest. His name is Thomson."

"Son of Tom." said Isabel. "Can we go down and look through the gate?"

And that is what they did next. Above the gate on its outer side they could see carved in the stonework and brightly painted, the Arms of the Nevills, a white saltire on a red background, and three other arms, two surrounded by the garter received by the Earl of Westmorland in 1402, and the two others by twisted wreaths. There was no barbican on this gate, unlike the one at Warwick which was firmly etched on their memories, just as there was none at Middleham, and they found that the middle court was quite small. Through another gate with its mantill wall they came to the large outer, or base court where were the brewhouse and horse-mills, and all the farm buildings, the granaries and barns, another well, and most important to these two children, the stables where their ponies were kept in winter. And there they also found the blacksmith in his leather apron and gloves, busy as ever not only with making and fitting horseshoes, but fashioning all manner of arms of war, and repairing others. He had a lad working with him, and another whose job it was to work the bellows which swished the fire into a blaze. The clanging of his hammer on the anvil echoed constantly all round the court, accompanied by a shower of sparks spraying out over the earthen floor, and the loud sizzling as he dipped the red hot iron into his trough of water. This was the most exciting place they visited, and they were loath to return to their own apartments which seemed very tame by comparison.

"Where are all the arms kept when they are not in use?" they wanted to know.

"In the safest places possible." replied Ella. "In the vaults of the towers; guns, arquebuses, bows and arrows, many barrels of powder and hundreds of iron shot. But that is all locked up by the armourer, so we shall only see them if they are taken out for battle."

Life for Isabel and Anne quickly settled back into a routine similar to that with which they had become accustomed at Middleham, but it was refreshing to be in a different castle and a different nursery where even the tapestries covering the great high walls of their apartments were a different set. This time they had scenes of a Flemish market with a multitude of people. But it was reassuring to have their own beds with their specially-made hangings embroidered with their initials entwined with the Bear and the Ragged Staff, their own oak travelling chests with all their clothes and treasures, their own stools and table from Middleham; even their own porringers and horn mugs with the silver edging and escutcheons with their initials, and their own spoons that Grandmother Despenser had given them one New Year.

Most of the servants were their own too, having come with them from Warwick and then from Middleham, and it was comforting in this huge castle to see familiar faces on the pages and attendants, and even the retainers downstairs going about their work. This castle, like Middleham, doubled as both a nobleman's home and the manor house for his lands, and so in the same way there was a constant stream of visiting yeomen and tenant labourers to see the steward, Sir William Chamberlain, on their own business, the payment of dues or of fines, to deliver goods they had grown for the lord of the manor, or to grumble over their conditions or their neighbours' behaviour. So there was continual hubbub in the different courts, such as they had heard in the town square at Middleham or in the courtyards of the castle there, with the everyday exchange of gossip whether it be the effect of the weather on the crops, the price of goods at the market at Easingwold or York, or the latest scandal or heresay, local or national. News arrived by word of mouth. Letters were a rare commodity confined to the rich who had their own messengers, but the peddler produced more than his trinkets to whet intense interest and bargaining; his chit-chat even more so from other places far and near produced insatiable curiosity.

As they had soon realised, the children found that they lived so high up in their tower, that they were able to look down from the windows into the inner court very little inconvenienced by the roofs of the dwellings within the curtain wall below. Moreover, the entrance gate was visible from their tower, which produced non-stop entertainment all day and much of the night as people came and went, arguments were settled - or not - even brawls, and they saw prisoners admitted by the guard on duty before being sent to one of the vaulted basements to be held for who knows how long. They saw also the supplies for the castle arriving in farm wagons from the tenants or from York and beyond.

Over the weeks of Spring the children learned to ride their ponies which had been brought from Middleham. At first they merely walked them along the High Street with the grooms in charge of the leading reins, until they arrived at the Church of St. Helen's and the Holy Cross at the far end, and then urged their ponies to walk round the edge of the graveyard to scan the country to the east. Nearby the land fell quite sharply away and a track disappeared from view before re-appearing on its way to Bulmer. A large rounded hill arose to the north-east with buildings just visible on its summit and away to the north. These were the home and stables at Stittenham of the Gower family whose present head, Sir Thomas, had welcomed them to castle at Sheriff Hutton. Other hills arose to the east, on several of which there were windmills with their sails turning in the western breeze. One day when they had become more proficient on their ponies, they would hack over those hills, and go to visit Lady Alice Gower in her ancient home that had belonged to the Gowers since Sir Alan Gower had been Sheriff of Yorkshire under William the Conqueror. Here legend had it that a Gower killed one of the last wolves in England in Stittenham Woods, the incident from which the family took the wolf as their crest. Ben had the children entranced with his tales, and when they had returned home they made him promise to tell them more stories about their ride next time.

There was plenty for him to tell for on their next ride they dismounted at the church, and wandered into the nave of the old Norman building. Crossing themselves at the holy stoup as they had been taught, they first lit a candle each, according to Ben's instructions. Then he told them to look at the wall paintings all around them, as they gradually became alive in the flickering light. Rather eerie in the gloom, the pictures of the crucifixion, the Last Supper, of the Virgin Mary and St. Joseph and the Baby in the

53

manger, all had a familiar ring, and reminded them of the church of St. Alkelda at Middleham. More scary was the painting of the Great Reaper with his ghastly face and his scythe ready to cut off the lives of sinners. In the newly built side aisles there were square-headed windows just like the ones at Middleham, and likewise filled with coloured glass which produced its own mysterious light into the church.

"Look!" said Isabel as she spied the white Nevill saltire on its red ground at the top of one window. "There are our Arms."

"And look here" said Anne, gazing at the stone effigy of a knight in armour with crossed legs. "Is he a Nevill?"

"No" said Ben. "He is Sir Edmund Thweng from Cornborough Manor, and he died over a hundred years ago. He was an ancestor of the present Sir William at Cornborough."

When they arrived back at the castle, Ella met them at the bottom of the spiral staircase up to their apartments, and was eager to hear about their ride, especially to the church, thinking that next time she would go with them to make a better job than Ben of explaining about the places they would visit.

"I expect you would like to visit the old Norman castle next to the church. Did you notice the ruins up the hill at the side of the churchyard?" She could see by their bright faces that they had, so the following week Ella also mounted a fine horse to accompany the girls but instead of riding as far as the churchyard, they turned up across the Green, then eastwards along the brow of the hill until they came opposite the church which was below them to their left. At first they were surrounded by a maze of ruined walls which marked the outer bailey of the old Norman castle. Much of the stonework had been carted away to build the new castle they now lived in, which had been begun by their great-great-grandfather, John Nevill, once he obtained permission from King Richard II in 1382 to do so. Old John had died in 1388, and his son, Ralph Nevill, lst Earl of Westmorland[3], carried on with the construction of his new castle at the same time as he was making all sorts of improvements to Middleham Castle to bring it up to a comfortable standard in which to live.

"But here we are now amongst the ruins of the old stone castle probably built about 1140 by Bertram de Bulmer who was lord of the manor, and became Sheriff of Yorkshire - " explained Ella.

"Which is why this is called Sheriff Hutton" triumphantly chorused Isabel and Anne.

"Quite right" said Ella. "And what sort of a castle was it?"

"Motte and bailey; here's the motte on this little hill, and round it is the inner bailey, and where we came through was the outer bailey, wasn't it?"

It gave them quite an odd feeling to think that their great great grandfather had actually lived within the ruined walls on this mount only about eighty years ago, and how he had had to await a reply from the king to give him permission to build his new fortified demesne at the other end of the township. At last a horseman had come galloping up the road from York and in at the castle gate with the reply - "Go ahead with your castle - we shall be pleased to have a further defence in this part of our realm."

So it was that the great new castle with its corner towers which could be seen right across the Forest of Galtres grew up at the west end of Hoton, on the spur overlooking the Vale of York, designed in much the same manner as the Scrope's new castle of Bolton in Wensleydale. Here too the domestic buildings in the inner court were constructed as part and parcel of the curtain walls, and with no central keep as at Middleham. The days of the formidable keep built solely for war, were over, but this did not detract from the sight of this vast pile set up on its crag to the north of the Forest, and as visible proof of Nevill power to all those around.

Gradually the children learned proficiency at handling their ponies, and their hacking sessions increased in distance and complexity. They learned to trot, to rein in the ponies, to spur them on, to guide them on one way or the other, and to stop when directed. Instead of riding locally and mainly on the level, they attempted hills, both up and down, which were available in every direction from the castle. Then one day they rode down the track towards the Forest of Galtres, the mysteries of which had held them in thrall ever since they had come through Brafferton and Easingwold on their journey from Middleham, and along its northern edge to Hoton. There was something magical and mysterious, elusive and even fearsome about the very name of Galtres. As they rode to the top of Bracken Hill, the whole expanse of it was laid out infront of them in a great flat plain punctuated with sparkling areas where the bogland gave way to ponds and flooding. To the east and west much of the old Forest was assarted and now farmed; to the south-west stood the towers and spires of York; but between them and that great city was a thick blanket of trees, now just changing into its Spring-time splendour; oaks and birches, alders and beeches. But the woodland, thick and almost impenetrable as it was in parts, had dispersed amongst it the green launds with their rich grazing and wild flowers, and between these again were the natural ponds and wetlands of the forest floor. The sounds were those of nature almost exclusively, the twittering of nesting birds, the calls of a jay and cooing of wood pigeon; there was the baying of a fox, the clashing of deer's antlers, the snuffling of wild boar and the more domesticated pigs hunting for beechnuts amongst the trees. Here and there the riders came across foresters clearing the undergrowth to use as fencing or to strengthen the clay walling of a cottage, or a peasant burning wood for charcoal in the beehive ovens of turf, gently and lazily smoking away hour by hour. The smell of the burning wood reached far, as did the occasional human voice or barking dog, but in the main it was a peaceful place where the deer were allowed to roam and the appearance of the descendants of the last wild boar did not surprise. Dangers there were though from robbers who could waylay travellers and steal their jewels or money, could kill or maim to carry out a threat or repay a wrong, so a wise person never travelled alone through the shadowy remoteness of Galtres, and the Warwick children were fair kidnap material and could never ride without an escort.

As they approached the lower slopes of Bracken Hill on this present occasion, the track became less and less steep as it ran towards the old wooden bridge over the River Foss which creaked and groaned as they crossed.

"Will those peasants never keep this bridge in repair?" grumbled Ben, making a mental note to complain to the Steward, who would refer the matter to the manor court which in turn would fine the men responsible for maintaining the highways and bridges in good trim, in this case the church wardens and tenants at Sutton-on-the-Forest.

After the bridge, the track divided, one branch continuing south to Strensall, and the other abruptly turning west towards St. John's Well. But first they passed a turning to the lord's warren where his keeper bred rabbits for the kitchens at the castle, in artificial mounds soon taken over by the implanted conies. The children listened with their mouths open in disgust while their grooms enlarged on the production of rabbit meat, and felt rather more at home as they approached the pilgrim centre of St. John's Well. This was an ancient site with a constant upsurge of beautifully clear bubbling water from a spring on a branch from the nearby White Carr Beck. It was a holy place, so Ella told them as she crossed herself and bade them do the same. The Well had healing powers of both mind and body which was no doubt why the White Carr Beck was so named. People came here from near and far when they had any troubles in order to drink its waters and pray for a miracle cure. There was a square stone parapet on which one could sit and take in the beauty of the place in its surrounding woodland, and only the sounds of the Forest and the gurgling of the water broke the silence. A causeway ran off to the north-west connecting the Well with Moxby Priory less than a mile away across the East Field and the moor. This was a Benedictine (later Augustinian) nunnery between the Well and Stillington, an offshoot of the 12th century Priory of Marton, and doubtless both religious houses were connected to the Well by prayer and intercession. Ella quickly crossed herself again three times, and the children, looking rather overawed, did so too.

All around them ranged the woodland of birch and oak, some alder, and occasional great beech trees under which snorting pigs raked for last Autumn's beechnuts. Among the trees were largish patches of grass and wild flowers, the lunds where the deer grazed and at a single sound, leaped back in their dainty fashion to the safety of the woodland to hide. Sometimes the children saw the animals of the forest drinking from the pools, and the wild duck, the moorhens and coots swimming around with their young, little fluffy bundles of liveliness; even herons flying overhead with an eye to the fish in the streams and ponds, suddenly swooping down to attack their victims with their long sharp beaks. If one sat quietly for a little while the whole forest came alive with birds' song or movement, rustling in the undergrowth, the rutting of deer in season, the barking of foxes, the monotonous croak of frogs, and sometimes the whistle of a peasant calling his dog to heel. The reeds and rushes of the bogland which alternated with the firm and partly assarted ground, hid the homes of bird and mammal, and the early efforts of their young to swim and dive. Isabel and Anne though so young, sensed the peace of the forest, and yet its industry and never ending activity. Even the frightened screech of a baby rabbit under attack was all part of the forest's pattern of eternally changing season, just as the woody smell of the charcoal burning, the perfume of the wild flowers, and the distinctive sweet loamy fragrance of wet leaves were part of the sequence. It was a magical, busy place, but which over-awed and mystified the children by its secrets and size.

The forest was very quiet today, and they hardly dared to break the holy silence to ask their string of questions which felt as if they were bursting open their heads trying to come out. Why? How? When? Where? And around it all an aura of mystery and other worldliness was almost palpable. They were for once in their lives, silent.

And that, said Ella afterwards, was a miracle in itself, and now they must return home before they were exhausted. Yes, they would come again another day, and ride on over Thorpe Hill to Sutton-on-the-Forest to see where many of the Castle retainers lived, and the providers of their food laboured.

"Why do you keep turning round?" Anne asked her sister as they started homewards, this time splashing through the shallows of the River Foss and up a diagonal path past Cornborough manor.

"I think the Well is rather a ghostly place" Isabel answered. "It's both holy and ghostly, and makes me a bit afeared. I hope we don't ever meet the spirits of the water when we ride in the Forest. I shall gallop away very quickly if I see them, and I shan't wait for you," she declared as they both jerked at their reins and gave little kicks at the ponies' flanks until they broke into a canter only deterred by the steepness of the hill up to Cornborough. They only met one traveller as they mounted the hill, a nun in her black Benedictine habit walking down from the chapel of St. Giles at Cornborough towards St. John's Well. She bowed her head as she passed them, and when they turned in order to watch her descend the hill, she had disappeared.

"That's odd" said Isabel. But Ella only humphed, and again crossed herself energetically.

"It's the Forest that causes it," she said.

"Tell us!" the children clamoured, but she only humphed again, and hurried on.

From that moment the children grew more and more curious about the Forest, and nagged at Ella until she promised to take them into it again.

"We'll go to Sutton-on-the-Forest today," she at last announced. "We'll ride to Foss House below Mill Hill, and then down and across to Thorpe which is the hamlet just this side of Sutton, and then see if you are too tired to go further."

Once Mass and lessons were over, the page came to announce that the ponies were saddled and waiting. This time, once through the gateway to the Castle, they turned onto a steep path along the south side of the Castle, descending diagonally down the rocky mound on which the Castle was built until they could look almost vertically up to their own windows in the tower high above them. On their right there was a small postern let into the vaults below the Great Hall. On their left, far below, was a defensive waterway which doubled as fishponds. The vast stone walls of the Castle glowered above them, until they reached the level ground west of their own tower, and the track levelled out towards the outer gateway near the highway to York. They breathed a sigh of relief. It had been a difficult slope down which to negotiate their ponies.

Now they crossed onto a small bridle path, riding along towards Cornborough, just below the summit of the ridge for a short way, and then diagonally down the hill below the windmill, to the Foss where they found stepping stones leading to Brown Moor which had common grazing rights, and through St. John's Well plantation. They passed Thrush House along one of the balks separating the groups of furlongs, to the tiny hamlet of Thorpe on its low mound. Here there was no church and no inn, but a view westwards along the townstreet of Sutton-on-the-Forest with its thatched cottages lining each side of the muddy track through the village.

Sutton-on-the-Forest Church of All Hallows in 1987 AMM

At the far end of the townstreet the land rose a little before falling towards the village green, and also all along the north side of it ran a ridge on which were the crofts of villagers, which obscured the hills to the north. Where the street rose, ("the dead centre of Sutton" said one wag!), to the north was the church, whilst opposite it was one of the largest houses in the area, that of the bailiff. Both house and church were thatched, but whereas the bailiff's house was timber-framed with wattle and daub infill, the church was wholly built of soft sandstone. Standing back from the street, and at a higher level, with its churchyard infront of it, and with a farm to one side and the vicarage to the other to form a walled courtyard, it made an impressive sight.

"Can we go inside?" the children wanted to know, and when the grooms had helped them to dismount and tied the reins to a metal ring in the church wall, they saw that the vicar, Thomas Birtby, was coming towards them from his glebe where he had been hoeing his crops. With his black clerical dress tucked up in his leather belt, he could have been one of his own peasant parishioners, his lined and grimed hands hurriedly rubbed over with damp leaves on his way to greet his august visitors. Bowing respectfully, and mumbling a few words of greeting, he led the way into church.

Inside it seemed very dark after the sunlight outside, and it took several minutes before their eyes were accustomed to the gloom. Then they gradually became aware that the entire building was covered in wall paintings, many of bright and crude colours, toned down by the earthy terracotta and the soot-black of some of the characters in the pictures. Even the pillars between the north aisle and the recently build nave were patterned with swirls and bands of colour, and the coloured glass in the windows transferred its brilliance across the interior. The painting which transfixed them immediately was one on the wall opposite the entrance door, between the small early 15th century windows. There was a frightening figure in black, with his long hair tousled, his ugly face lined with fearful grimace, and in his hands he clutched a scythe ready to cut down mankind. Indeed, below him there was a painting of a skull, and also an hourglass to time the life left to some poor human being. Around this Father Time, lay sprawled, figures writhing in purgatory, and to the east of the church there were pictures painted on the whitewash of saints and angels, the Last Supper, the Baby Jesus with his Holy Mother, and over the rood screen the Crucifixion.

There was little furniture in the church except for the stone altars, a large one under the great east window given by their great great grandfather, John Nevill, and sundry other smaller altars around the nave. All were marked with small crosses, as was the water stoup near the door and near each altar. Only the parson had a desk from which to read the Rites, and the clerk to assist in the readings. Mostly the congregations stood or kneeled, or even sat on the mud floor, but around the edge of the nave were wooden benches for the old and infirm to use. It all was very reminiscent of the church at Middleham, especially the Decorated east window which had also been given by Grandfather John for the original east end, now a chantry chapel to the Nevills.

While Father Birtby lit the row of candles along the front of the roodscreen to form a flickering glow below the Holy Cross, and the wax dripped from the iron candelabra above the chancel step, the children gazed around at the impressive and rather eerie little church, asking questions to Ella, "Why? Why? Why?" and of Father

Birtby who tried to give erudite answers for which he was hardly qualified. But as to the saints, he reminded them that this church was dedicated to "All Saints", and hence the multitude of portrayals, but that the east window glass specially showed the head of the Virgin Mary, adorned with a blue veil, and surrounded by a halo, whilst also there were John the beloved disciple and Saint Joseph, surrounded by pinnacles and spires, arches and Decorated stonework more typical of the fourteenth century in England.

Following Ella's example they fingered the holy water in the ochre painted octagonal stoup near the doorway, and crossed themselves, mumbling Hail Marys, and genuflecting with each repeat. The floor of compacted mud was covered with rushes which had seen and smelt better days. The children were glad to emerge back into the sunshine and fresh air of the churchyard with its yew trees, its many memorials in sandstone or wood, and its stone cross on a plinth from where Father Birtby sometimes taught his flock. Here also the bailiff organised the cultivation of the open fields, or the constable the repair of the highways through the village. This was the social centre of the community where bargains were made, and sales of corn or animals agreed, marriages of sons and daughters arranged, and meetings of all sorts occurred, whether for business or pleasure.

Isabel and Anne were impressed, and not least by the villagers who were wandering into the churchyard to look at these fine young ladies in their splendid riding habits, and their grooms and servants and even the ponies, all with the Bear and Ragged Staff emblem on their apparel. They stood back as the Castle party moved off, some touching their forelocks respectfully, the women bobbing a curtsey, the small children sucking their fingers in awe, the bigger ones running to keep up with the ponies. Opposite the church they could see the large house of the bailiff, and down the slope of the High Street to the west, the village green with its grazing cows and scattered chickens and ducks, its pond, its well, and its blacksmith's shop. A group of old men sat on benches smoking their clay pipes, and women were returning from the church to fill their leather buckets at the well before going back home to their never-ending labours.

As the party made its way back along the townstreet, the children stared into the open doorways of the tiny cottages, often two-roomed, or some with an addition, the "netherend", built back into the garth behind, and some with a tiny window in the gable to give sparing light to an attic room under the eaves. To Anne it all looked as dirty as at Middleham. The people to her eyes were filthy, and the houses mere hovels with the floors of mud like the church, and many of the windows without glass, but covered with thick hemp sheets to keep out the cold. The roadway was muddy too, and uneven though some patches had been infilled with sand to flatten the ruts. In winter it must be either a mire or a mass of hard furrows.

Anne shivered. She had seen enough for one day, and wanted to get back from the smelliness and the poverty of it all to her own home. Thank goodness she did not have to live like that and work on the strips of land hoping that the wheat and the pulses would flourish and the family cow would continue to give milk, the hens to lay. But then, these peasants were stupid and anyway they belonged to the manor, and really they were nobodies and didn't matter.

On the way home they passed wagons of root vegetables being carted to the castle to feed its numbers of retainers and their families, just as they had seen the wagons loaded high bringing grain to the castle from the mill near Cornborough. Life seemed to continue for these people as a never-ending treadmill of dullness, but they did not look unhappy as they worked. Only the vagrants they met on the road had a hopeless heaviness of step and appearance as they trudged along. Other peasants had known no other life than they now endured.

CHAPTER 4

IN JUNE 1460 word went round that Anne's grandfather, father and cousin, the three Earls, of Salisbury[4], of Warwick[11], and Edward of March[18], the eldest son of the Duke of York, had returned from France to invade Kent and had then occupied London. In July a horseman came galloping up Bracken Hill from York to announce to Sir Thomas Gower that the Lancastrians had indeed been defeated at Northampton, and King Henry VI had been captured by the Earls. Aunt Cecily, Duchess of York, and her younger children had been released from the custody of her sister Anne, Duchess of Buckingham, and were lodging in Southwark at the house of Sir John Paston. The Duke of Buckingham[7] had been killed in an affray at Northampton, so poor Aunt Anne of Buckingham was doubly bereft. Meanwhile the Duke of York[6] felt it safe to return from Ireland in September, and the Duchess joined him at Hereford in October, leaving her children at the York's house, Baynard's Castle on the Thames just east of where the River Fleet flowed into the great river. They remained under the watchful eye of Sir John Paston, and were visited daily by their older brother, Edward, Earl of March. Baynard's Castle was an exciting place to live, not only for its marvellous views of the activity of the Thames, but also for its innate design. It had been re-built only thirty-five years previously by Humphrey, Duke of Gloucester in 1428, but because of his attainder, which meant his outlawing, it became the property of the king who gifted it to the Duke of York. From 1457 it was used as the Duke's London home. A characterful façade fronting onto the river displayed a striped effect by its many narrow turrets, augmented by hexagonal towers at each end. It was very impressive, and rumour had it that it was suitable for a king, and that the Duke of York meant to be the next king, the successor to King Henry VI.

The Nevill children heard many of these whispered reports even though they were so sheltered away in the North Riding of Yorkshire. And then one day in the Autumn when they returned to the castle after a ride to Cornborough, it was noticeable how many people were out and about in the town-street and the outer court at Sheriff Hutton. The excitement was palpable. Wagons and horses vied with each other for space. Ben, the groom, stopped a Warwick man to ask what was happening.

"The Earl[11] and Countess[12] are here!" was the shouted reply.

It was true, and soon after Ella and the children arrived up in their apartment, a servant entered with a request that as soon as they had washed in the rosewater which had been poured out already in pewter wash bowls for them to refresh themselves, they were to attend on the Lord and his Lady in their private suite in the south-west tower. Isabel and Anne grew wide-eyed with nervousness, and a mixture of pleasure and reserve. They put aside their riding clothes, and donned clean gowns and white cotton caps, dainty slippers over white hosen, and along they went, Anne holding Ella's hand very tightly, Isabel leading the way, but making sure they were following behind. A servant at the Earl's door bowed and admitted them. They had not seen their father since before Ludford, and their mother only briefly since, and it was always nerve-wracking to meet them again after such a long gap.

The Earl was in travelling clothes and high boots, his sword still in his belt, and Anne noticed that he smelt of a mixture of sweat and horses. He stood with his back to the fireplace, feet firmly apart, and inclined his head slightly in acknowledgement as they approached. Isabel curtsied to him without prompting - she was, after all, already nine and a half years old, and used to the conventions of a great house. The Earl responded in a distant manner as if his thoughts were far away, as indeed no doubt they were. But when she bobbed a curtsey to the Countess, she received a warm welcome and was immediately taken into her mother's embrace.

"Oh Madam, it is so good to see you!" the child exclaimed, tears in her eyes as she added "it has been so long."

"But you have been happy, child? Ella has looked after you well?"

65

"Oh yes, Madam. It has been fine to live here, but we have missed you". And then, turning to Anne, she directed "Come Anne. Curtsey to my Lord and my Lady - and stop sucking your fingers like a babby". Holding Ella's hand, Anne dared herself to obey, but briefly to the Earl, and with more enthusiasm to Countess Anne whom she only dimly remembered. Questions were asked as to their activities, their lessons, their ability to recite the Catholic Beliefs and the words of the Mass, and lastly about their riding forays, and in a short while the interview (for that was what it amounted to) was over, to everybody's relief.

The next few days were full of bustle and hubbub down in the courtyards. The smell of new bread arose from the ovens, the neighing of horses as they were newly reshod, the clanging of the blacksmiths' anvils as weapons and armour were repaired, the frantic stitching and cutting to repair leatherwork and boots. The Earl undertook inspections several times a day to ensure that all was to his satisfaction, though he hardly saw his children except by accident at their window. Their mother came up to see them every afternoon as the candles were being lit, and talked to them of the bravery of their father and uncles in battle. It all seemed very remote to Isabel and Anne. And then very soon, they woke one early morning to the clip-clop of horses, the grinding of wagon wheels on the cobbles of the courtyard as the soldiers and their followers left in an orderly fashion for Warwick. Countess Anne left in her litter a few days later with her own retinue of retainers and bodyguards. Once she and her train of servants had disappeared over the brow of Bracken Hill, everything at Sheriff Hutton gradually returned to normal as the local servants set about clearing up the rubbish and mess left behind the departing throng. All was quiet once more.

Christmas 1460 was a rowdy affair at Sheriff Hutton. Even when the children attended early morning Mass in the castle chapel there was unwonted merry-making to be heard within the precincts. It seemed to Isabel and Anne that Christmas was a grown-up's festival, and everyone except themselves and their Ella was tipsy and loud-mouthed. They could even hear the boisterous behaviour from their nursery, and it was rather frightening, so that they preferred to stay up in their own apartments which they decorated with branches of holly and streamers of ivy from the woodland

66

below the hill. When the sun was high in the sky they walked with Ella for company along the ridge to the old Norman castle, and then visited the parish church to admire the Christmas decorations and the many festive candles on the altars. Then home by the Highstreet, past the noisy Castle Inn where jollifications were already under way, and outside on the Green a tremendous snow-balling battle was in progress to the cheers and boos of onlookers. The villagers smiled at the Warwick children in friendly fashion - and perhaps with pity, mixed with envy - and some curtsied or touched their forelock. They were all enjoying their day's holiday until they were called back to the milking or feeding the stock. Next day they would be back at work on the land. Anne could not imagine such hardship, but they all seemed so happy, even those with crippling illness or disability. There was an unmistakable air of family cohesion that she envied and longed for. It made her uneasy, and surprised that such poor people could be so contented.

They had a special Christmas dinner alone with Ella in their nursery with the shouts of hilarity sounding from the courtyard. The spit-roasted wild duck was brought up on a big gold dish especially for the occasion. The feathers decorating the birds were covered in gold leaf, and it was stuffed with onions, parsley and "powdor douce" which contained ginger, cinnamon, nutmeg and a little sugar as a treat. It was garnished with rounds of boiled eggs coloured brilliant yellow with saffron. That was followed by jellies layered in different colours, together with a curd flan, and milk in gold cups. When they afterward said grace together, Anne really did feel thankful for being able to have such special fare rather than what she imagined most villagers could afford. But her thoughts were soon lifted when Merryman appeared and danced with the children, and did his own particular tricks to make them laugh. It was not such a bad Christmas after all.

At Sandal Castle near Wakefield, also a noisy party was in progress, where a very much smaller keep was housing the Yorks for a family celebration, Duke Richard and his Duchess Cecily, and most of their large family except the eldest, Edward. Yorkshire was a wild place anyhow at present, and Queen Margaret of Anjou, wife of Henry VI, was gathering together a large mob of fighting men, undisciplined but enthusiastic Lancastrians. Marching down towards York's army, a battle seemed imminent.

Anne Nevill's grandparents, the Earl of Salisbury[4] and Countess Alice, arrived at Sheriff Hutton in mid-December, but within a few days were off again to be with the Yorks at Sandal for Christmas, and his men to join York's army, bringing with them a succession of foot soldiers and their wives and sweethearts, their weapons and baggage trains. The Earl left behind him a necklace of white jasper stones for each of his Warwick grandaughters as his New Year gift, great foresight, as it turned out, and the only indication that these two young children figured at all in his plans for the future except as heirs to the fortune which their grandfather still hoped to amass, even the throne of England.

The week after Christmas was eerily quiet for Isabel and Anne, who carried on with their usual routine of Mass and lessons and meals, dancing and embroidery, and riding when the ground was not too frosty. The castle was empty of all but its skeleton staff now. The wagons continued to arrive from the fields, piled high with root vegetables and logs from the tenants, and return empty for further loads. Then on New Year's Eve once again a horseman wearing a ragged over-tunic bearing the Warwick emblem was to be seen galloping towards the gateway of the castle. He was mud-stained, exhausted and breathless, and his horse was in a similar state. Sir Thomas Gower saw him immediately he arrived, to hear that the Duke of York had emerged the day before from his castle at Sandal to challenge the Queen's[13] army at Wakefield, and had been bitterly defeated. Both he and his second son, Edmund,[19] Earl of Rutland had been killed. Later it became clear that the Earl of Salisbury had been captured, beheaded next day at Pontefract Castle, and now the heads of York[6], Salisbury[4] and Rutland[19] were being impaled on the east side of Micklegate Bar at York as a warning to others. Paper crowns were pulled over York's bleedy pates, which faced into the city, so that "York graced York" in this manner.

This was a rough and violent era, but even so, to lose your grandfather, an uncle and a cousin in this frightening fashion, was difficult to accept or to forget, however great and courageous one might think them, and Anne Nevill did neither. She was four and a half years old and her young mind was aware that this sort of obscenity occurred in war, but that great ladies such as herself were above such behaviour as openly to grieve. She was only acquainted with these men in a conventional way; there was no affection between them and this child of Warwick, and as long as she did not allow her imagination to visualise the actual scene on the scaffold or the gateway out of York, she could blank out her mind to the horror. Otherwise she would surely have nightmares about those dripping heads. On the other hand, men wounded and dying on the field of battle were only carrying out their duty, and the less said and thought about them, the better.

Isabel also took the news with remarkable equanimity as befitted the elder daughter of the Earl of Warwick. Death, natural or violent, happened so often - at St. Albans, at Northampton, and now at Wakefield, every few years, and it would go on repeating itself for ever. It was the way of things in the natural process of life. Only the most superficial emotion could be allowed to intervene. Feelings were to be kept out of it. Death was very near to everyone in the fifteenth century, and the Great Reaper's scythe always at the ready with fatal disease or accident. The retribution of purgatory after death was by far the most dreaded aspect of dying, and had to be atoned beforehand if possible. Was not this a reason for Ralph Nevill[11] to act with his brother George[28], future Archbishop of York, to found St. William's College in this fearful year of 1460 in order to save their own souls from perdition?

Christmas festivities in the 15th century usually lasted for a fortnight in the great houses and castles of England, until at last the junketings concluded after Epiphany. This Christmas of 1460 was curtailed almost at once as the fighting men left for Ferrybridge in order to cross the River Aire to join up with the rest of the White Rose armies gathering near Wakefield. No one had much heart for merriment that week, and once the news of the slaughter came through on the last day of the year, a gloom settled on the Yorkists.

The City of York, where King Henry[8] and Queen Margaret[13] and their son, Edward[14] were awaiting the news of the battle was thickly covered in windswept snow. At Sheriff Hutton on its hill some thirty miles away, the snow was even thicker, reflecting light into the castle windows so that the candles did not have to be lit quite so early, but the intense cold froze the water in the washing bowls and across the surface of the fishponds. Everyone's fingers and toes were almost frozen as well, even indoors, and the men wore leather jerkins and trousers with long leather gaiters, and thick boots and headware. The women changed into thick woollen over-mantles, kirtles and hosen, with wooden patons to lift them above the worst of the snow. Extra layers of hessian and wool coverlets on beds, and ember-filled warming pans between the sheets or the blankets helped to keep out the cold, and the log fires kept burning all night by a servant in attendance, was a mercy to the Nevill children. Still the staircases had to be tackled with determination and fortitude to endure the severe drop in the temperature which swept up and down them.

Edward of March[18], eldest son of the Duke of York, had been in the south-west at the time of Wakefield, dealing with the Welsh Lancastrians, and using his family home at Ludlow Castle as his headquarters. His efforts culminated in winning a decisive battle at Mortimers Cross on 2nd/3rd February, some eight miles south-west of Ludlow, against Jasper Tudor[9] Earl of Pembroke and the Earl of Wiltshire. Nearby was a crossing over the River Lugg adjacent to his old tutor's house at Croft, which he had thought to use as a backup. The story that filtered through to Isabel and Anne was of a miraculous vision of three sparkling suns suspended in the sky over the battlefield which was taken as an auger for victory - and which it turned out to be. From that day Edward took this picture of the "sun in splendour" to be his own special emblem, as Anne was soon to see in the newly inserted coloured glass windows in Sheriff Hutton church. After that she often noticed it on belongings and portraits of her cousin, the King, who immediately after the Battle of Mortimers Cross rode up to London where he was welcomed and proclaimed Yorkist King Edward IV on 4th March, to take the place of the weak Lancastrian King Henry VI.

Meanwhile Ella told the children that the Queen[13] had gathered up the Lancastrian forces after Wakefield, and was adding to them as she travelled south, where only a short time later, on 17th February there was yet another clash between the two sides, the Second Battle of St. Albans where the Lancastrians fought against the Yorkists under the Earl of Warwick, once again severely defeating him. But he survived, although his cousin, John Nevill, only son of the 2nd Earl of Westmorland was killed, so the sadness and misery which Anne could not understand, continued, White Rose and Red Rose at each other's throats, and the whole country taking the opportunity to settle scores on their neighbours, to pillage, rob and thieve.

"Duchess Cecily has decided that the situation is very dangerous," said Ella loftily, while her charges listened to the account of their elders' exploits open-mouthed. "She has sent your cousins, Edward's youngest brothers, George[21] and Richard[22], out of harm's way to the care of the Duke Philip of Burgundy, a very grand and wealthy court." said Ella, as if she had been there herself. "I wouldn't wonder if their sister Lady Margaret of York[20] joins it one fine day."

While Queen Margaret of Anjou[13] busily engaged the armies in a "Guess Where Next" competition, the household at Sheriff Hutton was packing up to move up to Middleham where they planned to celebrate Easter on 5th April, and to give time for the Castle of Sheriff Hutton to receive a thorough spring-clean and particularly a cleansing of its garderobes which had given heavy service over the winter. The Spring was beginning to appear, and the days becoming longer. Trees and bushes were showing green, the birds were starting to sing as they gathered material for nesting; doves in their cotes were cooing desultorally, and there was some warmth in the air. Light ploughing was being repeated on the furlongs, and great sacks of seedcorn were being dragged from barns and cottage attics preparatory to sewing immediately there was a sign of settled weather. At Middleham the ewes were being herded into stone-walled pens on the lower slopes of the hills in readiness for lambing, when all at once the turf which had become green with the shoots of new grass, was covered once again with a sprinkling of snow.

The journey from Sheriff Hutton was long and rather tedious for the Nevill children, cosy though they were tucked in their litter together for warmth. Their mother, Countess Anne, accompanied them in her own litter but kept the curtains drawn most of the way. Perhaps she was snoozing the hours away, wondered the children. Their personal servants rode beside them, sheltering them from unwanted attention from local people. This time the countryside was alive with men and women who had returned from Wakefield, and were either recovering from wounds, or preparing to return south with the York forces. Theft and assault were real possibilities for travellers, who dared not journey after dark. It was rumoured

71

that the Lancastrian forces were roaming the country, and the Nevill's great rivals, the Percys of Northumberland, were on the march. It was exciting, but frightening too, and the party from Sheriff Hutton had their own fighting men ready with swords and battleaxes, bows and arrows, to fend off any attack on their train. Infront rode the vanguard on the lookout for trouble, and behind an equally important rearguard to defend those coming last in the procession north.

After a long journey, slowed down by rising winds and flakes of snow, at last they saw the towers of Middleham Castle along the valley, until they were hidden by the houses surrounding the narrow entrance to the marketplace. Opening up before them unfolded the majestic picture of the castle's curtain walls, with the towers and the gateway enlarged and beautified by statues of armed men by their grandfather only a few decades ago.

It was up to this passageway into the inner courtyard that they were now driven, through the great heavy oak door already opened by the guard on duty as soon as the travellers were identified by the man surveying the approach road from the roof. The portcullis clanked up, and soon they were at the foot of the south-west tower and being helped down from the litters. When they at last climbed up to it, nothing seemed to have changed in their nursee, and especially the familiar views over Wensleydale, and within the castle their secret view across the inner court.

As the week progressed towards Palm Sunday, snow began to fall in earnest, and the wind whipped it up into thick drifts against the curtain walls and beyond the moat. The outline of the hills became blurred by the accumulation of snow on the ridges, and the sheep pens and shepherd's cotes out on the slopes were blotted out as they sank beneath the white blanket. Isabel and Anne were soon out there with their leather boots securely tied above their ankles. Playing snowballs was fine as long as your hands in their thick leather gauntlets remained warm and dry, but very soon Anne was crying with the pain of frozen fingers, and they had to go back to the big fire in the nursee. The next day they went out again for a short while, but it was clear that the thoughts of the whole household were with their comrades, husbands and sons, who would soon be battling with the Lancastrians somewhere near the crossing over the River Aire. Messengers arrived every few hours, having struggled through the snowdrifts, with updates on where the battle was being fought, and at last, on Palm Sunday the final location was a moor between two small villages near Tadcaster, called Saxton and Towton. It was turning out to be one of the biggest battles ever fought on English soil, "perhaps 40,000 Yorkists and 60,000 Lancastrians" took part.

Edward Plantagenet, eldest son of Duchess Cecily and the Duke of York, who had recently been proclaimed King Edward IV had arrived from London to lead the Yorkist armies, together with the Earl of Warwick[11] and Warwick's brother, the Earl of Fauconberg from Skelton Castle near the Tees. King Henry VI and his queen remained in York with their son, and the Lancastrian forces were lead by the Duke of Somerset.

"Poor souls" said Ella, crossing herself, when she heard the size of the encounter, the weather conditions and the likely number of casualties.

The snow was now falling heavily in Uvedale, and Anne wondered if when people were wounded in battle, the blood dropped onto the snow, turning it red. That night she did have a nightmare. She sat up in the big bed she shared with Isabel, screaming at the top of her young voice: "The sun in splendour has turned red with blood" she kept repeating, and Ella came rushing over to reassure her, and tuck her down again with the frightened Isabel. The next morning it all seemed unreal and the white light streaming through the nursee windows was reflected from the pure white snow on the hills around Middleham, making their room seem even more eerie.

But the following days brought back the feelings of fear and shock when fugitives from the battle soon began to struggle through the snow, those on horseback soonest, then wagon-loads of wounded men, some still with their breastplates strapped on, their clothes soaked with blood and snow, their cries of pain gnawing at the children's heart-strings, most groaning as they died, the freezing conditions releasing the poor souls all the sooner from their hell. Every now and then a weary group of women trudged after their men-folk to give what comfort they could, and at last to see them laid to rest in bed or grave.

Terrible stories were told of the battle, which continued from first light until the night fell, how the arrows of the Lancastrians fell short of their target because of the strength of the wind, and how the fighting soon became hand-to-hand, with the greatest ferocity; how the wounded were finished off by sword or knife as they lay in the snow. And then in the early afternoon when it seemed that a decisive victory could never be reached one way or the other, the Yorkist Duke of Norfolk brought in over 5,000 fresh soldiers who had hidden behind the hill crests, and attacked the Lancastrian lines of weary men, forcing them down the steep slope of the battlefield to the River Cock which they stumbled across or slumped down in its flooded waters, already turning red by the savagery of the fighting. Over their bodies struggled their comrades, fleeing from the horrors on the hillside behind them, only to find that the River Wharfe at Tadcaster had to be crossed - by its bridge if they were lucky - and so pursued by their foes all the way to the outskirts of York where King Henry[8] and the Queen[13] and Prince of Wales[14] were anxiously based, but were now preparing to escape north to safety.

Near 40,000 Englishmen were killed in miserable conditions that day on Towton Dale. Many of them were later buried where they fell, others in mass graves north of Saxton Church or near the chapel of Saint James at Towton, some near the little Church of Lead, the other side of the blood-stained Cock, the mounds still visible many centuries later. The bodies of the noblemen wrapped in their banners, were taken back to their homes by their widows for burial; only Lord Dacre receiving burial in a known grave near the battlefield. The Dukes of Somerset and Exeter, commanders of the Red Rose force, fled to the King at York; the triumphant King Edward and the Earls of Warwick and Fauconberg, also first rode to York to remove the decaying heads of Edward's father and brother, the Dukes of York[6] and Rutland[19], and that of Warwick's father, the Earl of Salisbury[4], from Micklegate Bar, after which they rode on north to Middleham to rest and celebrate the victory.

Only parts of these reports came to Anne Nevill's ears; such as she heard she could only partially comprehend. Even the numbers of the dead were beyond her understanding; one thousand signified a great many; forty thousand was unimaginably more. To her it meant a blur stretching as far as she could conceive, of poor mauled men, hurt and cut about, bruised and bleeding - and dead, that grim word, God rest their souls. And, following Ella's example, she crossed herself whenever she thought of it. Ella tried to explain, but a small child, not yet five, found it difficult to see why such dreadful deeds were done. Isabel, at nine was more sophisticated, and born at the beginning of a decade of civil war, she had learnt to protect her sensitivities by the realisation that life was of no value unless it could be used for the glory of the Country, England. The peasant was an expendable and very small cog in the machine of government, and his family little better than the animals on his own crofts. The most important result of the battle at Towton Dale was that their father, the great Earl of Warwick, was now the most eminent person in the country after King Edward, whom he had put firmly on the throne of England. The old king, Lancastrian Henry VI, would have been imprisoned by the new King Edward of York, had he not fled north with his queen.

Gradually the names of the fallen lords became known at Middleham; most of them either relatives or neighbours: John Lord Nevill, brother of the 2nd Earl of Westmorland, newly given custody of Sheriff Hutton castle after Wakefield; Lord Fitzhugh of Ravensworth, a few miles north of Richmond; Lords Fitzwater and Scales, Lord Willoughby whose daughter Maud had married Thomas Nevill; and on the Lancastrian side, Lord Shrewsbury who was thought to have cut down the young Earl of Rutland at Wakefield, Sir Anthony Trollope and Henry Percy, Earl of Northumberland, whose head was subsequently taken to adorn London Bridge, and many others whose names came trickling in during the days after the battle.

Countess Anne, who had remained at Middleham over the preceding weeks, ordered that the Nevill children come across the connecting bridge from the nursee every afternoon to her apartment in the keep, and sometimes to the Ladychamber in the west range of the castle, and there she asked them what they understood about the Battle of Towton. She found that they were very hazy, although Isabel knew how important it was to the Yorkist cause, and that her cousin Edward Plantagenet[18], eldest son of the widowed Great Aunt Cecily, Duchess of York[5] was now King Edward IV. Later that week they were excited to be told that their father was bringing Edward up to Middleham to celebrate the victory, and the beginning of his reign. It was also Edward's nineteenth birthday on 28th April, so there was plenty in which to rejoice, and the chill of fear which all those wagon-loads of helpless men had provoked in Anne's imagination was exchanged for happiness. She never remembered having seen her cousin Plantagenet before.

Very soon the sound of the Earl of Warwick's horsemen clip-clopping into the outer ward from where the snow had been cleared, followed by the baggage wagons, could be detected, and the cheers echoing from the town as more and more of his followers arrived from Towton. Anne and Isabel watched the main gateway as the King and the Earl slowly entered into the inner-ward on horseback, and then, as the grooms held the bridles, each man slipped to the ground. How young the King looked! And how tall! Like most of the Plantagenets, Edward was immensely tall - 6ft 3 inches, it was said - upright and slim, fair-haired, and of a fair countenance, with bright intelligent blue eyes which sometimes drooped down lazily when disinterested, augmented by a winning smile. Born in Rouen in 1442 where his father, the Duke of York, was then King Henry VI's lieutenant-general in France, and where his brother, Edmund, was born the following year, he had had the chequered career of being eldest son of the Pretender to the Throne of England, having been only thirteen at the time of the first Battle of St. Albans in 1455 when the King was first captured and the War of the Roses began in earnest. It was fuelled by the years of feuding between the two noble families of Percy and Nevill, leading to wide-spread disorder and lawlessness, particularly in Yorkshire.

Edward's eldest sister, Anne, was born at Fotheringhay Castle, her mother's favourite home, in 1439; she later became the Duchess of Exeter. Henry was the York's eldest son, but died in infancy, and then came Edward and Edmund, both born in Rouen, followed by Elizabeth, born in 1443, who became Duchess of Suffolk; then three more sons who died in infancy, Margaret[20], born in 1446, who eventually became Duchess of Burgundy, and lastly George[21], later Duke of Clarence, Richard[22], ultimately a King, and the youngest Ursula, born in 1455, the year the War of the Roses commenced, and thus only a year older than Ann Nevill.

Edward and Edmund were mainly brought up at Ludlow Castle, first under the care of their Norman nurse, Anne of Caux, who remained with the family until old age, but handed over her responsibilities as the boys grew older to a tutor, or "governor", Robert Croft of Croft in Herefordshire. Although mainly concerned with the boys' lessons in general, he also had to see that they received instruction in law, religion, etiquette, and the martial arts - everything that they might need to know in their future lives as heirs to their Ducal father and his aspirations to the throne.

When Isabel and Anne first saw their cousin Edward, they instantly took to this handsome and attractive young man, who already had several times been through the heat of battle, and survived with distinction. It even crossed Isabel's mind that her father might be considering whether a marriage between Edward and herself should be arranged, so naive was she and so unaware of her father's rabid ambitions, regardless as to whether she would be happy as Edward's wife. That was of secondary importance. In fact it would not have deterred the Earl from the arrangement if it suited his purpose. Had not Elizabeth Paston at Caistor in Norfolk been flogged again and again when she refused to marry the choice of her father and mother who was a battered and ugly widower of fifty? But nothing was said about a betrothal now, so instead of feeling neglected, Isabel reminded herself that there were other fish in the sea, even though Edmund had been killed, as Edward still had two brothers who were very eligible.

Later that week Edward asked to meet his host's two daughters, so, having changed into their best gowns and caps, especially made for the occasion from pink silk damask embroidered with white roses, and soaked their hands in rose water which they hoped would waft out its perfume enticingly to their cousin, the girls tripped across the wooden bridge to the keep where their father and mother were awaiting them in the grand audience chamber, accompanied by the dashing Edward, the heir to the Yorkist Plantagenet fortunes. Feeling rather nervous, they curtsied in their very best style, and he with knightly gallantry, raised them to their feet as if they were great ladies. He was so very tall, and they were so small, that he seemed to dominate the Great Hall even before he spoke, but his eyes softened as he said he hoped they would dance with him at the celebrations being prepared. In fact he decided to come riding with them as soon as the snow had disappeared, and Countess Anne looked pleased when she heard about this as if her little plan was coming to fruition, but warned the children that Edward was the King, and that he had much work to do in council before he returned to London for his coronation in June.

Family of the Duke of York
1411 - 1460

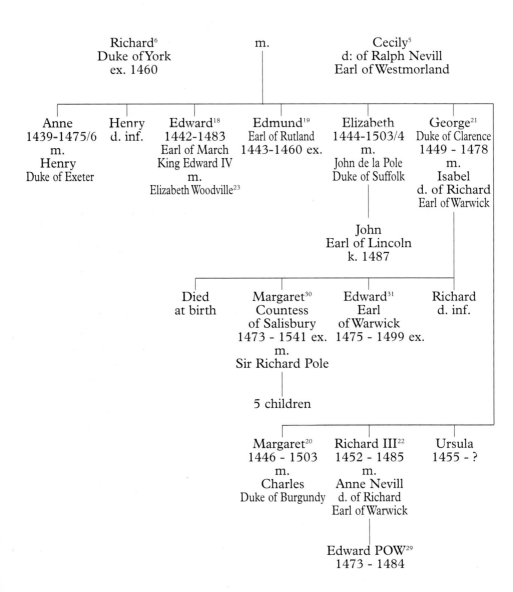

Richard[6]
Duke of York
ex. 1460

m.

Cecily[5]
d: of Ralph Nevill
Earl of Westmorland

Anne	Henry	Edward[18]	Edmund[19]	Elizabeth	George[21]
1439-1475/6	d. inf.	1442-1483	Earl of Rutland	1444-1503/4	Duke of Clarence
m.		Earl of March	1443-1460 ex.	m.	1449 - 1478
Henry		King Edward IV		John de la Pole	m.
Duke of Exeter		m.		Duke of Suffolk	Isabel
		Elizabeth Woodville[23]			d. of Richard
					Earl of Warwick

John
Earl of Lincoln
k. 1487

Died	Margaret[30]	Edward[31]	Richard
at birth	Countess	Earl	d. inf.
	of Salisbury	of Warwick	
	1473 - 1541 ex.	1475 - 1499 ex.	
	m.		
	Sir Richard Pole		

5 children

Margaret[20]	Richard III[22]	Ursula
1446 - 1503	1452 - 1485	1455 - ?
m.	m.	
Charles	Anne Nevill	
Duke of Burgundy	d. of Richard	
	Earl of Warwick	

Edward POW[29]
1473 - 1484

That day the aroma was of roasting beast and baking bread, spices of great value, pepper and ginger, cinnamon and nutmeg, mace, cardamoms and cloves, galingale, grains of paradise and cubebs. Luxuries such as sturgeon and porpoise, deer and boar, waterfowl and bustard, were on the menu, and the beautiful white bread called pandemaine. The triumph of the meal was the stuffed swan dressed up as a processional centre-piece for the top table. Dish after dish was brought in from the vast kitchens under the Great Chamber, perhaps as many as twenty different items, all beautifully presented with decoration of gold leaf alternating with yellow from saffron, red from sandalwood, and green from parsley.

Although the children sometimes sat down with the household at the daily meal, which was a state occasion when the earl was in residence, they had never been to a celebration meal except for Christmas, and not always then. Last Christmas, just before Wakefield, it had been a subdued affair, but now in late April 1461, there was everything to rejoice in, not least the presence with them at Middleham of the new king. Isabel and Anne on this occasion sat with Ella at the Rewarde table, the table nearest below the High Table on its dais where the parents and the king sat under a canopy, and as many of the nobility as could be accommodated - Scropes and Fitzhughs, Dacres and Darcys. Then, down the long hall sat, strictly in order of distinction, the large numbers of the Earl's henchmen, including the chaplain, the constable of the castle, the steward (to keep an eye on his underlings). The Rewarde table was served with dishes from the High Table, except for the red meat which was thought to be bad for children who were given simple fare and plenty of milk. Opposite was the Second Messe, and then tables facing each other down as far as the gallery at the far end of the hall, and the partition which enclosed the service area and the spiral stairway down to the kitchens. Since the recent alterations carried out by Grandfather Salisbury to form an additional hall above the Great Hall, the steep-pitched roof with its fine timber beams and braces, was obscured by the new ceiling which was painted with all sorts of heraldic devices in gold and red and brilliant blue and green. The walls too were painted and whitened and hung with rich fabrics on which the Bear and the Ragged Staff were dominant. The old central hearth had also gone and a few braziers took their place, but were allowed to burn low as the company

Great Hall

exuded its own heat, fuelled by the wine, the ale (for the lesser ranks) and the spirit of joviality. Finally, after working through as many dishes as possible using bread trenchers as plates, spoons and pointed knives to manipulate the food, grace was said, and a toast (one of the many that night) drunk to the new King - "King Edward of England", after which the great feast rolled to its conclusion. Those that could still stand, staggered to their feet and made for the large round-headed doorway in the east wall, and half-slid, half-collapsed down the monumental staircase to find themselves in the fresh air near the north gateway. Meanwhile the pot-boys and scullions, spit-boys and bottle-washers began to clear up the debris, and to eat what remains they could scavenge. Then like everyone else in the castle, over-come by sleep, they retired to a corner of the kitchen or cellar, and collapsed on a sack of flour or pheasants. It made no difference what.

Next day the castle woke up fitfully and the atmosphere was grey and grumpy as it recovered from its excesses. The Warwick children knew better than to argue with Ella when she forbade any visiting to their parents. Certainly the Earl would be tense and his temper brittle with the responsibilities for the King's welfare and good opinion of his host, and the plans for the coronation looming up. As the sun warmed the hills around Uvedale, the horses were saddled and the falconers arrived with their birds hooded in anticipation of a day's sport, and soon the hunting party moved off with a couple of retrieving hounds to the sound of the horn.

A few days later the King left Middleham on his long ride to London to prepare for his coronation, and the Earl set off with his retinue to Sheriff Hutton from where he could conveniently hold conference in York with the Scot's representative in a rather hopeless effort to obtain peace in the Borders. Ella told the children that there would "never" be peace with the Scots. They were far too wild and forever sending raiding parties into England - just think of the damage and fear they had continued to create ever since the Battle of Nevill's Cross that old John Nevill had fought in 1346, and they would go on doing so for ever and a day. Meanwhile, she told them, the household at Middleham would soon be moving south, first to Sheriff Hutton, then probably to Fotheringhay to visit Great Aunt Cecily, and then Baynard's Castle in London where they would stay during the coronation festivities.

81

"Your cousins, George and Richard, will be returning from Calais," she added in an off-hand manner. The girls' faces brightened - anything for a change, they thought.

And so it was, and on the eve of the great ceremony in Westminster Abbey, they heard that George and Richard had both been created Knights of the Bath the previous evening at the Tower of London, and George[12] had even become a Knight of the Garter and Duke of Clarence. The girls were mightily impressed.

The coronation passed in a mist of excitement and noise and activity. Their father was obviously, after the King, the most important person present, and so of course the Countess of Warwick and her daughters received preferential treatment and respectful prominence. Anne, who was just five, hardly took in what was happening. The journey from Middleham had left her with a hazy memory of continually changing scenes which became mixed and muddled in her tired mind as a conglomeration of recollections which she was unable to sort out. For Isabel there was a clearer picture, but at ten even she found the continual clustering of events difficult to assimilate, the clearest probably the few days at Fotheringhay, where they were able to be free and roam the river banks and wander around the college south of the parish church, and the new house that Aunt Cecily was building for her family. London was noisy and unreal after the warm atmosphere of the Plantagenet household, and Isabel was still very much a naive girl with little experience of court. The most memorable happening was as the singing in the Abbey was soaring into the great roof, she spotted her two cousins, George and Richard in the group surrounding their brother, Edward, as he sat in King Edward the Confessor's great chair to be crowned. George ("we must call him Clarence now" she whispered more to herself than to Anne) was tall and fair like Edward, but Richard was much smaller, dark, and held one shoulder higher than the other - indeed he would have seemed insignificant was it not for his bright intelligent eyes. Both boys were dressed in court robes, coronets, and long white gauntlets as befitted brothers of the King.

Coming back to Sheriff Hutton was almost a relief after the bustle of London over the last few weeks. Middleham was receiving a spring-cleaning in anticipation of its being used much more in the future as the seat of the Court in the north of England, now that its master, the Earl of Warwick[11], was so powerful. Sheriff Hutton on its hill, and the lovely rides to the friendly villages around, was a real home to the girls, a comfortable welcoming place. This time, however, there was a change. The Earl seemed suddenly to have realised that his daughters were not only marriageable, but largely untrained in the niceties of court etiquette. Isabel especially was of an age to be betrothed - her mother had been far younger - and now a governess had been hastily engaged to teach the girls some French, a little Latin and history, and music, singing and recitation, dancing and embroidery. Some of these subjects they already had learned with the faithful Ella, but now they needed polishing by someone with personal knowledge of what was required by such heiresses. Their reading was to be pursued further than it had so far achieved, and although mostly from manuscripts, and often of religious relevance, they were to read Chaucer, the meditations of Saint Bernard, and such as Piers Plowman. Their governess was to be a cousin of their dear friend, Sir Thomas Gower of Stittenham, a widow who had no dowry to back her into further wedlock, and without this employment, would have joined the community at Moxby. Very soon after her arrival at the castle to fulfil her duties, she found that the girls were not always attentive, and she would sigh, even hide a yawn, and complain that she would soon be having a word with the prioress to arrange to join the Order, whereupon Isabel and Anne, dreading someone more strict in her place, would raise their voices, pretend to cry, and wriggle about in a silly way, protesting that they "would be good, truly, dear Mistress Gower."

From now on, riding across Mill Hill towards Moxby held increased interest for them, and if the nuns were working in the fields with the lay brethren, they would rein in their ponies, and stop to see what they looked like.

"Surely you will not be labouring like that if you become a nun?" they asked Mistress Gower.

"Of course not," she replied. "I am a lady and shall be doing lady's work - I shall be reading and embroidering, and such-like things."

Just after they returned from the coronation, hay-making was in full swing, the men were scything the meadows and the Sisters stacking the hay in haycocks, round in shape like beehives, and as tall as themselves. Then the wagon, drawn by two hefty oxen, would come along to be loaded and hay taken up to the barn to feed the cows through the winter, or to refill the mattresses and bolsters of the Sisters and the families of the lay workers. It was supposed to be infra dig for the young ladies from the castle to join in this work, but the young ladies themselves thought otherwise and slid to the ground from their ponies amongst the sweet-smelling hay and dried meadow flowers, and shyly started to gather armfuls of it to add to the nearest stack. The nuns working there smiled encouragingly, but Ella felt this was not quite as it should be and anyhow they were hardly dressed for the job, and their young arms would soon tire from the unaccustomed work. Besides, the sun was hot and would be burning their high-born white features to a common pastoral bronze, and that would never do. There was every reason to recall them back to their ponies, and return to the castle, grumbling under their breath as they went.

However, when they arrived home, a surprise awaited them as Mistress Gower came hurrying down to greet them.

"My Lord Richard[22] has this day been created a Knight of the Garter at a most splendid service in the Chapel of Windsor, and" said she in a voice full of mystery, "What else but that my Lord has been raised to be Duke of Gloucester! There now!"

Isabel smiled with pleasure. She was fond of her young cousin, even if he was not very handsome. But Anne clapped her hands together and jumped for joy.

"Hurrah!" she shouted in a most uninhibited and vulgar fashion.

"Hush!" Ella hissed. "Madam will not approve if she hears." Anne did hush, with something like "Phooey!" under her breath - which was more or less audible. Now Richard was equal in rank to his brother, Clarence.

CHAPTER 5

LIFE FOR CHILDREN in the 15th Century varied from extreme dullness and lack of variety, let alone excitement, to events that were so extremely exhilarating or agitating that sometimes they were anticipated for weeks beforehand. For peasant and tenant-farmer children, domestic chores and routine filled at least six days in the week, and even Sundays had their duties about the home such as feeding the hens or the family pig, milking the cow or bringing in the logs and kindling for the fire, and hanging the cooking pot on its tramel over the blaze to stew the vegetables for dinner - whilst the family went to Mass at the Parish Church - the water should have been fetched in the day before. The high days were Saints' days and other religious festivals, Easter, Christmas and Michaelmas (which coincided with the hirings), and especially Corpus Christi, when there might be plays and mummers to watch. Lent was a gloomy time, but again came the hirings on Lady Day, usually accompanied by archery contests and visits from travelling jugglers, Punch and Judy shows and peddlers with their packs of goods for sale.

For the nobleman's children there was a parallel divide between the day-to-day routine such as Isabel and Anne experienced and was quite normal in their eyes, and the particular events that punctuated their families' lives, often too great for children to comprehend, including national or special religious episodes of importance. For these they had to be appropriately dressed, their gowns and shawls of the finest lawn or lace, or of the warmer saye in winter, with embroidery worthy of the occasion. Heraldic figures and devices were interwoven with national emblems, often flowers or birds, or weird animals, all of beautiful colours and design, far different from their plainer everyday clothes. Jewels in necklaces, coronets, rings and bangles were shown up in the paintings of the subject, which later lined the walls of their halls and castles. For youngsters it was a game of dressing-up and make-believe come true.

King Edward's coronation had provided one of these opportunities, and there were others to come. Now in 1464 the year started off in sombre style with troubles in Northumberland and perpetual fighting between the Rose factions. The King was in York early in the Spring, so word had it, on his way north, and this was soon confirmed with news of the Battle of Hexham in which the Lancastrians were roundly beaten by King Edward's Yorkist force, and Henry VI[8] taken prisoner and ridden to London to be lodged in the Tower. His Queen once more fled to France for her own safety and to plan for further action. Edward returned to York in early May triumphantly flourishing a royal cap called an abacot, which had been found in Henry's baggage on the battlefield, and which was richly decorated with two crowns. It seemed to Edward to be just the thing in which he could be crowned in a second coronation to compliment and flatter the people of York - and to cement their loyalty. Accordingly, on 4th May a splendid ceremony took place in York Cathedral, to which the Warwicks all proceeded, much to the joy of Isabel and Anne, who once again could dress in fine raiment and jewellery, giving them enormous pleasure now they were becoming older. The journey from Sheriff Hutton was relatively easy as it was early summer, and they were able to change into their best attire at the Archbishop's Palace in the Cathedral Precincts. Festivities continued at the King's Manor adjacent to St. Mary's Abbey, but the evenings were light now until late, and they rode home to Sheriff Hutton under a moonlit sky and a warm night.

Nobody at that time realised that the King had ridden the long journey from Stony Stratford for this coronation at York, and nobody really discovered the reason for some time, and then all fury broke out in the Warwick household when it was disclosed that King Edward had been secretly married to Elizabeth Woodville[23] - an "upstart" family not popular with the Earl - at the small church of Grafton on the Northampton/Bedfordshire border. Only Jacquetta, Duchess of Bedford (the bride's mother), the priest and two gentlemen were present, and in addition a young man enlisted at the last moment to help the priest with the singing. Elizabeth was the widow of Sir John Grey, son of Lord Ferrers, who had been killed at the 2nd Battle of St. Alban's in 1461, and very few people knew of this present marriage at the time, which was evidently a love-match. However, the event was emblazoned on the minds of the Warwick girls by the rage which the news aroused in their father who stormed and stamped around the castle, frothing with vituperative curses and slanders against the entire Woodville family. The very floors seemed to reverberate with his terrible language, which embraced not only Elizabeth, but her four brothers headed by Anthony Lord Scales (to become Earl Rivers on his father's execution in 1469) who took a prominent part in the political upheavals which continued the War of the Roses. All her sons by Sir John Grey took a hand in the undercurrent of intrigue and plotting which went on, posing a threat to the Earl's own plans. Outraged though he was by what he considered the underhand manner of the King's marriage, by dint of Countess Anne's calming influence, Warwick non-the-less controlled himself sufficiently (in his own interests) to agree to become sponsor to the eldest baby of the union when the Princess Elizabeth[24] was born the following February, and was baptised at Westminster. "What a fuss!" thought the Countess, but knew that if she said anything she would only be told that women didn't understand these things, and be cursed for her pains.

Next year (1465), Elizabeth Woodville[23] was crowned at Westminster on Whit Sunday, 26th May, in great splendour. Countess Anne related details of the spectacle next time she stayed at Sheriff Hutton, much to her daughters' fascination. Obviously the Countess had been very impressed by the grandeur of the arrangements, the trumpets, the singing, the huge and august assembly, and not least the colourful robes and dazzling jewellery, a subject near to her heart. The new queen's gown stole the show. It was made of cloth of gold, "and" said the Countess in awe "the material alone cost £280." All the cups and vessels used in the ceremony of anointing and crowning were moreover made of gold.

Warwick, although calmer would on no account allow his daughters to attend the coronation, nor did he himself, and his language on the subject was memorable, but somewhat appeased by the good news that his younger brother, George Nevill[23], Bishop of Exeter, had been appointed Archbishop of York at the early age of barely thirty. Already Chancellor of England, and therefore a most influential and powerful person, the two brothers working together planned to hold England in the palm of their hands.

This autumn the King placed his younger brother, Richard[22] in the household of the Earl of Warwick. This was a normal process in the education of sons of the nobility so that the youths could receive instruction in the etiquette and ways of the aristocracy, in the martial arts and advanced horsemanship, and a little about commanding and governing, as well as generally maturing. He would gain much social kudos from meeting important personages who would be useful to him by their patronage all his life. Much of Richard's time would be spent at Middleham which so often held what amounted to the Court, but he also travelled frequently between there and Sheriff Hutton, Warwick and even Penrith, depending on his master's movements and wishes. Late in this same year, the Earl of Warwick was granted £1,000 towards Richard's maintenance, a huge sum, which covered his expenses for the next three years. Richard was thus able to attend not only the new Archbishop's enthronement in York Minster, but also the great feast at Cawood early the next year. He arrived at Sheriff Hutton a few weeks beforehand, still a very naive youth, and made Isabel giggle when he tried to be courtly or to dance with her. He blushed scarlet under his dark skin at her taunts, turning away with his one shoulder even higher than the other as was usual. He felt more comfortable with his little Warwick cousin, Anne, who was rather shy and in awe of him, even though he was not very much taller than herself.

He saw his cousins again on 22nd September at the enthronement of George Nevill through the crowds that stood packing the vast interior of York Cathedral, and the haze of incense which made him feel light-headed. The coloured light shining through the window glass gave an ethereal aura in which he could hardly recognise the girls in their finery and their outwardly dignified calm, but as they proceeded through the throng, to the singing of the choir, and out of the great west door to the joyful cacophony of the Cathedral bells, he felt proud and happy. It was good that the waiting rabble outside should see and respect these two daughters of Warwick.

To celebrate his preferment and all its power and wealth, Archbishop George was bent on holding perhaps the most enormous banquet ever described, probably in the whole of England, certainly ever at his seat at Cawood Castle. It was to be held on St. Maurice's Day, 15th January 1466 and would be open to all-comers, though the first days would be devoted to his most aristocratic and influential acquaintances. The locals and anyone who wanted, could join the party later in the week to finish up the left-overs, which, it being winter, would remain edible for days. The actual number of guests, invited and uninvited, was very large, some reports citing as many as several thousands, and the staff to deal with this massive invasion perhaps two thousand. Vast quantities of fish, flesh and fowl were consumed, washed down by colossal quantities of ale, and wine, complemented by thousands of custards and tarts and jellies such that Cawood Castle became legendary for this gargantuan party.

Cawood had belonged to the Archbishops of York from the tenth century, but most of the present fortified manor house had been rebuilt in the thirteenth century. Subsequently, the Kingmaker's great great uncle Alexander Nevill, Archbishop of York, had repaired the structure in the late fourteenth century, and laid out the gardens. His successors rebuilt the Great Hall and added a gallery in the early fifteenth century, as well as further "offices" which included accommodation for every trade required at the Castle. A new residential range was added on the southern front to the east of the entrance, linked to the older existing arm to the west by a splendid new gatehouse of white magnesian limestone which glowed and sparkled in every degree of sunlight. The whole complex reached down to the river bank except for a walkway between the water (which was tidal - up to twelve feet) and the north boundary wall of the castle outbuildings.

The resulting palace, resplendent with towers added by Archbishop Alexander Nevill, some way down the River Ouse from York, rose with magical grandeur as one approached round the bends of the river to the ferry landing quay at the head of the town Highstreet. Visitors alighting here were then transported a few hundred yards along to the Market Place, across a bridge over the Bishopdyke, to the drawbridge and gatehouse which overlooked the Castle land and fishpools to the south. The magnificence confronting them so unexpectedly after traversing its surrounding flat fenland and forest, was indeed appropriate for the new Archbishop to celebrate his elevation to the throne of Saint Peter in York.

Cawood Castle

The Earl and Countess of Warwick entered into the spirit of the Cawood banquet as if it were their own, which in fame and advancement of their family interests it certainly was. Their daughters went by state barge down the River Ouse from York at the beginning of the feasting, but the whole thing soon became so noisy as the company mellowed, that they felt overwhelmed. Their cousin, Richard, was quietly sitting with some of the Fitzhughs, and seemed contented. He smiled vaguely at the Warwick girls and then took no more notice of them. It was hot and rowdy in the Great Hall, and after a few hours, Ella could see that her charges were wilting, and took them out onto the terrace beside the Ouse where they revived. It was very frosty outside, and the shouting and bawdiness followed them onto the river bank where it echoed up and down the waterway.

"Please can we go home now?" Isabel asked. "We don't like this very much." And although their Uncle George was now almost as important as their father, and with their Uncle John, Lord Montagu (now raised to his new title drawn from the Percys, of Earl of Northumberland), they were at the very peak of Nevill power in England. But this meant little to two very tired young heiresses, who had hardly seen their father in months because he seemed more interested in the Crown than his children, except for their value as barter, a subject which was beginning to exercise his mind.

When Warwick was feeling more clear in his thoughts after the effects of his brother's beneficence at Cawood, he decided to suggest to the King that for the strength of the realm, Isabel should become the wife of young George of Clarence, whilst Anne was not too young at eleven to be betrothed to Richard of Gloucester, and then married as soon as his period of training with the Warwick household was over. But Edward would have none of it; Warwick was far too wily for his taste, and his ambitions were limitless. If he could not become king himself (although he had several irons in that fire) at least he could expect one of his daughters to give birth to a future monarch - if only that Woodville woman could be attainted or cast adrift, and her daughter, Elizabeth, caught up in some web of scandal.

However, for the time being Edward put down his foot on such schemings with a firm refusal.

Life now settled back into its old routine, with time being spent mainly between Sheriff Hutton and Middleham. Sometimes their stay at one or other coincided with cousin Richard's visit, sometimes with other young sons of the nobility. In August 1467 they were introduced to a new ward of their father's, Francis Lovell, who was two years younger than Richard, but already married, although at the time barely twelve. His wife was Anne Fitzhugh, whose mother, Alice Nevill, was sister of the Earl of Warwick; her father, Henry Lord Fitzhugh of Ravensworth would die in 1472, an adherent of Henry VI, such was the confusion of family relationships during the War of the Roses. Francis was an attractive young man who remained a trusted friend of Richard's all his life. He loved the North Riding, especially now that he was part of it by marriage, and even held the advowson of Bedale Church. The Lovells owned a number of lordships in the area, for which Sir Thomas Metcalfe of Nappa in Wensleydale was receiver - or controller - during Francis' minority, and the two youths spent much of their free time riding or striding over the hills of Wensleydale and Swaledale taking in the glorious scenery and the hospitality of the innkeepers and cottagers. The Vales of York and Mowbray and the valleys to the west were rich farming country with a tiny population, their nearest town of any size being York itself. Threat from Scottish invasion and raids was ever present, and did much damage to crops and cottages when they came, but could not counteract the fine harvests and herds and the wealth that the land brought. Lovell taught Richard a love of the Dales, and Middleham especially gave them never-ending pleasure.

Yorkshire was heavily influenced by the Celtic traditions of Lindisfarne and Jarrow, and Saint Cuthbert had left a legacy of Christian worship as far south as the Humber, especially around the little area of Crayke near Sheriff Hutton which remained part of the Diocese of Durham. Robert Nevill[27], the Bishop of Durham and uncle of the Earl of Warwick had rebuilt the castle at Crayke for his own use on his visits to York in the 1430's, and Isabel and Anne often rode over to its craggy magnificence from Sheriff Hutton to enjoy the marvellous view from the heights over the Vale of York with the Cathedral standing up far above the distant trees of the Forest of Galtres. Bishop Robert had died in 1457 but they enjoyed also the refreshment from the old bishop's store of Lindisfarne mead that they would be offered. Riding back to the Castle, whichever way they took, whether along the high ridge which carried the ancient drovers road with views to north and south, or the lower route across the farmland below Mill Hill and Cornborough, was always a delight. It varied with the season, but always there were groups of labourers sowing or reaping, or preparing the ground for the next crop. The scene was never without the interest of people, be it sunny or cold, wet or parched, whatever the season. The two girls on their fine horses found themselves, like their cousin Richard, developing a deep fondness for this countryside, something quite in spite of themselves and very deep within their souls.

The year after the Cawood feast, to the surprise of most people, the Archbishop's fame suddenly received a jolt. The Nevill family had become threateningly powerful, and to dent this potential for complete domination, the King dismissed Archbishop George from the Chancellorship of England. This was a crushing blow not only to the Archbishop's self-esteem, but also to his influence on affairs of state for both himself and for his brother, the Earl of Warwick. Anne could see that Ella had her own opinion about this development, but she kept it to herself and merely sniffed in a dismissive way when she was asked about it.

Richard was back at Sheriff Hutton in February for a meeting in York, one of his first official duties, when he acted as Oyer and Terminer ("to hear and determine") for the City of York. He was still under what was considered the age of majority for a nobleman, but he was pleased of the opportunity to build up his image in the region which he was beginning to know intimately. The responsibility of this new position was not as arduous as it seemed, and it was honorary in so far as it only lasted one day. Moreover there were his official advisers there to guide him. The Nevill girls were duly impressed and enquired of Mistress Gower what he would have to do.

"Well" said she, "he will sit in the assize court and judge each case as it comes, and determine what justice demands, whether anyone should be punished, and how to settle claims and arguments."

In truth she was a little unclear herself, so they made a mental note to ask Richard when he got back, but when they did, he was altogether evasive, and although he had enjoyed being so important for the day, and having the aldermen doffing their caps to him, and seeing the passers-by stare and curtsey or bow as they recognised who it was on horseback clattering along the street, he refused to discuss details - just that it was "important". He tended now to go to York whenever the excuse arose as he wanted to feel that the City associated him with his brother, King Edward, rather than with the Earl of Warwick, and in the year when he finally became of age at sixteen, he was officially received by the City of York, its Lord Mayor and Aldermen to their mutual benefit, and it served Richard well in the future as he became more and more at one with the district.

So for a few months Anne saw more of him, and liked his restrained kindly manner, especially as she felt that covert movements were being made in the marriage market, and that soon Isabel would go away and leave her much more on her own. The Earl had withdrawn partially from the public eye for the time being, but she suspected that it was to free him for his planning and contriving by undercover plotting which she was sure would end by embroiling them all in warfare.

The thought of the changes this might involve, scared her. Ella tried to calm her, Merryman to make her laugh, and Mistress Gower to interest her in her lessons. Her mother was often with her, either at Middleham or at Sheriff Hutton, and talked to her about the splendid future that she and Isobel would have as wives of great noblemen, perhaps of Dukes and Kings, and might even become the mother of a future king. This piece of information gave Anne much food for thought. She both disbelieved it, but then as she digested the idea, began to believe it, and find it exciting and important that she, Anne Nevill, a younger daughter, had such dazzling expectations. And then she wondered if perhaps her father would wish her to marry a foreign duke, French or Dutch, even Spanish, and then she became scared all over again at the idea of being in a strange land with a foreign language, and vowed that she would work really hard at her lessons to make up. The Countess bethought her of all the compensations that would accompany such privilege, and it occurred to her that she herself might quite enjoy the position it would give her as the bride's mother, and later the mother of the enciente wife.

Family of the Earl of Warwick
1428 - 1471 k.

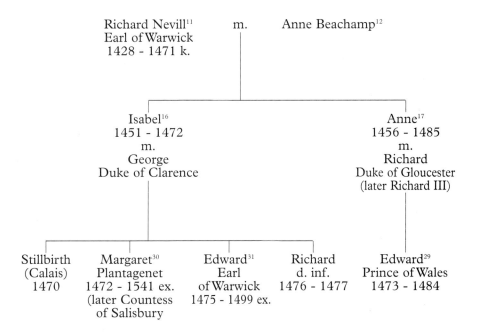

Richard Nevill[11]   m.   Anne Beachamp[12]
Earl of Warwick
1428 - 1471 k.

Isabel[16]   Anne[17]
1451 - 1472   1456 - 1485
m.   m.
George   Richard
Duke of Clarence   Duke of Gloucester
                                         (later Richard III)

Stillbirth   Margaret[30]   Edward[31]   Richard   Edward[29]
(Calais)   Plantagenet   Earl   d. inf.   Prince of Wales
1470   1472 - 1541 ex. of Warwick   1476 - 1477   1473 - 1484
               (later Countess 1475 - 1499 ex.
               of Salisbury

"I will always come to you when you give birth, so never fear," said she sympathetically if rather mechanically.

"But Madam, how shall I know when I am going to give birth?"

"Your woman of the bedchamber will tell you" said the Countess serenely.

"I don't understand how the infant will climb into my body" Anne pursued in a puzzled voice, crinkling up her forehead at the mystery, "or indeed how it will get out" wailed this child of twelve, condemned to her naive ignorance until she could discover the truth by her own experience.

"You will soon understand" answered her mother, "and now you must refrain from asking all these questions like a peasant girl. Surely it is enough that your son will be a great heir, and you should not bother with all these queries. Before you marry, I shall give you an Agnus Dei which will protect you from all evil, and see that your little one is born safely."

The Countess often wore her own Agnus, but particularly if some danger raised its head, or a long journey was to be taken, and it always accompanied her when she went to supervise a childbirth, which was a speciality of hers. She would have gone to give succour to the Queen when her eldest baby was born, only she knew the Earl would burst a blood vessel in fury had she done so. Anne had often admired her mother's Agnes when, on a wet afternoon she had gone to play with the Countess' jewellery or her chess set, and knew the details of the fabulous lozenge-shaped pendant hung with pearls very well. She knew its engraving of the Trinity which she found awe-inspiring and cruel, but was dazzled by the huge sapphire built into the top of the scene. The other tiny etchings on both sides of the jewel were so beautiful, her favourite always the Nativity with the naked little baby Jesus lying in a halo of light with his mother kneeling beside him in case he awoke frightened, the ox and the ass meanwhile munching their hay in the stall in the background while St. Joseph looked on in an attitude of concern. The minute figures of saints bordering the picture seemed to protect the baby. There were Latin words from the Mass, and a magic Greek word 'Ananizapta', which was a charm against drunkenness and epilepsy, while the sapphire protected against all manner of ills including those of childbirth. The Countess usually wore the Agnus on a chain round her neck with decoration suitable to her husband's inclination at the time, be it Lancaster or York, or the safest, the Warwick Bear. Most of her highborn female relations had similar Agnuses and often had them showing in their portraits.

Not long after this interesting conversation Anne heard that Richard had been recalled to Court by King Edward. She also gleaned from her ladies that the reason was that her father was known to be continuing his plotting and had managed to draw Richard's elder brother, George Clarence, into his circle opposed to the King.

"How awful" she thought, "to have brothers plotting against each other, and their older brother, the King, trying to decide between the two of them. Poor Aunt Cecily, having so much friction and bitterness separating her children, and her daughter just gone away to France to marry Charles Duke of Burgundy." And then she remembered that Sir John Paston had gone with Margaret of York to witness her marriage at Hamme Castle in the hinterland of Calais, so she felt that all would be well because Sir John was such a nice man and so honest.

Little did she and Isabel know just how much wheeling and dealing was going on amongst the different factions, and how their lives were being woven and re-woven to suit these men, and indeed how completely they were in the hands of such ambitious persons. Whisper came through to them via Sir John Bulmer who owned property near Sheriff Hutton, that the Earl wished to marry Isabel to her cousin, George Clarence, but that since his mother, Aunt Cecily, Duchess of York, was both Isabel's great-aunt and her godmother, this could only be allowed with the Pope's dispensation for the near relationship, and at this very moment messengers and ambassadors were engaged in interminable wrangling over Isabel's fate.

"King Edward does not approve of the match," remarked the Countess of Warwick when the girls egged her on to explain what was causing the delay, "but I expect" she continued resignedly "that my Lord, you father will get his way. He usually does."

In fact Clarence's marriage to Isabel was part of a plan for insurrection against King Edward and to restore Henry VI to the throne. The Earl of Warwick, who previously had been so strongly behind the Yorkist cause, found that his nephew, the King allowed him less and less influence over the throne, and moreover, Edward's marriage in 1464 into the grasping Woodville family who were anathema to Warwick because of what he considered their low standing, filled the Earl with rage. He was only too well aware of the large number of dependants of the queen - her two sons by her previous marriage, her five brothers and six sisters - who would all demand advantageous marriages and good dowries from the King. Next came the dismissal by the King of Warwick's brother George, Archbishop of York from the Chancellorship of England in 1467 as a further curb on Nevill power. And the following year Edward's sister, Margaret of York[20] was married to Duke Charles, a move which added to the Woodville confidence since Burgundy was an enemy of the hated French and an old ally of England, and could be relied on to back King Edward against the French conniving with the Lancastrians.

Warwick however refused to accept these rebuffs, and arrogantly planned to remain in control of the throne, but now (as he hoped) the Lancastrian throne of Henry VI. Renewal of civil war was now inevitable, with Edward leading the Yorkists, and Warwick the Lancastrians.

The Spring was shining through the misty air of the mornings and the fields of Sheriff Hutton were coming alive with the shouts of peasants as they harrowed the good earth which had been well marled with clay the previous autumn. Very soon now the sceps and sacks of seedcorn saved from last year's harvest would be brought down from cottage garrets and yeomen's granaries to be gathered into leather pouches to tie round the waists of the labourers sowing it anew. Several men at a time walked the common fields spraying handfuls of seed as they strode backwards and forwards endlessly up and down the furlongs, their arms and hands rhythmically showering the seed, first to left, then to right, whilst each man sang to himself in time with his movements. Behind him came a flock of birds to pick up the welcome food; some of it fell on the strips belonging to his neighbour, some on the balks and headlands where it could not be tended but most fell on the good ground. The trees were already beginning to show green, and the bushes of hawthorn and blackthorn were coming alive again as the weather grew warmer and the days longer. On the moorland of Mill Hill, and in the dales around Middleham, the ewes were grubbing up every blade of grass to feed their expectant hunger, and were being driven into pens for their lambs to be born.

Once again a king's messenger galloped up Bracken Hill to the gates of Sheriff Hutton Castle to be received by Sir Thomas Gower, who shortly afterwards asked to see the Countess and her elder daughter. His orders were to prepare the Countess for the journey to Calais where Isabel was to be married to the Duke of Clarence. Anne of course would accompany her mother and sister to France.

Isabel's eyes opened wider and wider as her mother relayed this news. She knew this was very likely to have been arranged while her father had been so secretive, but even so it came as an exquisite, an almost painful, shock of delight. She hardly knew her cousin George, but she remembered him as very tall and broad, fair-haired and good-looking - quite different from his brother Richard, but not unlike the King. She had only seen him on the few state occasions to which she had been, and hardly spoken to him at all, but this was a dream come true, and once the facts had sunk in, she gave way to her joy, grabbing Anne by both hands, dancing round and round the room in a sort of polka, head thrown back, eyes shining, and her long fair hair floating out behind her.

"Isabel, Isabel, calm yourself," called her mother. "There is much to do, your wardrobe to renew, gowns to be planned, everything for the journey, and all that is needful for a royal Duchess of England." And then a pause, "Thank heaven I purchased all that cloth of gold and the fine Flanders cloth last year...and the scarlet damask and the silk and the tippets .....," as an afterthought, her mind working overtime as to what they would all wear.

"Duchess of Clarence! Duchess of Clarence!" sang Isabel over and over again as if she was seeing what it sounded like. "Duchess of Clarence; the Duke and Duchess of Clarence," and she put her hands up to the sides of her head as she tried to force herself to believe it.

And then the questions began; when would the marriage take place; who would be present; where would she and Clarence live when he was not away on official duties; and so on, and so on until a different thought struck her.

"But, Madam, why am I to be married in France?" she asked.

"Because of course my lord your father and the Duke are now in Calais making arrangements (by which she meant awaiting the Pope's blessing), and the King of England (she sniffed her disapproval at events) does not approve and will remain in his island fortress."

Anne had very mixed and muddled feelings about Isabel's marriage. It seemed to promise a brilliant future for her as a royal duchess and sister-in-law to the King, but on the other hand my Lord Warwick was at present hand-in-glove with Clarence against the King, and how, she wondered, would this place her sister? She envied Isabel her role as the bride, and all her new clothes hurriedly being cut out and stitched by every available seamstress and tailor. She envied her self-confidence and joy at the prospect of becoming a royal lady, and no doubt soon a royal mother. And that is where her envy waned, and she felt a disgust that Isabel was being used as might a prize ewe or a mare, to produce heirs for the royal household. Battles and skirmishes were there many in the continuing struggle for the throne, for power of the nobles, for land and status. How would Isabel fare in this tempest of intrigue and greed?

At thirteen Anne had seen too much of the pain and heartache of war, although she knew that being a great heiress she should be above and unconcerned with the misery it caused. She could not remember Towton very well but she knew of the continuing troubles of the families who had lost their main breadwinner in the slaughter, or the agony of lost limbs or eyes or health of the peasant soldiers. She hated the misery, especially the nonchalance which she as a high-born lady was supposed to air to such suffering, and she was forced to hide her true feelings or be ridiculed or scorned. Isabel seemed completely at one with the way the world was, and could override emotion with joy in her own success. It made her appear hard, toughened her views, and in doing so eased her way through life. Anne felt that this might change now with a new future opening up before her sister, and very probably all too soon before herself.

The journey to Calais by land was long and tedious. As it was Summer the decision was taken to travel by water, by river from York and then by sea. York was a busy port, and river traffic was used for all the considerable commercial trade both to London and beyond, and to the continent. Some of the vessels were tied up alongside the Merchant Adventurers' wharf a little way up the River Foss and the lower reaches of that river. The ship taking the Warwicks to Calais had to accommodate their servants and some armed guards, so it was larger than most, and had to berth on the main River Ouse. It set sail at high tide, and thereafter it had to keep to the centre of the river until they reached the Humber. As they passed Cawood, Anne's thoughts turned back to the great Feast, as Archbishop Nevill came aboard to travel with them.

After nearly a week and mostly favourable wind, they found themselves at Calais under the Earl of Warwick's governorship. It was the beginning of July. The Duke of Clarence had already arrived from England, and now Isabel had a day or two to rest from her journey, and to get to know her bridegroom. Anne was glad of the interval to gather up her strength for whatever emerged, and to back up her sister who was by now an explosive mixture of nerves and excited anticipation.

"He is very gallant and courtly," she told Anne after her first meeting with Clarence. "I know he will be kind to me, and everything is going to be lovely" she said as if to convince herself.

The marriage was duly celebrated on 11th July with the minimum of pomp consistent with the importance of the participants. The ceremony was performed by the bride's uncle, George Nevill, Archbishop of York at the Cathedral of Notre Dame, in the presence of the Earl and Countess of Warwick and her sister, Anne. Isabel wore her coronet for the first time, and her Agnus Dei that her mother had given her just before they set out from Yorkshire. She fingered it nervously as if it was an icon, which in truth it was - a superstitious jewel of great beauty and significance. It went with her now through every day and every problem and hurdle, and truly for a few months it did protect her, in spite of great troubles ahead, as she was to realise as the party hurried back to England as soon as she and Clarence were bedded.

The Countess once again accompanied her daughters back to London, to the Archbishop's stately home, York House on the north bank of the Thames between Westminster and the City. There a messenger arrived with the news that the Earls of Pembroke[9] and Devon were riding with a force loyal to the King to foregather against a rebel army led by Lord Warwick near Banbury, and about to do battle at Edgecote. Other rebellions were brewing, notably of northern Nevills, Sir Humphrey of Branspeth and his brother, Charles, in favour of Henry VI, and another in the East Riding headed by a mysterious person who was popularly known as Robin of Redesdale but who never unequivocally disclosed his identity. Ella said she thought he was Sir John Conyers of Hornby, but was never certain. Instead she hinted at executions which duly followed battle as usual after Edgecote, but that it had all by-passed King Edward who was struggling to join his royalist forces as he made his way from the north.

The Countess had had enough of all the upset - the country seemed topsy-turvey - and she escaped with her personal servants to Beaulieu Abbey in the New Forest for a rest and temporary sanctuary. Isabel, for her part, found she was not now her own master or even a chattel of her father's, but had to follow her husband's instructions, which were vague because he did not himself know where she should go, so he sent her up to Warwick. Poor Anne was on a limb because no one wanted to be bothered with her, or undertake the journey to Yorkshire in the uncertainties of the marauding forces in the Midlands, so she was lodged at Baynard's Castle with her own servants and one or two of Warwick's fighting men to guard her. She was still worth a ransom. Aunt Cecily was at Fotheringhay, and it seemed that Edward would make for Woodville land near Stoney Stratford in the Midlands.

Anne was very happy to be in London for a short while, as Baynard's Castle was on the most exciting site possible, with the busy river and the crowded wharfs surrounding it, and the water-borne traffic, especially the grand pleasure barges passing up and down the river between Westminster and the Tower, and Greenwich. The working barges and fishing smacks and ferry boats continually plying their trades just below her windows at Baynard's gave her unending interest. But she missed her Yorkshire countryside and the kind peasant ways and the peace of the land with its round of renewing seasons. And then, just as she was becoming really homesick, she heard from Ella that the King had been captured at Olney in the Midlands by Archbishop Nevill who had taken him to Warwick Castle and then to Middleham where Sir John Nevill was now constable, as Warwick's prisoner. From this northern imprisonment, he was in theory to rule England. This was Warwick's intention anyway, so that he, the Earl of Warwick, could keep control of the government. But Anne then heard that Edward was too popular in the country to be isolated in the north and there was clamour for him to come back further south where he was accessible to his subjects.

By 10th September Warwick had had to free him, and Edward was in York, where later that month the two traitorous Nevill brothers who had taken part in the northern revolt, Humphrey and Charles, were executed in the King's presence. "Robin of Redesdale" was never captured.

Cousin Richard kept a low profile after Edgecote, but remained true to the King, so Anne heard, and she was overjoyed when the King was freed and had rewarded Richard with the position of Constable of England in succession to Earl Rivers, (the queen's father who had been executed following Edgecote). She could well imagine Isabel exclaiming "How grand!" Moreover Richard was given various pieces of estate by the King previously belonging to the Hungerfords on the Welsh borders and some of the Duchy of Lancaster estates, to bring him an income, as well as the lordship of Sudeley Castle in Gloucester, and to represent the King's authority in Wales to replace Pembroke who had been executed after Edgecote.

Anne was constantly thinking of Isabel, for she had never been apart from her before, and the two girls had always shared a big double bed except for the few nights when they were travelling. Their lives had inter-knit, and now she missed her desperately. Even Isabel's whereabouts were dubious because like most of the ladies in her family, she tried hard to accompany, or at least follow, her husband on his journeyings, just as did her mother and Aunt Cecily when their husbands travelled.

In the early Autumn, a few months after Isabel's marriage in 1469, Anne received a note from her, written at Richmond Castle in Swaledale where she was staying briefly. She was obviously in a state of great excitement, and it was to tell Anne that she was pregnant "by my lord", and the baby was due in the Spring. She was feeling very sick, but hoped that would soon pass, and that she would see Anne before long, perhaps in London.

Anne let the note fall into her lap, and thought about Isabel in her new situation, and a baby on the way, and wished she could comfort her in the difficult times, and rejoice with her at the advent of this child. The present antipathy between the King and his brother George Clarence made it problematic as to where she and Isabel could see each other, and London or Warwick seemed the most likely places. She confided as usual in Ella about her anxieties for Isabel, and together they talked it all over, and in the end she persuaded her father by a tearful letter to let her go to Warwick to be with Isabel as soon as possible. In the early year Edward was at Baynard's Castle with her, and in his understanding way he saw how much she missed her sister and arranged for her to go up to Warwick at once. It so happened - perhaps Edward had heard rumours of yet another uprising against him - that a group including Warwick and Clarence, hoped to lure the King into a trap near Lincoln, and then to free the imprisoned Henry VI. Edward received a message in London in early March, and quickly galloped north, spending the night of 11th March at Fotheringhay to see his mother, and next day face the rebels at Losecote Field near Stamford, where he decisively dispersed them, and Warwick and Clarence had to flee to the south coast at Dartmouth to escape by sea to France. Richard was ordered to march south via Gloucester and Hereford to raise fighting men, whilst Edward tried to consolidate his position in the north, visiting York and Lancashire and finally riding post-haste to Exeter with his troops in eighteen days (a journey of 209 miles).

Anne was by this time at Warwick with Isabel, both of them sitting over their sewing for the baby and gossiping as hard as they sewed. Such a happy scene could not last long, and in early April Isabel was commanded by her father to meet her mother at Portsmouth where they would join the Earl's ship as it rounded the coast from Dartmouth, and sail with him and Clarence to France. However, in the last moment an urgent order came from the Earl that Anne must accompany her sister to France, so there was a hurried packing up of clothes and possessions and poor Isabel was heaved onto a litter and off they went to Portsmouth, stopping on the way at a different venue each night, wherever there was a friendly country mansion or manor. They finally picked up the Countess's train at Beaulieu before the last stretch of the long journey to Portsmouth where they were able to rest until the Earl's ship hove into view around the Needles. There was a kind of stability for the two girls now the Countess was with them to direct affairs and make any decisions required.

As soon as the ship had rewatered and revictualled, they were off on an eastward tack with some anxiety at the lowering clouds and increasing winds. The threatened storm broke as they reached Beachy Head, and with the first roll of the vessel, Isabel let out a scream as the preliminary pangs of childbirth assailed her. Anne stood transfixed in their cabin, wondering what to do, but the Countess was in her element; this was a situation after her own heart. She loved to comfort a woman in travail, and this was her own daughter in such a plight on this rolling cork of a boat. Out came her Agnus Dei as the Countess got down to work and the agonised Isabel clutched her own Agnus that her mother had given her before her marriage. The Countess drew the jewel down poor Isabel's body over and over again to aid the infant in finding its way into the world, while the young mother screamed and screamed, and the ship's sails flapped noisily, the wind blew, and the sea roared in the most terrifying manner, whilst the waves crashed against the sides of the cabin so that the Countess could hardly hear herself speak over the din. As they neared the French coast it was apparent that the baby's appearance was imminent, and as soon as they were almost in-shore, the commander ordered the sailors to furl the sails and to drop the anchor just as Anne thought she could not bear another second of this horror and her sister's torments. As the noise of the ship's battle with the storm began to die away, Isabel let out one further prolonged yell, and her son was born.

Silence.

It was immediately obvious he was dead. The little boy who would one day have challenged the Crown of England, was no more, and all Isabel's efforts that awful day were as naught. The cry which had been one of agony now became a wail of misery, and the Countess wrapped the little figure in fine lawn, and took it up to the Earl on deck so that he might have it buried at sea. He held the bundle disdainfully which reminded the Countess so vividly of his manner when its mother was born at Warwick Castle all those years ago, as he handed it over to a sailor for disposal. After that, Isabel cried and slept alternately until she could be lifted up to be carried ashore at Calais from where in a few weeks' time she followed her father and husband to Bruges. But Anne and the Countess remained at the citadel of Calais while she regained her strength and Anne thought about marriage and childbirth and how she would ever bear either.

CHAPTER 6

ISABEL DID NOT RECOVER from her pregnancy and delivery of the stillbirth for some time, and she was low in spirit although she began to talk about a 'next' baby. So the sisters remained in France, with their mother to oversee their care. The Earl came and went, and with him Clarence, and the ladies lost track of their journeyings. As May merged into June and then July, the beautiful Summer of northern France brought back bloom into the girls' cheeks, and they were able to visit the castles in the area, walk in the gardens of the noblemen, and practise their French.

One day in mid-July, they received a note from the Earl. Anne's heart sank as the messenger handed it to the Countess. She knew in her innermost soul the likely contents. The Earl and Queen Margaret of Anjou were in Angers, the capital of Anjou on the River Maine. Louis XI of France was also there scheming together with them how they could rid England of Edward IV, and replace him on the throne by Henry VI. Agreement had been reached with Louis that he would materially help with Henry's restoration, and as part of the deal, Henry's son, Edward of Lancaster, Prince of Wales, would be married to Anne Nevill.

Anne's fingers holding the missive seemed to weaken as she read in disbelief that this was indeed what was planned. She did not personally know the young prince, or really anything about him, except that he was almost three years older than herself, an only child of Henry of Lancaster and of Margaret of Anjou whom she had heard was bossy and autocratic. Henry, on the other hand seemed so pious as to be weak and slightly deranged and not nearly so effective a king as Edward IV, and certainly not so attractive. She wrung her hands in anxiety, not even able to cry at the awfulness

107

of her fate to be married to this Lancastrian who would surely rival her cousin Edward for the throne. How could she bear it? And yet she knew full well it was not for her to decide on a husband for herself. She was obliged to do as her father wished in these matters. Oh, and the horror of having to be bedded by a man she had never before met, be mauled by him and her body be at his disposal and possession, and to bear the indignity of it all.

There was no wonder that poor little fourteen-year-old Anne felt so confused and upset about her father's plans for her marriage. He had been an ardent Yorkist, and largely instrumental in assisting the accession of Edward[18], son of the Duke of York to the throne after Towton. But now Warwick's influence with his young monarch carried less and less weight as Edward recognised the growing danger of the Earl's strength. Warwick was now bent on confirming his own change of allegiance from the House of York to that of Lancaster in his attempt to return the weak and useless Henry VI to the throne, and taking George Clarence, Isabel's husband with him in his efforts. This new marriage of Anne to Henry's only child, Edward, Prince of Wales[14] brought Warwick into close liaison with Henry and his queen, and would drive Anne irrevocably into the Lancastrian camp, and away from her previous adherence to the Yorkists, to which she had learnt loyalty from her cousins Edward[18] and Richard[22] during their visits to Middleham. Her own loyalties were now to be mercilessly divided, and she was being driven to marry a youth[14] who would certainly challenge King Edward[18] in the future, and one or other of the two Edwards would eventually be overcome and probably killed by the other.

This was Anne's predicament and sadness, and was the very basis of this hateful civil war which brought families into conflict with each other, becoming themselves fractured between the two sides; battles brought relatives to attack each other, even killing a brother, a cousin, an uncle, and any one of them would think nothing of changing sides if it suited them personally, though such treason risked execution.

To the Countess this news of the arranged betrothal was no surprise. She knew full well the political value of her daughters, and she lost no time in getting down to work planning the trousseau for the girl who was to be the wife of the Prince of Wales. She called for silks and satins, laces and linens, and then for dressmakers and tailors, just as she had done in England for Isabel, and together they settled down to the business of concocting everything the three Warwick ladies would need for the occasion. No time could be lost as the betrothal on 22nd July would quickly be followed in August by the marriage in the cathedral at Angers, once again to be presided over by Uncle George Nevill of York.

Again Ella was there, this time officially in the position of Anne's personal maid, to comfort her, to discuss her anxieties with her, to put things in perspective, especially regarding the wealth and honour which this marriage would bestow on her and her family, and how she now would almost certainly become the mother of a future King of England if God wished.

"But how can that be when Edward is on the throne and is so well loved by his people?" she cried, and to that Ella could only rock the girl, whom she now had to call "My lady", on her knee as she had done when Anne was a small child in tears. Well Ella knew the hurdles that lay in the path of this daughter of Warwick, and how much she feared for her in her role of puppet which could so easily end in her ruin.

"Dry your eyes now," she said after a while. "Madam has a special gift for you. Let us go and tell her you are ready for whatever may be in store for you."

The Countess was still choosing between the damasks and fine lawns which the merchants had brought for her to view. When she saw Anne, her attention strayed to a small casket of finest gold on the chest beside her, and out of its recesses she extracted another, most beautiful Agnus Dei similar to that which she had given to Isabel. This must now be worn by Anne at all times to protect her from evil, devilment, disease and misfortune, particularly when travelling, whether by land or water. "And," breathed Ella under her breath "from all the humiliations and heartbreaks which are in store for her."

This lozenge-shaped gold jewel with its exquisite etchings of the Trinity, the Nativity and the Saints, also (like Isabel's Agnus) was enhanced by the most lovely sapphire of penetrating blue. Within the locket, there was a wax medallion stamped with an icon of the Lamb of God, which had come from the Pope as a gift. A most wonderful object which Anne would value all her life, not only

Lady with Agnus Dei AMM

for its protective properties, but as an aid to Catholic worship. It had been crafted by the goldsmiths of London for a great lady, and now was Anne's own. She passed the chain over her head to admire it in her metal mirror.

"Very well!" said the Countess with satisfaction.

At last, working well into the night, the seamstresses and embroiderers completed their task, and the Warwick party set off for Angers, that beautiful old town from where Geoffrey Plantagenet had fathered the royal line of England through Henry II, and where the last Duke of the Duchy of Anjou was Rene, father of Queen Margaret, wife of Henry VI.

Anjou was a "black" town where building materials of flint had been quarried from time immemorial. It was, by contrast, surrounded by fertile land which grew vines and vegetables and good pasture. The huge black castle rose above the town with its seventeen drum towers, at this time over two hundred years old, and the great flint ramparts enclosing it in a black wall of formidable strength. Now in addition a moat was being hacked out of the underlying rock to give further protection, and it was across the bridge over this ditch that the Warwicks rode up to the castle, where they were able to rest, and Anne could meet Prince Edward[14],

Next day she was presented to him. Her first thought was how young and shy he was. Very unsure of himself, and yet in an effort to seem older than his sixteen years - nearly seventeen - he was stiff and formal and all too obviously had difficulty in finding anything to say to his betrothed. After a few halting enquiries regarding Anne's health, her journey to Angers, and his wish that she would "enjoy her stay", he bowed, she dropped a slight curtsey in reply, and the interview was abruptly over.

The following day they tried again, and he had apparently been advised to walk her round the ramparts from where he could show her the town, and loosen their strained relationship. This worked a little better as he pointed out various places of interest, but as he handed her back to her own quarters in the castle, she still felt she barely knew this diffident young man, and wondered how it would be when they were left on their own on their wedding night. She dreaded the prospect even more now she glimpsed his hesitant and self-conscious manner. The strong overbearing personality of his mother, whose word was law, had completely undermined his confidence apparently.

The days passed with some little progress in their intimacy, and by their wedding day he was able to smile nervously at her though was still often at a loss at what to say. At last the day arrived on which she could don her jewel-encrusted gown of silk, and a veil held high by stiffenings in a pointed creation above her head, and ride with her mother and father to the Cathedral of St. Maurice. Here she was almost transfixed by the immensely high and beautiful west front of the building with its two spire-topped towers to north and south. Within the dark bare interior, the coloured glass filling the windows reflected their patterns on the black stone floor from the rays of the summer sun. To left and right were transepts with newly built Rose Windows such as she knew at her own York Cathedral where the one in the south transept was fitted with grisaille glass like its opposite number, the Five Sisters, in the north transept. Following her mother's example, she dipped her fingers in the large holy-water stoup of verde antico, recently given by King Rene, and crossed herself slowly and deliberately, and with conviction before processing up to the high altar where Edward appeared flustered and uncomfortable until the Archbishop pronounced them man and wife, and he could lead her by the hand back down the long dark nave to the great west door and the sunshine outside. There a few cheers from the populace greeted them as they entered their conveyance to take them back to the feasting at the castle.

Together the young couple sat in their finery at the top table trying to look relaxed and happy, trying indeed to find something at all to say to each other. Anne ate and drank very little; Prince Edward also ate little, but drank a great deal, and by the time they were accompanied by the parents and attendants to the state bedchamber, and their attendants had undressed them into their nightshifts and drawn the curtains of the great bed, Edward was a dead weight, snoring and unconscious.

"Thank God" thought his little wife as she curled up under the coverlet as far off as she could to avoid the fearful stench of his breath. It was plain that there would be no consummation of the marriage that night, nor was there on subsequent nights, whether from an excess of Dutch Courage in the form of wine, or from nervousness and inability on Edward's part. In the daytime they rode the countryside, walked in the orchards and vineyards, lunched at country taverns served by startled inn-keepers, and dined and wined each evening at the castle where the proceedings became progressively more riotous as the hour grew later, and Anne quietly slipped away to her bed almost unnoticed. Hours later in the night, the servants more or less dumped her husband beside her, rolling him into bed like a hank of rope, and drew the curtains on the pathetic couple.

In September Warwick and Clarence boarded ship at La Hogue in Normandy and crossed to Devonshire, where they were soon joined by John de Vere, Earl of Oxford, and Jasper Tudor, Earl of

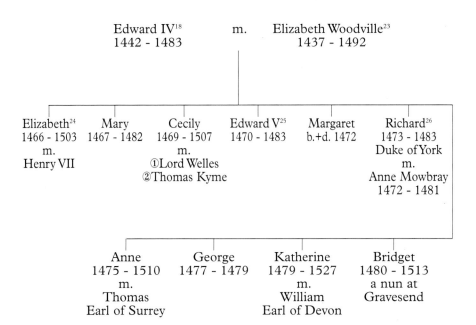

Edward IV[18]   m.   Elizabeth Woodville[23]
1442 - 1483   1437 - 1492

Elizabeth[24]	Mary	Cecily	Edward V[25]	Margaret	Richard[26]
1466 - 1503	1467 - 1482	1469 - 1507	1470 - 1483	b.+d. 1472	1473 - 1483
m.		m.			Duke of York
Henry VII		①Lord Welles			m.
		②Thomas Kyme			Anne Mowbray
					1472 - 1481

Anne	George	Katherine	Bridget
1475 - 1510	1477 - 1479	1479 - 1527	1480 - 1513
m.		m.	a nun at
Thomas		William	Gravesend
Earl of Surrey		Earl of Devon	

Pembroke, to commence their planned restoration of King Henry to the throne. Anne and her husband remained in Anjou under the watchful eyes of their mothers, the Queen and the Countess. Life settled down to a quiet domestic pattern, and because Isabel was still convalescing with them, the subject of babies was carefully avoided, and without too much difficulty as both girls knew that there was no possibility of pregnancy for either of them at the moment. Prince Edward gradually became more relaxed, but remained more of a friend to Anne than a husband, and she felt sorry for him under the constant eagle eye of his overbearing mother.

From time to time the party at Anjou received messengers from England, and knew that the two Rose factions were busy manoeuvring their followers into position to defeat each other, but solid facts were more hard to come by and impossible to confirm. In September they heard that Warwick and Clarence had landed safely in Devon. King Edward had been in the north trying to disperse the rebel Fitzhughs and promote Richard as Warden for the West Marches. He had restored Henry Percy to the Earldom of Northumberland and Laurence Booth, Bishop of Durham, to the lordship of Barnard Castle, thereby consolidating his position in the north. News came through that Lord Montagu, who always looked to his own advantages first, had changed sides in the struggle for power, and now joined his brother, the Earl of Warwick. As a result, they were trapping Edward's forces between their own armies in the south west, and Edward and Richard were obliged to flee to King's Lynn where on Richard's eighteenth birthday, 2nd October, they were at Anthony Woodville's castle at Middleton. From here they embarked for the Low Countries as exiles at Alkmaar in the care of Louis of Bruges who was governor of Holland for Charles, Duke of Burgundy, now Edward's brother-in-law since his marriage to Margaret of York[20]. Simultaneously, Henry VI found himself back on the throne of England, to his own mild surprise and approbation.

That winter the exiles remained in Holland, planning a return to England to retake the throne from poor Henry once more. When Elizabeth Woodville heard of her husband's departure to Holland, she hurriedly gathered up her three daughters, Elizabeth[24], Mary and Cecily, and took them and herself into Sanctuary at Westminster Abbey. This was an enormously strong building of stone, between the Abbey nave and St. Margaret's Church to the north. It had a tower of two stories, the upper room a church with a belfry in the roof, and a lower floor which was quite impregnable so that she could feel safe as she awaited the birth of her next baby. This little boy, a future king, came into a troubled world and a short life on 2nd November, later to become Edward V.

Now that he had a pause to review his situation, Edward[18] saw very clearly that most of the Warwick wealth which surely would be used against him by the Lancastrians, in fact belonged to the Countess of Warwick, Anne, who had inherited much of the Beauchamp and Despenser fortunes. This would all go at her death to her two daughters, Isabel and Anne, who were now both married to Red Rose adherents, Clarence and the Prince of Wales[14].

Somehow this eventuality must be stopped before either the Countess died - life was very uncertain in the 15th Century - or the estate was transferred forthwith by unscrupulous hands to the two girls, and thus to the mercy of their husbands. Edward knew his rights as King of England, and hastily dispossessed the Countess, leaving her technically with no estate or belongings of any sort.

The news soon filtered through to the gathering at Anjou, causing enormous anger and vilification, but to Clarence particularly, and to Queen Margaret for her son, a whole range of possibilities came to mind as to how to turn around this decree. Anne and Isabel heard much of the heated discussions, and thought they understood the situation now that their father had been dishonoured though not attainted, but they were very young and under the thumb of their elders, and this was an affair above their heads.

By March plans were complete for the Lancastrians to return to England. Queen Margaret[13] collected her son and his wife, and poor Isabel, and the party travelled in stages up to Honfleur at the mouth of the Seine where they rested and waited for the Spring storms to abate. It was exciting to be contemplating a return to England, and hoping against hope there would be a chance to travel up to the places they loved in the north. But there was much to do before then as they knew that Warwick and Montagu were mobilising troops as quickly as they could right across the southern half of the country from Exeter to London. Anne also knew that dear Edward and Richard had already sailed from Flushing and up the eastern coast of England, hoping to land with their followers in Norfolk. However, at Cromer they were repulsed by local Lancastrians, and went on to the mouth of the Humber where they landed at Ravenspur, the very same place where Henry IV had landed nearly a hundred years before. From there Henry Percy from his castle at Wressel aided their journey to York, where they found that memories of Towton were too strong to allow a hearty welcome or recruitment of troops. Consequently they turned south to call instead at Sandal Castle for a brief rest. Next it was to Coventry where there was no castle but very strong town-walls, and lastly to the Palace of Westminster, a straggle of impressive buildings with turrets and pinnacles, towers and gables and very steep roofs, by the side of the Thames. Finally they went to Baynards Castle where Edward was able to see his baby son for the first time, and his wife and little girls.

Back in France, at last on 24th March, Queen Margaret was able to escort her party on board a ship at Honfleur. The Countess of Warwick, now destitute, and her attendants travelled on a different ship to Portsmouth from where she rode to Beaulieu Abbey to be given sanctuary in these wild times. The whole of southern England was alight with the fever of war, though where further battle was to be no one yet knew, but the dark clouds were rolling across as the Queen's barque came into Weymouth harbour on 14th April. It was good to set foot in England, but there was a sense of rush and anxiety and impending tragedy, and the crowds on the quay had heard that opposing forces were gathering north of London. When they realised this, the Queen immediately took Anne up to Cerne Abbas in Dorset, where they could rest in the guest house of the Abbey. Isabel returned to her husband's care, but in fact probably was taken in by Aunt Cecily at her castle at Berkhamstead, to be away from the fighting. This was the stage of battle Anne could not bear. All her nearest relations were involved, and though for some, such as her father, she had no very close feelings, she could picture them all in the midst of the fighting, hour by hour as she told her beads and attended masses for the living and the dead, and wondered who came into either category. Here among the peaceful rolling hills of Dorset, with the ancient giant overlooking the Abbey, before nightfall the news which Anne had been dreading, arrived. The Battle of Barnet had been fought on the previous day, Easter Day, in atrocious weather of rain and dense fog. Victory had gone indubitably to Edward and Richard and their Yorkist forces. On the Lancastrian side, Anne's father, the powerful Kingmaker, had been hacked to death and his brother, Lord Montagu had also been killed. Clarence had saved himself by reverting to the Yorkists only a fortnight before, when he weighed up the odds and evidently thought there was less danger for him in treason than in this battle. Edward and Richard, although in the thick of the fighting, had come through unharmed. So had King Henry, who had been captured and was being escorted back to his apartments at the Tower of London in the care of Archbishop George Nevill. The naked corpses of the dead Nevill brothers were also being taken to London to be exhibited at St. Paul's before being transferred to Bisham Abbey in Berkshire which was the burial place of the family. What other fatalities had befallen, they were yet to hear, but before long it was clear that Barnet had been an appalling defeat for the Lancastrians. Queen Margaret was devastated, and yet so strong was she that Anne saw that the effect was to numb her into silence as she sat ramrod straight and glassy-eyed, trying to collect herself.

"This is the end" she breathed at last, but her advisers gathered around to persuade her that there was still hope, and she should hang on, continuing on to Exeter and Bath, and perhaps north to Cheltenham, collecting fresh troops on the way, before raising her standard in west Wales.

Anne, who had lost a harsh father who used her only as a saleable commodity, was dry-eyed as the details of Barnet sank in. She was only so thankful secretly that her dear Yorkist cousins were safe but dare not admit this. For Clarence she did not care except as Isabel might be affected. He was a dishonourable turncoat as she saw it, and now Warwick was no more, Clarence in returning to the Yorkist camp, brought with him 4,000 men. It was said that his sister, Margaret of Burgundy, had persuaded him back to his brother Edward's cause.

Gradually Queen Margaret[13] rode west from Cerne Abbas with Anne and then north, collecting fighting men as she went, arriving just south of Tewkesbury early evening on 3rd May. The gates of Gloucester had been closed against her so that she had to abandon the idea of raising further troops in Wales. She immediately sent Anne off with a bodyguard to the Malvern Priory where she would be cared for. All the next day Anne walked and fidgeted, and fidgeted and walked around the Priory, her embroidery left untouched on her board. She knew that Edward[18] and Richard[22] with Lord Hastings were leading the Yorkist forces, while her young husband, Prince Edward[14] with the Duke of Somerset and the Duke of Devonshire were commanding the Lancastrians. In addition, many of the lesser commanders were known to her, and the mental picture of the fighting seared her soul as she imagined the bloody hand-to-hand assaults once the cannons and the archers had done. Whoever was victorious she would lose some friends or relations. This was civil war at its most horrific. She wished so much that she could be like Isabel and blot it out, or like Queen Margaret who could put it to the back of her mind. Anne put her hands up to her ears as if to blank out the screams and the clash of steel, to try to stop her imagination and the sick ache of fear for those men. Well she knew that she should be above such childish thoughts; she had suffered them before as a small child when the Battle of Towton was taking place. Oh Mother of God, whenever would she be delivered from these thoughts. She was young and human and compassionate, gentle and intuitive as far as life would allow her to be in the rottenness and cruelty of the fifteenth century. God rest all the souls of those who had been lifted up to heaven that night.

It was 4th May when the two armies clashed between the little River Swilgate and the Avon, until the battle flooded over to the meadows in the west where the bloodiest fighting took place. Many of the Lancastrians were killed in attempting to cross the Avon near Tewkesbury Mill, and by nightfall the action was over except for the executions of traitors which were carried out in Tewkesbury on 7th May under the command of nineteen-year-old Richard in his capacity of Constable of England. Queen Margaret, who had ridden up and down the lines of her fighting men before the battle, transferred command of them to Lord Somerset, but as the outcome of the conflict became clear, she fled to Malvern, accompanied by her French lady-in-waiting, Catherine (wife of an English knight, Sir William Vaux) and the Countess of Devon, wife of John Courtenay. Anne, surprised, received her, and before she even spoke, could see the way of things. This strong, seemingly indomitable woman was broken, and sat shivering with shock as details of the battle arrived. When a messenger gave her the information that her only child, Edward[14], Prince of Wales, had been killed (though details varied), she and Anne clung to each other in fearful waves of sorrow. For Anne it was the loss of a young and harmless friend, but for the Queen it was the end of the Lancastrian cause and her son and to all intents probably of her dear, silly, weak, pious husband. The weeping by the Queen was all the more paralysing for Anne as she knew how self-controlled Margaret of Anjou had always been. Now her heart was broken, and Anne's own tears fell in sheer sympathy, forgetting that she herself was now a widow though not yet quite fifteen.

Any thoughts of Sanctuary were dispelled when some hours into the night the sound of galloping horses arrived at the Priory. Some soldiers had come to take the Queen prisoner, and would convey her to Coventry in the care of Sir William Stanley to confer with King Edward as plans were drawn up for the ordering of the country which the war had rendered so disorganised and lawless. Next week King Edward would ride into London in triumph, and Anne afterwards heard that Queen Margaret was compelled to ride in his train as part of the booty of war, but was then committed to the Tower of London to join her husband as a prisoner.

Everywhere at the guest house at Little Malvern Priory seemed to be wreathed in ghostly quiet after the Queen was removed. Anne clung to Lady Vaux and the Countess of Devon, in sad memories, talking little, occupied with their sewing or their beads, taking walks around the Priory garden and accepting meals as they arrived, but with little appetite. They knew that before very long the ladies would be fetched by their dead husbands' retainers, to be taken home. Anne was not afraid to be on her own in quietness to digest all the implications that were before her. She doubted she would be allowed to visit her mother at Beaulieu. Queen Margaret was in the Tower of London, and anyway Anne was not keen to see her and be under her rigid thumb at present. She realised now that, as a widow, perhaps a wealthy widow as heiress to Warwick, Beauchamp and Despenser riches, she was once again a glittering bargain - but for whom? Who would think it worthwhile to marry her than to leave her to someone else? Now both her parents were out of the picture, she supposed that Edward held her wardship, but she was not sure. Perhaps it was King Henry, her father-in-law? And then she heard the rumour, soon confirmed, that the pious old man had collapsed and died in the Wakefield Tower of the Tower of London the very evening that Edward had ridden so triumphantly into London. Gossip abounded, and it was said by Anne's maid-servant who had heard in the market at Malvern that King Henry had been murdered; even worse that Richard - or was it Clarence, or was it Sir James Tyrell, or some other name thrown into the ring - who had performed the deed?

Anne did not know what to believe, but could not think that cousin Richard could have done something so dreadful. She prayed to Holy Mary to tell her it was not so, and for the soul of the poor, pathetic old King[8], old in manner though not in years, so kind and well-meaning, whose body, revered by many as of a saint, was to be rowed up the River Thames to be buried at Chertsey Abbey.

Hearsay followed hearsay, perhaps some of it, such as the revolt in Kent by the Bastard of Fauconberg, was true. Then she heard that the northern estates of her father had been taken over by Richard, much to her joy since they included her childhood homes of Sheriff Hutton, Middleham and (less familiar) Penrith, while the more southerly ones, including Warwick Castle, were appropriated by Clarence. Richard, now raised by the King to be Duke of Gloucester, had gone up to Middleham already, to be welcomed by Sir John Conyers of Hornby, who was still steward there, and of whom Anne had happy memories. She also heard that Thomas Fauconberg - "the Bastard" - had been pardoned for his treachery, but still did not know whether to believe he was the mystical Robin of Redesdale.

In July, without warning, a horseman with Clarence's insignia of the Black Bull on his hat, was shown into Anne's room, and announced that he had orders to take her to the master's house in the City of London where her sister now was. Anne greeted this with pleasure, mixed with mild dread as she disliked George Clarence, and did not trust him. But it would be good to see Isabel again, and her belongings were rapidly packed into her trussing chest which would travel with other bulky items in a wagon pulled by a sturdy donkey. The journey was something of the order of 120 miles, and would take at least four days if the roads were dry. Clarence had already taken over the Earl of Warwick's London residence, Erber House in Dowgate, one of the watergates that ran down to the Thames, this one next to the Walbrook, just above London Bridge, and not far downstream of Baynard's Castle.

The first few weeks at Erber House with Isabel were spent quietly and without incident, and few people seemed aware of Anne's presence there. Certainly only official visitors and trades people seemed to call, and Anne spoke to no one but her sister and the servants. Even Ella had disappeared into the blue. It was almost as if the Clarences did not wish to advertise the fact that the widow of the Prince of Wales was resident there. She was never allowed to go out to roam the streets with her servant or her sister, nor even to visit Baynard's Castle; everytime she mentioned it, there was an excuse which prevented her. Edward and his family were given no access to her, and now began one of the most bizarre episodes of her life as she came to realise that indeed she was a prisoner. But why?

It was her Aunt Margaret[33], youngest child of her grandfather Salisbury and married to John Earl of Oxford, who did occasionally come to the house, and was willing to placate the girl by as much explanation as she dared to divulge, either by direct inference or by hints. From her, Anne gradually became aware that she herself was the centre of a bargaining match between the royal dukes, Clarence and Gloucester. Anne Beauchamp's wealth was the stake at the centre of the tug-of-war, and although it should legally remain with the Countess all her life, and then be divided equally between her two daughters, George Clarence was eager to have his hands on the lot, whilst Richard of Gloucester was just as keen to prevent Anne's share from being spirited away from her into the coffers of her brother-in-law. His reasoning was transparent although not brought to the surface, but Anne was now fully immersed in the marriage market because of her potential fortune, whilst Isabel's future was already as sure as it could be as Clarence's wife while she had breath in her body and Beauchamp assets in her richly embroidered poche.

Richard was often at the house in Dowgate, and voices were raised, the strident arguing easily heard by Anne, who, however, was never allowed the opportunity to receive him. And then in late August Richard's visits became more frequent and the shouting more urgent, and it was then that Clarence told her that "wicked men" wanted to kidnap her, and it was best if she found concealment by dressing up as a kitchen maid, and be banished to the great kitchen of the house, away from the Walbrook stream and semi-underground, where there were plenty of scullions and lower servants always scurrying about amongst whom she could hide.

Terrified of being stolen away, Anne did as she was bidden, exchanging her silken gown for a course linen dress and an apron of huckaback. Away went her silken veil, to be replaced by a common cap of rough saye. For shoes she had simple home-sown leather slippers and pattens. Cowed by all these orders, she persuaded herself to believe the ruse was necessary for her own safety, but she felt lost and forsaken as even Isabel did not seek her out. The servants in the kitchen were at a loss to know how to treat her but dared not do otherwise than helplessly stare at this refined creature in their midst, who obviously knew little of the work in a kitchen, and whose fine soft hands soon became rough and sore as she was given all the simplest tasks. They refrained from making a figure of fun out of her, fearing for their own safety since they were far from understanding the reason for her presence, and when they asked her name, she replied "Harriet", which is what they called her. Whenever a tradesman or even a beggar invaded the kitchen, Anne bowed her head into her work, hoping she would not be recognised, scared that she would be dragged away by some evil force. At night she lay on straw in the garret with the other girls, frightened to talk in case she gave herself away.

At last one day she felt a gentle tap on the shoulder, and turning round, to her astonishment, at the outer door she saw a man beckon to her. He had a white boar emblem on his tunic, the badge of cousin Richard[22]. Feeling that rescue was at hand, she went out into the courtyard as unobtrusively as she could, and there to her joy, was indeed Richard with his finger to his lips. Signing to her to follow him, they were soon out of the Dowgate, and she found herself riding pillion behind him, trotting west along Cannon Street, turning north just before the high steeple of St. Paul's, and without commotion into the Sanctuary of Saint Martins. A priest was awaiting them, and a young girl called Mary who had been allotted the task of looking after this lady, who she was to address as 'Madam'.

"You will be safe here" said Richard, "until I can take you further afield. Young Mary will look after you, and some clothes will be sent over from Baynard's Castle. But you should on no account go out for the present." And his kind smile warmed her poor heart for the first time for weeks, making her feel befriended and secure. Her little maid turned out to be about her own age, and if the truth be known, was from an aristocratic family herself. In fact she gradually told Anne how she had been admitted to St. Martin's as a novice since her elder sisters' marriages had absorbed all her parents' funds, leaving nothing for this daughter but life as a Religious. Together she and Anne were contented, Mary never admitting that she knew of Anne's royal connection with the Lancastrian Prince of Wales.

CHAPTER 7

RICHARD ONLY OCCASIONALLY visited Anne in Sanctuary, but he was one of her contacts with the outer world, and very soon after she came to St. Martin's, in mid February he told her that it had been decided by King Edward at a meeting at his Palace of Sheen that Anne should be married to "Richard, Duke of Gloucester"[22] soon after the end of Lent.

This piece of news was in truth no surprise to her, and she wondered if this could be the reason that he had extracted her from virtual imprisonment at Erber House, and correspondingly that Clarence had hidden her there to prevent Richard from marrying her. There was also, she knew, the quarrel between the two brothers over the Countess of Warwick's[12] tremendous Beauchamp wealth destined for her two daughters, and Anne thought her rescue had something to do with settling their claims. Whilst she distrusted George Clarence, she found Richard a much warmer character, and she felt that because he was so inferior in physique compared with his tall, fair, Plantagenet brothers, that one shoulder drooped, that his thin face was pointed instead of round, and his eyes dark brown instead of blue, all of which gave him a patience to endure, and an understanding of the problems of others. She knew he was ambitious both for himself and for England, but she did not think he would be needlessly cruel to achieve his ends. She was to learn very soon that he could indeed be pitiless if required, when she heard that he had ordered the Bastard of Fauconberg to be beheaded in his presence at Middleham that September, in spite of having been pardoned for his part in the uprising in Kent, his head subsequently placed on London Bridge "facing Kent". It was Anne's understanding that Richard had proved himself a fighter by sheer perseverance, and if she could bear him a long line of sons - and daughters too with whom he could bargain successfully in the

123

marriage market - he would perhaps be a worthy lieutenant to his brother, the King.

Once again as Anne and Richard were second cousins and therefore within the forbidden relationship of marriage, the Pope's approval had to be sought, but by July all was in order for their nuptials, and Anne had had her sixteenth birthday, so was considered well able to fulfil the role of Duchess of Gloucester which she would now become. This time George Nevill, Archbishop of York was not available to marry them - ("thank goodness" breathed Anne to herself) - having been arrested at his manor, The Moor, in Hertfordshire, in April for his treasonable goings on, and was now languishing in the Castle of Hammes in the Calais marches. King Edward had taken possession of George's large personal wealth including his fabulously valuable bejewelled mitre, which he immediately arranged to be broken up. And that was really the last they heard of Uncle George, except for his death back in England in June 1476, his release from prison largely due to Richard's intercession on his behalf.

This wedding was so completely different in every respect from her first one to Prince Edward, that Anne felt free of all the constraints with which the first had encircled her. For one thing she knew her bridegroom quite well, and had done so ever since the days he spent as a young boy growing up under the aegis of her father, mainly at Middleham. He had often arrived also on short visits to Sheriff Hutton, and they had enjoyed each other's company partly because they were so near an age, and were growing up together. They also had become very fond of each other's mother. Aunt Cecily, Richard's mother, had always treated Anne with warmth, and her household at Fotheringhay or Baynard's Castle were without fail welcoming and concerned for Anne. In return Richard had always admired Anne Beauchamp in her often difficult role as wife of the Earl of Warwick, a hard and ambitious man, frequently irascible. Both Richard and Anne were younger children, he of a large family which had lost their father in battle back in 1460. She was the younger of two girls only, but her father had also been killed in battle, and they shared a grandfather/uncle (the Earl of Salisbury) who had also suffered that fate. Both had had to play second fiddle to their siblings, and life had not been easy for either. Between them had developed a mutual affection,

A White Boar.
The Emblem of King Richard III

and Anne had confidence that Richard would treat her well. She knew he could be stern, but examples of this toughness were part and parcel of his military training and heredity. Perhaps, she thought, now Edward[18] is firmly on the throne, and so popular, and already has a son and heir, the country would be more peaceful, and civil war something in the past, so that Richard could busy himself in his various commissions in the north of England without interminable warfare.

As her mother was still immured at Beaulieu under guard, she was not available to plan details of Anne's wardrobe for this wedding, and could merely send messages by letter to her daughter reminding her of this and that. The Countess of Oxford (Margaret, a sister of her father[33]) was helpful, and Margaret Nevill, illegitimate daughter of the Earl of Warwick, herself to marry in the near future, gave her support and encouragement. With Isabel, relations remained strained since the kitchen-maid episode, and anyway Anne so disliked Clarence that she was not sorry to be independent of that household.

The marriage of Anne Nevill to Richard Plantagenet, Duke of Gloucester took place quietly at Westminster Abbey on 12th July 1472 in the presence of the King and a group of Woodvilles, Aunt Cecily, Duchess of York and her younger daughters, Anthony Lovell (an old friend), Sir Thomas Gower, and some other northern noblemen who were glad to support the young couple. Anne was just sixteen, Richard nineteen. After a minor feast in Westminster Hall and a night at Baynard's Castle, the young couple set off on horseback, surrounded by their retainers, for the north, visiting Fotheringhay for old times' sake on their way. Finally, a week later they arrived at dear Middleham in all its Summer glory, where, warned of their imminent appearance, the local folk gave them a tremendous welcome as they rode through the town and up to the north gate of the Castle. Here their quarters were in the keep with its wondrous views over Uvedale, warm and sheltered from the anxieties and sorrows of the last years. Sir John Conyers was there to welcome them, and Sir John Huddleston of Millom and Lord Richard Fitzhugh to make their homecoming as delightful as could be imagined, while Margaret Nevill was at hand to take on the position of First Lady to the new little Duchess of Gloucester.

Their quarters were in the west half of the keep, with access to the Great Hall on the east, and their bedchamber to the south, divided off by a wooden partition separating this inner chamber from the Great Chamber to the north. Both chambers had their own great fireplaces, their own wash places and latrines, and in addition there was a tiny privy chamber for use as a dressing room. Access to this suite of rooms was by a spiral staircase serving the Great Hall, but only recently and much more convenient, a wooden bridge had been built across the courtyard from the garderobe tower on the west of the keep to the western range of buildings of the Castle. The Great Chamber was for use as a withdrawing room and audience hall with big windows on the north from where one could just see the upper stretches of the northern hills, beyond which was the valley of Swaledale. The most extensive change in the keep, however, was the recent building of an upper floor in the huge roof space, which by lowering the ceilings of the first floor, made them much warmer, more intimate and domestic. It also gave a marvellous uninterrupted view of Uvedale in all directions, including a spectacular panorama across to the old Norman castle, the entrance to Coverdale and the northern hills. The furnishings of these rooms had been given some thought, evidently by Sir John. Bright coloured tapestries of hunting scenes covered the walls, rush matting the floors, and the furniture was of ancient local oak carved with rural scenes by local craftsmen, and blackened by age and smoke. It was a beautiful home for a young newly-married couple.

One of their first actions in their new home was to exchange presents. Anne was in possession of a gold ring which had been passed on to her by her father, and had originally been given by Henry IV to Ralph Nevill, 1st Earl of Westmorland for some service in which he was instrumental in placing his brother-in-law on the throne as Lancastrian King. The ring was of solid gold, decorated on the outer side by twelve letters S, denoting the word "sovereyne", with black enamel separating the S's. On the inner surface there was the word "sovereynly", which was Henry of Lancaster's motto. Anne remembered seeing shoulder chains being worn by Red Rose noblemen where the decorative feature had been a series of S's, even appearing on the effigies of their tombs. This interesting relic from the beginning of the century, perhaps naively tactless as a gift to a confirmed Yorkist such as Richard, was prized as one of the mementoes of the war, and one of the most valuable pieces which she owned. Richard showed his pleasure in his dark eyes, as he slipped it on his finger, and then turned to give her his gift of a jewel casket made of wood finely carved, on the top of which was affixed a circular metal plaque bearing the initials R and A, linked by a decorative strap. Around the rim of the boss was engraved the motto in French "A vo. plaisir" - "For your pleasure". It was a small gift, not of great monetary value, but one which this French-born prince had thought out with care for his new young wife, and she was quick to show how much she appreciated its special significance for her. With shining eyes she first looked him straight in the face, and then after a pause she bowed low, head inclined, long fair hair falling over her shoulders.

"Thank you, my lord" she said; "Thank you."

Middleham was indeed a true home to Richard and Anne now, and they spent much of their time remaking acquaintances both in the town and in the country around, enjoying the riding and falconry, the feasting and fun which the Dales could provide. For several months they hardly left Uvedale except to visit Richmond, though only briefly as Clarence's men were now in control of the Castle there. In the Autumn they rode down to Sheriff Hutton which was much more welcoming and had so many happy memories and old friendships to revive. They visited Lady Gower at Stittenham, Sir Thomas and Lady Bytham at Cornborough, the Sisters at Moxby who gave them huge beakers of milk to refresh them and took them round the cowsheds to admire the herd. Not least they went to Sutton sub Galtres and sat outside the Foresters Arms to drink local beer from horn beakers. Richard's servants were now attending to the Bishop of Durham's Castle at Crayke in his absence, and so to Crayke they also rode, and from the Castle looked out over the Forest of Galtres where in the far distance they could make out the great new west towers of the Cathedral at York.

This was a companionship that Anne had never experienced before in her young life. Richard was hers, and she knew that her affection for him was now growing into love, and she found herself wishing that time would stop still while this joy was such a real gift. For both of them this was perhaps the happiest period of their lives. There was only one remaining sorrow in her heart which was the far separation from her mother. This anguish increased when it became obvious that Anne was already pregnant. Thanks be to the Blessed Mary for that, and her Beads clicked along their flax string with even greater speed than usual.

Babies now became a favourite subject of conversation between her ladies and herself when they returned to Middleham to preparc for the birth. Her aunt Lady Fitzhugh came over on purpose from Ravensworth to discuss such an intimate matter with her, and Lady Scrope came from Masham with advice for the baby's clothes, and their needles embroidered as fast as their tongues wagged until the candles burnt so low that they could see their stitches no longer. The Queen had recently given birth in August whilst at Shrewsbury to another son, Richard[26], who greatly to her relief seemed likely to survive, unlike her previous baby who, in spite of her and Edward going on pilgrimage to Canterbury, had died soon afterwards, leaving six-year-old Princess Elizabeth[34] and her sisters, Mary and Cecily, and two-year-old Edward[25]. She needed at least one more son to assure the succession in case of further fatal illness amongst her children. Now another royal baby was expected by the King and Queen, and when she arrived very prematurely, but lived long enough to be baptised Margaret (after her aunt of Burgundy), Anne, who was very near her time, became restless and frightened of her approaching ordeal, longed for her mother, and fingered her Agnus Dei continuously to give herself strength and comfort.

Her mother's old midwife from Warwick, Mistress Raven, had already taken up residence at Middleham well in advance of the birth, even though in the end it occurred about a month before expected. Anne was making her way cautiously round the wall walks of the Castle, accompanied by Margaret Nevill, talking about the baby as usual, hoping against hope it would be a son, heir to the Beauchamp treasures and those of the Warwick estate which had not been commandeered by Clarence, when the first twinges of labour assailed her. From here Mistress Raven took charge, aided by a Middleham housewife, Mistress Shepherd who would be the baby's wet nurse, and a maidservant to run errands, and the preparations for the birth were hurried forward. Anne was dressed in a grey velvet gown decorated with finest white fur, just as her mother had been when she herself had been born at Warwick Castle less than seventeen years ago. She was then helped across the wooden bridge, and along to the Round Tower at the south-west corner of the Castle, and put to bed to await events. Richard came to see her, but evidently felt that this was a woman's world, and as his "son" was making slow progress into the world, he would go hunting with Lords Scrope and Fitzhugh to pass the time.

The time did indeed pass slowly, but at long last, to screams from Anne in spite of the mixture of poppy and myrrh with which she had been doped and which made her feel rather dizzy, and in spite of the linen rope tied to her bedhead for her to pull on with all her might when each pain nearly split her apart, the baby was pulled and pushed and turned and finally was dragged out into the world of the departing Middle Ages and the White Rose of York, accompanied by the Agnus Dei which Mistress Shepherd unremittingly passed down over Anne's body time and time again.

"It's a boy, Madam!" at last the midwife cried. "He's small, but he's lively" she added as she slapped him to make him cry, which at length he did in rather an off-hand manner. Then, wrapping him in linen and purple velvet, she showed him to his mother, who was totally exhausted, after which Mrs Shepherd took him over to the fireplace and tucked him into his wooden cradle.

"Thank God and Mother Mary" sighed Anne, and everyone present including by now Sir John Conyers and Sir John Huddlestone and the priest from St. Alkelda, Father William Beverley, repeated this sentiment in thankful relief, crossing themselves in unison, before a servant was sent off on horseback to find the baby's father up on the Fells.

The baptism was held directly Richard appeared, with a broad smile on his face. The baby seemed none too robust and one could take no chance on this score as to risk an early death without baptism leading to perpetual purgatory for the fleeing soul of this child. Father Beverley looked at Richard questioningly; Richard replied firmly "Edward;" the baby was quickly dipped in the makeshift font (a golden bowl) and a message despatched to his two grandmothers with the news. A further message was sent to Sir James Tyrrell at his house at Gipping in Suffolk asking him to try to persuade the Countess of Warwick to allow herself to be brought up to Middleham by Sir James under the custody of Richard, so that she could advise on the nurture of this precious heir of Gloucester.

The King's permission would be needed to remove the Countess from virtual imprisonment at Beaulieu - known euphemistically as Sanctuary, but closely guarded so that her wealth remained under King Edward's control - and persuaded by a personal visit by Richard both to Westminster and to the Countess herself. By June Sir James had fetched the Countess from Beaulieu and set off with her and their train of servants and guards on the long journey to Middleham, to the custody of Richard of Gloucester, and safe from the machinations of her other son-in-law, Clarence, and his greed. The welcome she received at Middleham was heart-warming to the poor woman. Not only was her namesake daughter, Anne, tearfully ready to hug her mama - quite ignoring normal protocol - but the sight of her first surviving grandson, little Edward[29], quite made her kind heart turn over as now at last she was receiving affectionate recognition. Richard too felt that "Madam" had come home. He well remembered her kindness to him as a youngster at Middleham when he still had to prove himself in all the martial arts and the ways of the Court, and now he was happy to give her shelter and a home for the rest of her life, or so he thought. In fact it was over a decade until the situation changed and the Countess returned south to the only Warwick manor left to her. Just now she was technically penniless, and thankful that Richard took over responsibility for her affairs. She could not bear to be part of the worsening squabble between her daughters' husbands over what she considered her own property stemming from the Beauchamps. Especially sad was her situation, though in the Summer she heard that Isabel had at last given birth to a healthy baby, a little girl named Margaret[30], after her aunt of Burgundy (a promising person on whom to keep the right side). Margaret was born at Farley Castle, near Bath, and grew up a happy, generous lady in spite of the indignity of her death in 1541.

Anne's baby was by no means easy to rear. Little Edward was fractious, sickly and failed to thrive in spite of the good offices of her wet-nurse. Mrs Shepherd was the personification of an ideal mother, capable, unflustered, rosy-cheeked and cheerful under all difficulties. She hummed while the baby fed, and she gently rocked him to sleep when he had had his fill, all the while thinking of her own six children being looked after by her sixteen-year-old daughter. She missed her own family intensely, but this job with the Duchess meant good money, and was not one to forego.

When she grew strong again, Anne started to accompany her husband to some of his visits around the north. One of these was to Durham to visit the Cathedral and the fraternity of the Priory, to attend Mass and to pray in the exquisite Nevill chantry in the nave for the souls of John Nevill and his wife, Maud Percy, and for John's father, Ralph Lord Nevill and his wife, Alice. John Nevill was of course most memorable to them as the builder of the Castle at Sheriff Hutton, but the entrancing gothic screen which John had had installed in the Cathedral also filled Anne with pride. The Bishop, Laurence Booth, however, never became a close friend although after he was translated to York as Archbishop in 1476, he was involved in Richard's plans for a college at Middleham. After this they often saw him when in York, when they would either stay at Sheriff Hutton or at the guest house of the Augustinian Priory between Lendal and the River Ouse.

Much to Anne's pleasure were visits to Coverham Abbey in it's beautiful little wooded valley, an off-shoot from Uvedale to the west of Middleham and an easy ride, during which they could see the ruins of the old castle on its mound. Coverham was quiet and unfussed, protected from the moorland winds and with a profusion of wild flowers, and a sparkling stream rushing and splashing over its stony river bed. As her son grew stronger, though always puny and prone to coughs and colds, she was able to ride with him the short distance to Coverham using his special supporting saddle that the tanner had made for him at Middleham, before Edward grew too weary. The monks always lifted him off his pony and carried him into the guest house for a mug of milk straight from the cow, and then a hot griddlecake from the oven. Edward would sniff the lovely warm smell of baking, and toddle into the Abbey kitchen where he made a great friend of Brother Anthony who was head cook. Then Anne would take her son's small hand, and slowly they would walk along to the old stone bridge over the River Cover from where the boy could throw in twigs from one side of the bridge, and if he was quick enough, could watch them emerge on the other side. This was a game he enjoyed from babyhood, and his thin features would become flushed with excitement, enabling him to face the ride home sitting up in front on his groom whilst his own pony followed behind.

This child of Richard's was a care to his parents. He lacked the vitality of a healthy robust little boy, his speech was slow and difficult to understand. He tired so quickly that Richard became impatient with him and gave up trying to teach him to use the tiny bow and arrows he had given him. Worst of all the child easily lapsed into tears and ran to his mother for comfort, a shaming thing for a Plantagenet to do. When the noble families of Swaledale sent their sons to play with him, he was shy and awkward, and one day when his father brought him home a tiny suit of armour from Calais, he was too scared to try it on, and when at last he was induced to do so, he drooped under its weight and was unable to support the minute lance that came with it.

Richard turned away in disgust and humiliation. The boy had a pathetic physique like his own - though his shoulders were symmetrical - but he had no tenacity or guts to overcome it, and certainly no interest in learning to wrestle or fence.

Anne silently watched all these scenes with a gnawing pain in her heart. Was this child never going to become stronger and more purposeful? Would he never take an initiative, and laugh and shout and roll about fighting like the little sons of her friends? And - most worrying of all - would he never be followed by younger brothers, or even sisters, as she had hoped for? Everything had seemed so good when she and Richard had first returned to Middleham after their marriage, but now a dark bogey was gradually bearing down upon them.

When Edward was about two, Anne had received a letter from Isabel who was at Warwick Castle where in February she had given birth to a healthy son, another Edward[31]. Her little girl, Margaret[30], was now eighteen months old and a lively walker and talker with fair curly hair as uncontrollable as herself, and this new baby came as a happy addition. Isabel hoped that the two Edwards might see something of each other as they grew up - perhaps Anne would visit Warwick Castle if Richard was coming that way; there was a truce between the two brothers at the present time, so she hoped old wounds could be mended.

"By the way" she ended, "you will know that my Lord is now the Earl of Warwick and Salisbury, so we hope in due course that our little Edward will become the next Earl of Warwick like his grandpapa, and turn out to be as great." Anne rehearsed to herself the fact that far more of the Warwick land and property was going into Clarence's grasping hands than into Gloucester's, but she kept her own counsels and scribbled a congratulatory note to her sister.

Another frustration and continual nagging worry was the deposition of the Warwick and Beauchamp estates. The Countess had written pitiful letters endlessly to the King to resolve the problem, as until it was, she remained utterly penniless, depending entirely on her Gloucester son-in-law. He and Clarence were continually at each other's throats over the issue, and the country was well aware of their quarrel. The King had taken both estates under his wing in rather an unorthodox fashion, but the antagonism which the situation produced, encouraged him to try to settle the whole business once and for all. So, much discussion and two Acts of Parliament later (in 1474 and 1475), Edward bestowed the northern properties of Middleham, Sheriff Hutton and Penrith irrevocably on Richard, to which were added subsequently Scarborough, Falsgrave, Cottingham, Skipton and Helmsley. The southern properties went to Clarence, including Warwick Castle and the Nevill manors in Essex, the Midlands, and the Erber in Dowgate.

The cadet Salisbury heir was the son of Warwick's brother, John Lord Montagu who himself had been killed at Barnet. This was George Nevill, Duke of Bedford, (vested in a moment of wild planning on 5th January 1470) who was unmarried and "still in his mother's care." A younger Montagu brother, John, a miserable weakly infant had died early and was buried at Sawston, south of Cambridge. George was stripped of his new title by the King when it was perceived that he was unlikely to produce an heir, and Richard had appropriated much of his property, and should inherit the title for himself and his male heirs unless John continued to be without legitimate offspring. This arrangement was to protect Richard Lord Latimer who was the heir of the senior branch of the family, but as yet he was only a minor and would remain so until 1491. Should John die, the title would revert to a life interest only for the Gloucesters.

Whilst all these wheels within wheels were turning, Clarence went over to Calais with King Edward, with Richard following on with his own force intending to settle a few old scores with Louis XI by invading France. Finally a peace treaty was produced which seemed to have been signed whilst they were all under the influence of plenty of good red wine, after which Louis packed all the English back over the Channel in exchange for generous payment and a promise of the betrothal of the Dauphin to ten-year-old Princess Elizabeth[24] and the release of Margaret of Anjou.

Much of the time in the 70's was given over by the Gloucesters to residence at one of their main castles in the north, particularly Middleham and Sheriff Hutton, and occasionally Penrith when Richard was carrying out his duties as Sheriff of Cumberland or on the Scottish Marches, and to begin with, when he was having Penrith Castle brought up to standard, they stayed at the Gloucester Arms in the town. Barnard Castle eventually was awarded to Richard as part of the Beauchamp inheritance, and they spent some happy visits there, as a copy of the White Boar carved under a soffit of an oriel window gives evidence. Richard also spent the winters of 1476-77 and 1477-78 in London, which enabled him to be present at the marriage of young Richard of York[26] (second son of King Edward) to Anne Mowbray, daughter of the Duke of Norfolk, in St. Stephen's Chapel at the Palace of Westminster on 14th January 1478. The bride was six - quite old enough to enjoy the dressing-up and grand festivities of which she was the centre. Her little bridegroom was only four, and inclined to be fidgety, but she held him firmly by the hand, and he behaved very nicely once the King, his father, (who "gave away" the bride) shot him a stern look. Anne Mowbray was an only child of a newly widowed mother, and the King was anxious to snap her and her potential wealth up for his son before someone else did so. The Duchess of Norfolk was indeed pregnant when her husband died, but the baby also died, leaving Anne as the only child, and sole heir to a large fortune. The Duke of York, young Richard, was now created Duke of

134

Barnard Castle

Norfolk and Earl of Nottingham, and rubbed his sleepy eyes as he tried to keep awake through the hours of feasting and jousting, but was soon sound asleep on his elder sister's knee.

Neither the child bride nor her little bridegroom had long to live; the marriage only lasted four years before she died, and was buried with enormous ceremony in Westminster Abbey, a sorry saga which was brought home to their aunt, Anne Nevill when her husband returned to Middleham to tell her about the wedding. Would her little Edward, still only five years old, have to go through the farce of child betrothal in order to amass a fortune like his cousin, Richard Duke of York? But nothing was said of it, and Anne kept her own counsel, dreading the future of her poor sick boy.

A few months later in June, Richard, Duke of Gloucester[22], was back in London briefly, to beg forgiveness for his brother, Clarence, who was by then imprisoned in the Tower.

CHAPTER 8

IN JULY 1476 Edward took advantage of a peaceful interlude to arrange for his father's and his brother's remains, which had been temporarily buried in Pontefract after the Battle of Wakefield, to be brought back to Fotheringhay for reburial in the Chantry College of secular priests attached to the parish church. This was a large cathedral-like quire to the east of the existing church, with cloisters and other collegiate buildings to the south between the church and the River Nene on the site of a previous Cluniac nunnery. The first royal burial in this quire, which was only completed by 1434, was of Edward Langley, Duke of York, who had been killed at Agincourt in 1415. Now the royal Dukes of York[6] and Rutland[19] were also to be interred here amidst great ceremony.

Richard departed for Pontefract several days before the procession set off, but dissuaded Anne from accompanying him because of the complications of stopping at five different locations on the way, at each of which a great crowd would gather to watch events, and where every person was given a penny with which to commemorate the occasion, and every pregnant woman twopence. At Fotheringhay they were met at the Castle gates by Great Aunt Cecily, the Duchess of York, and taken in to find their accommodation. The assembly included the King and Queen, Clarence, Earl Rivers (previously Anthony Woodville), Dorset and Hastings as well as Richard. Quite a large family gathering, and seldom that Cecily had her three remaining sons together. It was also the last time this would happen before tragedy once more overtook them, and thus a memorable occasion.

"The ceremonial at the church was spectacular," Richard later reported to Anne, chuckling as he told her "Edward was in the most amazing mourning robe of blue velvet reaching nearly to the ground, with loose sleeves and decorative embroidery. Quite old-

Fotheringhay Church

fashioned, but very striking!" He was impressed by his elder brother, who anyhow was a very handsome man, and he was glad to see his mother who herself was such a personable lady. But he was relieved when the huge feast which concluded the events was over and he could return to Middleham, having barely exchanged a word with Clarence.

During the Summer of 1476, Anne received another letter from Isabel to say that she was expecting her fourth baby. In the event Isabel was visiting the City of Gloucester when she went into labour, and was taken into the New Infirmary at Tewkesbury Abbey where the baby boy was born in October. They named him Richard as a sop to his uncle who did not rate Clarence very highly just now. At first the baby seemed strong and healthy, though premature, but

Isabel was very ill, and increasingly so, so that Anne was again reduced to anxious yearnings to see her sister. But Tewkesbury was such a long way off, nearly a week's riding for her, and she could not leave her own child with his continual winter ailments even though her mother was there to look after his welfare. With some temporary relief Anne heard that in November Clarence had taken both mother and child in a litter up to Warwick Castle, where they were now in the care of Ankarette Twyntine, an elderly dependant of the Queen and who had also worked previously as nurse to Isabel, and had been brought from her solitary dwelling in Somerset for the purpose. Old Mistress Twyntine did her best to restore Isabel and her little one, but slowly and surely they both declined, and just before Christmas Isabel became unconscious and died just as if poisoned. In January her baby, Richard died in much the same fashion.

Anne received the news of her sister with increased anxiety finding it hard to understand this morbid sickness in someone who had always been well. Her dislike of Clarence turned to suspicion as messages arrived via the servants at Warwick Castle who had known the Nevill girls all their lives. There was tittle tattle and rumour, hints and gossip. Surely this could not really be a case of poisoning? But that was indeed what Clarence professed to believe as he ranted about in a fury of profane mourning. He made no bones about who was responsible, accusing the poor old woman from Somerset of administering poisoned ale to Isabel. The old nurse in turn was horrified at the accusations, which by April had assumed fact. Now she was dragged to the Guildhall in Warwick, and in spite of her protestations or a chance of a proper trial, Mistress Twyntine was sentenced and immediately taken to the village of Myton outside the City, and hanged.

Anne was beside herself at the news. She fervently believed that these deaths were Clarence's doing, and the old woman had been innocently forced into the position of guilt. Somehow the fact that her sister was dead was now clear to her. Perhaps she had not really believed it before, only that she was terribly ill, and so was the baby. Now after the tragic death of the old nurse who had done all she could for her, Isabel was cold in her grave at Tewkesbury Abbey with her baby, and that murderous husband with his unquenchable greed was free.

Free for what? Why had these deaths been necessary? Why had Clarence got rid of Isabel? Then the light began to glimmer through to her as she gradually realised the implications. Of course it was all a matter of the battle for power. The Princess Elizabeth[24], eldest child of King Edward[18], had been betrothed, in the 1475 treaty of Picquigny between Louis XI and her father, to the Dauphin, that poor weak French boy, yet another pawn in the struggle for ascendancy. Clarence had had his roving eye on the little Princess Elizabeth, Anne knew, and while her father lived (and God grant him long life in spite of the interminable wine and the women, both of which were undermining his health and increasing his girth), the Yorkist princess would be safe from Clarence. But if Edward should be killed or poisoned or just die naturally, the Queen would be powerless to prevent Clarence's conquest of this very beautiful child.

Anne struggled for control of herself. A tear rolled down first one cheek, then the other. Thank God her own fate had not been to become Clarence's wife, to lead the miserable existence which had been her sister's lot. Even Richard was beginning to be less attentive than he had been, and his love-making with Anne had ceased to embrace the charm for him that it once did. She on her part felt inhibited and cold, and knew that Richard was unsatisfied. No further pregnancy occurred, which meant no brothers for little Edward. As hope of more babies faded, so she became more frigid and stiff at the realisation of the shame of her apparently barren state. Often now, even though not at court, Richard would be away for several days about his duties in the north, unwilling to specify where, and there was talk of a lady of the Haute family, a kinswoman of the Queen[23], to whom he went for consolation, and who was said to have borne him a daughter called Katherine after herself. He already had another illegitimate child, John of Gloucester, whom he later appointed Captain of Calais although even then a minor. Meanwhile their only legitimate child, Edward of Gloucester, continued in his weakly manner, failing to fulfil his parents' expectations, and seldom well enough to leave their homes at Middleham and Sheriff Hutton where he alternately played out his life.

Richard based his own life now on these two castle, Middleham for the most part, and Sheriff Hutton when visiting York, or when the garderobes at Middleham became intolerably smelly and in need of cleansing. Not until 1477 did he return to court to deal with the situation raised by the death in the Battle of Nancy against the Swiss, of Charles, Duke of Burgundy. This would inevitably mean that the northern counties of France - Picardy, Artois and Flanders - would pass to the French Crown, leaving Calais isolated and vulnerable. King Edward's sister, Margaret of York[20] was the childless widow of the Duke, and her step-daughter, Marie, was one more heiress on whom Clarence[21] cast his voracious eye, and could now very well be promised to Anthony Woodville, Earl Rivers. Clarence had already committed more than one treasonable offence, notably when he changed his allegiance before Barnet, and the latest one, his support for the Earl of Oxford's attempt to invade southern England. His answer now was not only to engineer riots in Cambridgeshire and Huntingdonshire, but to resurrect once again the old rumour that King Edward[18] was a bastard. This piece of spite was for Edward, who was usually so jovial and good-tempered, happy to make up a quarrel over a haunch of venison and a horn of ale, the last straw. He had had enough of this graceless brother. Clarence must go. The Council agreed, and Clarence was sent to the Tower and a messenger despatched in haste to acquaint Richard with this fact. Richard's answer was to beseech the King for his brother's life, but in June Clarence was tried by the Lords in Parliament, prosecuted by the King, and condemned to death for treason. The manner of his execution was his own choice, which was to drown - not in any common way, but to this bibulous, erratic and power-mad nephew and son-in-law of Warwick the Kingmaker, by the memorable employment of a butt of Malmsey wine, showing thus his scorn of the court. Within a few days he was dead, and his body on its way to Tewkesbury to be buried in the Abbey near the Lancastrian Prince of Wales, young Edward[14], and his own wife, Isabel Nevill and her baby, Richard.

"He was only twenty-eight" wept Anne as she mourned her poor sister and her two children, ground down with the news of Clarence's fate. Her little niece, Margaret Plantagenet[30], was not quite four years old, and Margaret's younger brother, Edward[31], the new Earl of Warwick, two and a quarter. For nights thereafter, Anne sorrowed for these orphans, crying herself to sleep in her loneliness when Richard was away, but when he was with her she

141

could see that he too was overcome with grief at the tragedy. He remained in Yorkshire all Summer, finding contentment in ruling the northern counties as Edward's[18] deputy, whilst Henry Percy recognised his authority as long as his own rights were maintained in the area over which he himself had jurisdiction, in the East Riding and Northumberland. Westmorland, Cumberland and the West Riding came under Richard's personal aegis as did Richmond Castle now. He especially cultivated the City of York which already was favourably disposed towards him, and was quite the most important commercial centre in the north. With a population of about 12,000 and a broad navigable river connecting it to the Humber estuary, York was in close association with the Hanseatic towns across the German Ocean, through close ties with the Company of Merchant Adventurers. York considered Richard as their friend because of his many activities for their welfare; keeping an eye on the municipal elections to see that they were fair, the control of potential riots, and even on occasion commuting of taxes. One particular aspect which placed the citizens in his debt was his willingness to use his influence and patronage to benefit them as in the question of fish-guards. There was an increasing number of these traps in the River Ouse, belonging to various nobility and ecclesiastical notables, leaving little space for the ordinary folk to fish. One day in March, Anne was sitting by her window overlooking the inner courtyard at Middleham when she saw a group of villains and yeoman with, amongst them, one in more official dress and with an insignia round his neck.

"Who were those men?" she asked Richard that evening when they were sitting quietly, listening to the castle music makers.

"They were the deputation from York to ask for yet more help in approaching the King about those wretched fish-guards on their river. Yes, we shall make a survey of the Ouse, the Wharfe and the Aire to report exactly to the King the number of fish-guards, and who owns them." And this is what happened, though it took two years to complete, and even longer to send a report to Westminster but at least the citizens knew that Richard had their welfare at heart, though the argument simmered on.

This attitude to the people made Richard enormously popular in the north, and when the Merchant Adventurers of York asked him if he and the Duchess would become members of the Guild of Corpus Christi and join in their celebrations each June, they were glad to accept, and as long as they were able, he and Anne attended these festivities which included parades and fairs and the famous Mystery Plays. This was a time of great delight to Anne, and she could see that Richard was enjoying the informality and warmth of the occasion as they walked through the old streets with the crowds falling back to let them through - sometimes with friendly, but always respectful, quips.

Another interest of Richard's just now, as was common with the noble and titled families in England, was in the several chantries which he planned to inaugurate. At both Sheriff Hutton and at the Chapel of St. Giles at Cornborough there were chantries endowed by Ralph Nevill and his son, John, victors against the Scots in 1346 at what became known as the Battle of Nevill's Cross. As a reward Ralph was given £100 by the King (Edward III) and a licence to endow two priests, one at Sheriff Hutton, the other at Cornborough for masses to be said in perpetuity for the souls of the King and Queen and for the present lords of those manors. Chantries were frequently built at the east end of the north aisle of a church, and this occurred at Sheriff Hutton, where masses were to be said for Sir Edmund Thweng (killed in the Scottish war) and his wife, Isabel, daughter of Sir Robert de Mauley. The building of the chantry was ordered by Sir Thomas Bytham, who was currently Chancellor of the Exchequer to Edward IV. His wife, Agnes was co-heiress of William Thweng, all friends of Anne and Richard. At Sutton-on-the-Forest a chantry had already been formed out of the east end of the old original church in place of the chancel when the whole church had been doubled in width towards its south earlier in the century by Joan Beaufort, wife of the Earl of Westmorland. None of these three chantries had colleges attached, and nearest to Richard's heart was the one he planned at Middleham, the place where he had grown up, where he and Anne had been happy, and where his son had been born. Here he hoped to instate a dean, six chaplains, four clerks and six choristers, so that cathedral-type office could be said regularly in the choir, and there would be also one clerk in charge of divine service at the parish altar in the nave for the laity. "Perpetual masses would be said in the College chantry for the King and his Queen (Edward and Elizabeth) and for Richard and Anne and his heir, and after their deaths, for their souls and those of their father, brothers and sisters" - thus including Clarence.

Middleham Church was of Saxon origin and dedication (to St. Alkelda, a local saintly martyr buried in the church). The present church had been erected in Early English style by Mary of Middleham about 1280 when she brought the Castle and Lordship into the Nevill family by her marriage to Robert, Lord of Raby and Brancepeth. Her great grandson, John the Builder, had added 14th century alterations in the decorated manner, notably the east window, exactly as at Sutton-on-the-Forest. Richard ordered that the normal college seating arrangement using facing lines of stalls should be used, each priest's stall assigned with an appropriate saint's name, starting with Saint George of England. He applied to the present Archbishop of York, now Laurence Booth, for approval of his plans, and then for parliamentary sanction for the finances, and at last, on 29th January, 1478, the Archbishop's commissioners and others gathered at Middleham for the ceremony of inauguration of the College. It was dubbed a "Royal Peculiar," thus not under the jurisdiction of the normal ecclesiastical officers. It was well endowed by Richard, and would have become more so had he lived longer, for it was one of his pet personal projects, as Anne well knew, and proud she was of her still young husband the day of its formal beginning. She looked forward to the completion of its clergy house, the foundations of which were already laid in the neighbouring pasture, but she was to be disappointed.

At the same time, Richard, who now had control of Barnard Castle as part of Anne Beauchamp's estate, obtained a royal licence for a college to be set up in the parish church there. He hoped also for a much grander project at York, with the endowment of a college of a hundred clergy. He had given a number of gifts to the Cathedral, and Anne always thought he would want to be buried there and benefit from the prayers from a chantry in the Cathedral. But the plans never came to fruition as they were overrun by events. However, the projects kept him busy in the dark evenings of 1478 when the candles and the roaring fire were burning low, the musicians had departed to their beds, and he felt disinclined for merriment. She would glance at him as he sucked the end of his quill seeking inspiration, but so often over-ridden by the many sadnesses of the year, the most hurtful the slow progress of his son.

Quiet evenings were, however, in the minority this winter, a more usual pattern the incessant feasting and drinking, as the northern nobility made merry at their host's expense. On these nights, before the participants gradually slithered beneath the tables, loudly snoring the sleep of the heavily drunk, or became belligerent and foul-mouthed, Anne would slip away to her chamber in the west range, from where the noise of the rollicking was muffled by the thick stone walls. If it had not been for the presence of her mother, the Countess, to whom she could creep in her nearby chamber next to the Prince's Tower, she would sometimes have been drained of courage. Seldom now did Richard come to her in the night as she slept on her own in the Lady Chamber across the wooden bridge from the Privy Chamber in the Keep. Surrounded by retainers and hangers-on, her loneliness gnawed at her more and more. The hoped-for baby to join little Edward, never materialised, until even she gave up hope, and Richard sought consolation elsewhere, usually in the arms of his neighbour's wives and daughters.

In the daytime Anne played with her little son, whom she adored in spite of his problems. She took him for walks in the town, which being immediately outside the entrance gates of the castle was within his range even though he and Anne had to climb up the hill on the homeward journey. They would sometimes go to inspect the new college stalls in the Parish Church, or just wander round the town square. Sometimes they would venture down to the river to see the wild fowl, though usually they did not manage to go the whole way on foot and had to send for Ben to bring ponies for them to ride home. Other times they walked up the hill to the old Norman Castle, from where there was an exciting panorama of the town and the distant hills. Edward liked it best when his mother ordained that they would ride to Coverham to visit the Abbey kitchens, and the child, without fail, was given a bread bun warm from the oven and slit open to be packed full of honey from the Abbey bees, or thick creamy butter straight from the churn. Her other joy was to visit Edward at bedtime to hear him say his prayers, letting him use her rosary as an aide memoir. Anne would tell him a story from the Bible, adapted to his grasp, and feel like a real mother, and not merely a duchess. Just occasionally she visited the nursee at mealtimes, to watch the boy as he nibbled a little morsel here and there. His appetite was tiny, but she herself rather enjoyed the nursery fare such as a bowl of gruel, and the sweetmeat that came after it. And then came the time to tell him stories of his forebears right back to the Conqueror. Just now William Caxton, an Englishman who had worked in Brussels for many years, had set up his printing press near Westminster Abbey in far-off London, from where the first books in English were beginning to appear. Perhaps Piers Plowman or Aesop Fables would appeal to the boy if suitably adapted by his mother as she read. Her friends, she knew, considered the way she played with Edward, and told him stories, very demeaning, but for Anne it was one of the joys of her empty life.

Richard had interests other than the King's, some of which were close to Anne's heart. After Clarence's execution, he inherited control of Warwick Castle which was where she had been born and spent happy days growing up with Isabel. The building enthusiasm which held him at Middleham College now influenced him to commence work on a mighty tower house set in the centre of the north curtain wall at Warwick. It was to have two towers, the Clarence in memory of his brother, and the Bear in deference to the Warwick insignia, and he planned that both should be as high as the much older Guy's Tower built in the early 14th Century, rising to 128 feet, and with five storeys. But the work was slow, and although the master mason came up to see Richard at Middleham for instructions, the towers only progressed gradually. He was not only fearful of an attack from without Warwick Castle, but also from mutiny within, a distrust which increased over the next seven years. Moreover, he only visited London four times in the next four years, which was in keeping with his duties in the north which left him fully occupied.

Anne felt he was nervous and suspicious, almost paranoid. She was surprised to hear that George Nevill[32] had lost his recently acquired title of Duke of Bedford, but Richard still could not induce him to marry and beget children, without which the title to the northern Nevill property would revert merely to a life interest for Richard. That poor duffer, George was thought to be putty in Richard's hands, but he evidently stood firm on the question of marriage, and Richard Nevill, Lord Latimer, still only a child, remained heir to the estates.

The Woodville Plantagenets continued to multiply within the King's own family. A little girl, Anne, was born in the Sanctuary of Westminster in 1475; George who died in infancy was born there in 1477; and in 1479 another girl, Catherine arrived. And then in November 1480, the youngest baby was born at Eltham Palace, her parents' favourite home, quite near Greenwich. Edward had made several improvements at Eltham, and in 1478 built a splendid Great Hall there to accommodate his social life of wining and feasting. Standing on a knoll of its own, well back from the river, the architectural result was impressive for all to see. This last baby was baptised at the Palace; her godparents were her grandmother, Duchess Cecily, her sister Princess Elizabeth, and old Bishop Waynflete who was now about eighty-five. The baby was carried by Margaret Countess of Richmond, (mother of the future Henry VII), "assisted by" Lord Dorset, and a whole concourse of one hundred knights and esquires. She was named Bridget at her paternal grandmother's wish, after the Swedish saint who was patroness of the rich Bridgetine Nunnery at Syon Abbey, much favoured by Aunt Cecily. Cecily was very pious and left numerous gifts to another grand-daughter who became Prioress of Syon. This present baby was also to become a nun - at the Dominican Convent at Dartford, perhaps because she was mentally retarded and therefore of no value as marriage barter.

Preparations were now in hand by the King for an attack on Scotland, and Richard rode off north from Middleham to inspect the borders, and particularly Carlisle to the west and Berwick to the east. In May 1480 Edward appointed him Lieutenant-General against the Scots, and an army was raised in York and towns to the north. Edward was in London and in poor health. Though still barely middle-aged, he was now suffering from the years of feasting and whoring. He had grown very fat, pasty-faced and was short of breath, and his good looks had been dissipated. Still he persisted with his jaunty social life, but he was no longer fit to lead an army. He left the Scottish War to Richard's more capable fighting prowess, and was not disappointed when first Berwick and then Edinburgh fell, and the land between the two laid waste so that Border raids were impossible. He rewarded Richard with permanent and hereditary wardenship of the west Marches, ownership of the Castle and City of Carlisle, and the King's manors and revenues in Cumberland.

Anne was suitably proud of her husband, but she missed him as she stayed on at Middleham with her son and her mother, and waited impatiently for news from the north, with the ever-present threat of injury or even of death to Richard. Somehow his coolness towards her of late, and his frequent absence in the north, had not completely extinguished that flame of affection, and even love, which she had for him. For her it would have been easy to return to the close tie which bound them when they were married, even as the boss on her jewel casket showed their initials strapped together. Little Edward was becoming more and more of a concern, and now found it difficult to run or even remain in the saddle without falling off, so much so that Anne arranged for the carpenter at Middleham to construct for him a little cart to ride in, drawn by a pony which was well-trained and amenable. She would walk beside the vehicle as they went into the town to enjoy especially the new market and the occasional fair which had only recently been granted to Middleham. On these days the open square would be filled with peasants and labourers from the country around, buying and selling goods, bargaining for their cows and sheep, chickens and goats, cheeses, curd and butter, not to mention their daughters, each agreed contract completed with a slapping hand-clap between the parties. Edward was transfixed with curiosity at the scene, and never wanted to go home when it was time. He seemed to wake up with the excitement, but relapse when he left it behind.

During this same year of 1480, Richard at last gained control over George Nevill[32] to the extent of ordering his whereabouts. His mother who had previously looked after him, had now died, and he still posed a threat to Richard's title to the northern Nevill wealth. Now Sheriff Hutton Castle became a repository for various youngsters who had lost their parents. Part prison, part home, George was transferred there under the jurisdiction of the Earl of Lincoln, but in fact became another responsibility for Sir Thomas Gower, who, alas, was failing now. To Anne, when she next visited the Castle, George did not seem too intelligent, and her son Edward and he made a pair of lost souls. Up the hill to Sheriff Hutton also came the young Earl of Warwick[31], aged five, and his sister Margaret Plantagenet[30] aged seven, orphans since their father's (Clarence) execution in 1478. This Edward was a dull boy, but Margaret was as bright as a button, pretty and vivacious and lively. She enjoyed bossing the three boys about, delighted in riding and even hunting in the Forest of Galtres, quite fearless on her pony, and revelled in visits with Ella to Crayke, Sutton-on-the-Forest, and to see the Sisters at Moxby. Sheriff Hutton Castle echoed to the shouts and singing of these children, awoke from its occasional gloom, and reflected the youthful vitality which now assailed it. Ella had need of more assistance in the nursery, but invoked as her ally another lost soul, Catherine Plantagenet, a bastard daughter of Richard's, love child of Catherine Haute who was a cousin of the Woodvilles. A sensible girl in her early teens, Catherine was kind-hearted and quiet, helped to keep the boys in order, and became a real friend to young Margaret. Last but not least for the time being came another bastard child of Richard's, John of Pontefract, to join this group of unwanted children, just a young boy when he arrived, and perhaps the most loved by Richard of all the waifs at the Castle.

Anne's son, Edward found this sudden appearance of children puzzling; he had never before had to contend with more than one at a time. And they were so noisy, some more than others, but when they all came together the clamour and commotion made his head ache.

"Madam!" he would whimper to his mother, "please take me home; these children make me dizzy and my ears ring." But she only explained that they were children like himself and he must be glad to play with them. When they first arrived, each child (except the exuberant Margaret) was quiet and withdrawn, but gradually as they became familiar with their surroundings and the other children, they all relaxed and enjoyed the friendship which none of them had really known before. Dancing, riding, lessons with Father Birtby or Mistress Gower produced enthusiastic rivalry which enlivened them all, brought each one out of their closed self-centred little cells, and made life, at least for a while, worth living, exciting and safe. The only sadness during this time was the news from Westminster that the little bride, Anne Mowbray, still only eight years old, had died at Greenwich, and was to be buried in the St. Erasmus Chapel in Westminster Abbey. This beautiful child, so excited on her wedding day four years ago, delighting in the ceremony and her pretty gown, her hair braided with strings of pearls, now lay dead in her lead coffin.

In contrast, news of the death of Queen Margaret of Anjou a few months later filled Anne not so much with sadness, but a reliving of the horrors of Tewkesbury and the dreadful death of Margaret's only son, the Prince of Wales[14] who had been Anne's nominal but unconsummated husband for so short a period. Queen Margaret had lived at Wallingford Castle for a time after she was released from the Tower of London, but by agreement between King Edward and Louis Xl of France, had eventually been allowed home to her own Anjou, and died at the Chateau of Dampierre. A very strong woman, Anne mused, for whom she had great respect, but not love.

This year was an untroubled one in most respects for Anne and young Edward, though Richard was seldom with them, occupied with his affairs on the Borders, keeping an eye on James lll. It seemed afterwards that it had been a calm before the storm of 1483 when unforeseen events overtook them all and the speed of life quickened to extremes. But now at Middleham with her mother the Countess to confide in, Margaret Nevill to encourage her, Sir Thomas Gower (the younger) with a firm hand controlling Sheriff Hutton, and Sir John Conyers at Middleham still, her life was calm, predictable and to a great extent contented.

CHAPTER 9

DURING THE EARLY MONTHS OF 1483, George Nevill[32], imprisoned at Sheriff Hutton, was obviously ailing, and no amount of medical attention - bleeding and purgatives and herbal draughts - seemed to do any good. Sir Thomas Gower provided what comfort he could, and Anne came down from Middleham to see him. She had a soft spot for poor George who suffered for his father's treasonable behaviour culminating with his death at Barnet twelve years earlier. George was of no great shakes intellectually, and had been no trouble to Sir Thomas whilst under his care, and now at twenty-five years of age seemed completely to have given up the battle of life, and just faded away.

Towards the end of March, news of another illness arrived by messenger riding posthaste to Middleham where Richard was at the time home from his Scottish triumphs. King Edward had been at Windsor where he enjoyed a spot of fishing as a relaxing pastime, but unfortunately it was rather early in the year to be sitting about in a boat, and he had caught a chill which quickly threatened in this overweight, bloated, middle-aged man to become a serious threat to his life. The decision was rapidly taken to transfer him to the Palace of Westminster where he would be at the centre of government, and over several days, stopping at Chertsey and Syon on the way, he was taken down-river by royal barge to the steps of the private apartments at the Palace, more dead than alive.

He survived for another week before succumbing on 9th April, a few days before his forty-first birthday. A horseman, already awaiting instructions, was immediately despatched to Middleham, and others to Ludlow where the Prince of Wales[25] was with Anthony Earl Rivers and his tutor, John Alcock, the Bishop of Worcester. The King's mother, Duchess Cecily, was near at hand at her castle at Berkhamstead, and saw him off from Windsor, and his Queen

151

Windsor – St George's Chapel   EDWARD WHITELEY

was already at Westminster with her other six children. Her eldest son, Edward Prince of Wales was proclaimed Edward V[25] on 11th April at St. Paul's Cross, and the Queen immediately pricked up her ears, knowing that there would inevitably be a tussle for power and influence over the young King. An intelligent woman, ambitious for her family, she realised that this turn of events also put her second son, Richard Duke of York[26], in considerable danger as heir to his elder brother who was probably as safe as he could be at Ludlow. After a few days, with the funeral in view, and rumour and speculation rife, she gathered up her belongings, her one son and five daughters, headed by Elizabeth[24] who was already being sought as a marriage pawn, and decamped up the road to Sanctuary at the Abbey. This time she and her flock were housed in the Abbot's quarters, which no one, she thought, would dare to trespass.

The funeral arrangements went forward immediately, with considerable pomp in mind. Edward had been a popular monarch, kindly and jovial, and moreover the first English king to die solvent since Henry II. In addition the country had been more or less peaceful for the last twelve years, barring the everlasting petty squabbles between the nobility battling for land and power. His subjects bore him little ill will nor did they wish to deny him a fine send-off from this world, especially as the enormous cost of the projected funeral, amounting to £1,496. 17s. 2d. was met by the sale of royal jewellery. He lay in state in St. Stephen's Chapel at Westminster, having been embalmed immediately after death, until 16th April, and was then taken in procession to the Abbey with the Court in attendance. Next day he was carried in his finest barge and with a further procession of lordly barges, up-river to Windsor, stopping en route at Syon and Eton where crowds gathered to pay their respects, or just to stare. At Windsor the coffin was taken to St George's chapel, the Garter Chapel which he had built, and once more a watch was kept overnight. Next day, 20th April, the coffin was placed in the tomb he had prepared for himself, very near his infant children, Mary and George.

Richard and Anne received the news of King Edward's death with more surprise than shock. Life was so cheap, illness so rife, and in spite of the medical men, treatment of disease so unpredictable. At middle age, expectation of living much longer was always dubious, and those that did last longer were exceptional, even if they had avoided battle and murder. Richard was a mere thirty-two years when he died in 1485, Anne not yet twenty-nine years, and these were thought of as mature ages, and as much as many people could expect in the hazards of the period. But Edward's death was not exactly anticipated yet in spite of his increasing lack of fitness, and its reality was bound to mean a complete re-ordering of their lives. For one thing, the succession to the throne came into question as there were still those who would aver that Edward's marriage was illegal and his children bastards. There were many others who knew from experience that he had been a good king, and his consort was an intelligent, beautiful and loyal wife even if she was a Woodville who received so much opprobrium for being of 'inferior stock'. Moreover of the sons she produced for him, two survived as Prince of Wales and Duke of York, and Anne assumed that the royal inheritance would be smooth, and she had no concept of the troubles to come. The Countess of Warwick was clearly of the opinion that the throne was safe, particularly so when she heard that Richard was appointed Protector until the young King reached years of maturity.

Richard immediately left Middleham for the south as soon as the messenger arrived with the news of Edward's death, and Anne had no chance to talk things over with him. He stopped off in York where he stayed at the Augustinian Friary in Lendal. A dirge had already been sung in the Cathedral followed by a Requiem Mass next day to which the Dean invited the Lord Mayor and all the Council. Richard caused a solemn funeral service to be held also, after which he called on all the nobility and gentry in the neighbourhood to swear allegiance to the new King, Edward V, he himself leading in the pledge of loyalty to his nephew. He lingered on in York where he enjoyed so much popularity, for several days, and had left by 24th April.

The coronation was set for 4th May, for which Anne was expected to be present, and as soon as she heard this, she set about reviewing her wardrobe since there was little time left for dressmaking. Should she take her own Edward with her on the long journey to London and risk infection and sickness for the child? She could not make up her mind, but feared for him, and decided in the end to leave him at Middleham where he was happy and safe, and under his grandmother's eye. As for the funeral of the old King, she hated the idea of the long uncertain journey, the stages in different places on the way, the rush to get to Westminster unscathed, and her own position merely as the wife of the Protector, daughter of the Kingmaker Yorkist-turned-Lancastrian.

"What shall I do, Madam?" she asked the Countess.

"Do, child?" replied the lady firmly. "Do? Why, the funeral will be a-bobbing and a-curtseying, and a-pushing and a-flattering. You stay here and prepare for the coronation; that will take up all your time. Anyhow, who knows whether it will be on the day they say, by the time their lordships have finished all their arguing."

In the event, and with the Countess' prediction being realised, the coronation was indeed postponed, and 4th May was instead the day that "poor George[32]" died at Sheriff Hutton. As none of his five younger sisters took any interest in where he was to be buried, Sheriff Hutton Church seemed as appropriate as anywhere since he was a grandson of the Earl of Salisbury whose Arms adorned the Castle gatehouse. His only brother, John, who had died long ago in infancy at the house of Sir William Huddleston of Sawston, near Cambridge, had been buried at Sawston. It was a lonely end to a useless life, and a sad little cortége which accompanied George's coffin on its last journey to the village parish church next to the old Norman castle of the Bulmers. A chantry had just been completed north of the chancel at the bequest of Sir Thomas Bytham, Lord Chancellor and owner of Cornborough who had recently died leaving his armour and helmet as mortuary to the church. Perhaps George was buried in the chantry, but more likely before the chancel step - it was not clear which.

Letters and gossip intermittently reached Middleham, and Anne lost the thread of their continuity. The Countess shook her head and clucked disapproval. They heard that on 24th April young King Edward with his uncle Anthony Lord Rivers, his half-brother, Sir Richard Grey, Sir Thomas Vaughan, and a Haute relation, with a small armed guard had met up with Richard and the Duke of Buckingham at Stoney Stratford on their way to London. Richard and Buckingham and the new King, after some argument, advanced to London, arriving on the fateful 4th May, a date for ever imprinted on Anne's memory. The coronation was postponed as foretold by the Countess, and the boy was lodged in the palace of the Bishop of London near St. Paul's, but was not allowed to see his mother, which was rather upsetting. Instead he found Sir Edward Hardgill of Lilling who had been his father's Usher of the Chamber and had attended his funeral, and who would now take over care of young Edward. A few days later the King was transferred to the Royal apartments at the Tower, in its use as a palace, rather than a prison, so the rumours conveyed, though to Anne the very name of the Tower indicated something terrible and threatening. Earl Rivers, Lord Richard Grey, Sir Thomas Vaughan and Richard Haute were accused of treason, because of their support for the young King, though Anne could not understand why, and the Countess only shook her head again in disbelief. Earl Rivers was brought as a prisoner to Sheriff Hutton Castle, where he had often visited in happier times, but where he now wrote his Will. The other three prisoners were taken to Pontefract Castle, an example of the frightening power which Anne's husband now possessed, and which doubtless would rule her own life as he wished.

When she heard that these four noblemen, including the gentle poet, Anthony Earl Rivers, had all be executed without trial at Pontefract on 25th June, she was horrified. When she realised in

155

addition that Lord William Hastings had been summarily executed on Tower Green during the discussions over the accession, because he showed loyalty to Edward V, she sank with fear to the floor, and burst into bitter and fearsome weeping. Hastings was married to the Kingmaker's sister Catherine, and had always been a good friend of King Edward IV; indeed Edward had promised that he would be buried near him, which he was now at St. George's Chapel. What in heaven's name had happened to Anne's lord and master, she yearned to know? How had he allowed this terror to occur? And what of the young King?

And then it became clear that old Archbishop Bouchier, who was related to the Queen Mother[23] by marriage, and whom she no doubt trusted, had persuaded her that the boy Duke of York should be released from Sanctuary to be with his brother at this time. Perhaps the old prelate meant it in kindness, but in fear for all their lives and pity on her eldest child all on his own in frightening circumstances in the Tower, she gave in. So Prince Richard[26] came to the Tower of London where he and his brother lived in the Garden Tower - later renamed the Bloody Tower - and were seen from time to time playing in the grounds of the fortress, while the rest of their family remained in the Sanctuary of the Abbey. From Paul's Cross on 22nd June it was proclaimed that Edward IV's marriage was unlawful because of a previous marriage to Lady Eleanor Butler, therefore making all his children by Elizabeth Woodville into bastards. Whether the populace believed this, Anne never knew, but certainly she was shocked and scandalised at the thought, and terrified to think that Richard would now be King.

The last thing that the Countess had said to Anne before she left home for London was to be sure to wear her Agnus Dei on such a long journey with all its hazards, and travellers being the main target of thieves, wolves and thick mires - all of which proffered horrific possibilities. Anne was all too aware of these risks and hated to leave her dear North Riding where she and her retinue were well known and admired, and where she felt safe; very different from the wilds of the Midlands or the haunts of highwaymen, woodlands where gangs of robbers existed in Robin Hood enclaves. She hated to leave her Edward too, and waved all the way as she rode along the valley to Jervaulx where the turn of the river and the hills obscured the view of the Castle, even the pennants fluttering from the keep. She fingered her Agnus, slipped it inside the neck of her gown, and said the mass silently to herself as they rode along to Well for their first stop.

She arrived in London in mid-June, and went straight to the Palace of Westminster to where Richard then moved from Crosby Place in Bishopsgate which he had borrowed from Lady Agnus Crosby. In early July the coronation festivities commenced impressively with a review of 5,000 armed men from Yorkshire, Northumberland and Westmorland at Moor Fields to the north of the London city walls. People were travelling into London and Westminster from the country, hoping to see something of the new King Richard, shocked or surprised that the boy King Edward V[25] was judged as a bastard, and would remain in the Tower for the time being. A great throng pressed around the Abbey, many curled up asleep on their packs, or eating their rye bread, drinking their horns of bere. The path from Westminster Hall was the most popular for viewing the procession from the Palace, and the pushing and shoving was almost overwhelming, as the official ceremonials began on 6th July.

Anne felt tremulous and uncertain of herself as Richard lead her into the procession to the Abbey. She spent so much of her time normally in the country, that the ways of the town folk were unfamiliar, the noise confused her, and the terrible stench of unwashed bodies, bere and sewage was somehow much worse than on the wind-swept slopes of the Dales, perhaps because the crowds were packed so close together, craning forward to get a better view.

Cardinal Bouchier and his acolytes carrying lighted candles came first with his supporting clergy and the Abbot. The crown was carried by the Earl of Norfolk (which was strange when one came to think about it as the young Duke of York[26] had been raised to that Earldom after his marriage to Anne Mowbray, now alas dead). This new title was a creation only days old, and with hindsight an indication of events to come at the Tower. Margaret Nevill attended the new Queen (for which Anne was deeply thankful), and her enormous train of finest Venetian lace from Burano was carried by another Margaret, Countess of Richmond (whose thoughts, however, were secretly on her son, Henry, now preparing to land near Exeter on his way to claim the throne of England). The Duke of Buckingham[7] carried Richard's train, and

Richard's sister, Elizabeth, now Duchess of Suffolk was in attendance with the Duke and their eldest son, John Earl of Lincoln[34] who was rapidly being promoted to be one of Richard's closest aides. There also was an old friend from the Middleham days, Francis Lovell, recently raised to the Viscounty. Then came all the regalia, carried by personal servants, followed by the Earls and Barons of the Realm, the trumpeters and heralds: a splendid show. Duchess Cecily kept pointedly away, which was hardly surprising in view of the disloyalty of one son to the heir of another. Nor did the Countess of Warwick[12] appear for much the same reason, though her home was now so many miles away in Yorkshire and she was getting old to ride so far.

After the anointing and the crowning and all the obsequies, the praises sung by the Abbey choirs, and the professions of allegiance to the new King. Anne found herself struggling to absorb the fact that she, she Anne Nevill, was Queen of England. Unbelievable, amazing - and frightening. Overwhelmed by events, she could feel the tears pricking her eyes as the choir broke joyfully into a tumultuous Te Deum which soared to the very roof of the Abbey and rolled round and round the great building.

"Queen Anne" she kept repeating to herself as if to bring home the truth. "I am the Queen!" But the truth was that this very wonder struck a deep fear into her soul of all the hazards, the jealousies, the feuding, even surreptitious poisoning for personal gain. Had not Aunt Cecily demonstrated the consequences to a family of unlimited power; her brother executed after battle, her husband and her second son both killed in battle, her next son executed in the Tower, and her grandsons now in all probability in great danger. What should have been joyful anticipation of great occasions to come was obliterated by gnawing fear in spite of being surrounded by many courtiers that Anne knew she could trust, headed by her own lady attendant, Margaret Nevill (an illegitimate daughter of the Kingmaker), Francis Lovell and her dear Thomas Gower.

After the crowning came the feasting in Westminster Hall, and then a night to recover, after which she left Richard and went up river to Windsor to rest. Richard almost immediately set out on an extended royal progress to show himself to his people and covertly to drum up popular acclaim. Making his way up the

Thames valley, calling at Reading, Oxford, Minster Lovell, Woodstock, then Gloucester and Tewkesbury, handing out favours where appropriate and enjoying the goodwill of the inhabitants. At last he was in Warwick where he wanted to inspect progress on the Clarence and Bear Towers, still far from complete. He had also ordered the construction of a garden in the area between the Mount and the River Avon, especially for Anne to enjoy, so that the Court would cease its malicious gossiping about his treatment of her, and instead note how much he must care for her. He had largely planned the lay-out himself, and given directions for the list of plants to be submitted to him for approval so that cuttings could be obtained at once, and planting completed by the end of August, to be added to next Spring. The result was beautiful, and very feminine. Surrounded by a high stone wall for privacy, up which grew the sweetest honeysuckle and ivy on the landward side, it was divided into squares as in monastic gardens, each section bordered by low box edging, and raised from the ground by using supporting wooden boards. Mainly these flowerbeds contained sweet smelling herbs and lavender, lilies from France, iris germanica, raven's leek (orchis), slite or sowbread (cyclamen), feverfuge, yalluc (comfrey) and senecio. In one area there were fruit trees, pear, plum and cherry, and an arbour of trellis with climbing dog rose and honeysuckle. The walks were of grass, and the seats of green turf. In the centre was a bed of white roses. A small bowling green was planned on the least sloping ground, and in the meadow next to the garden as if to augment it, were cowslips, buttercups, celandines, dog rose, ragged robin, rest harrow, speedwell and many other wild flowers. Low by the river were willows and osiers, hiding in turn mallards and coots, moorhens and cygnets.

This simple garden provided peace and beauty as a refuge from the turmoil of Court and State, and when Anne joined Richard now from Windsor, he guided her towards the little guard tower below the Mound, which gave access to "Queen Anne's Pleasance". Although she had heard rumours of its creation, this came as a happy surprise, all the more so because she thought it confirmed his true love for her, never suspecting that there might be ulterior intention behind the plan.

After a few days at Warwick, they set out together northwards to Coventry, Leicester and Nottingham, and finally Pontefract where they paused for breath before going on to an enormous welcome at York. Here they were escorted by the city dignitaries in scarlet robes, who accompanied them within the Bar Walls to streets decorated with wall-coverings of arras, tapestry and silks and the usual concourse of people as well as their own household and no less than six bishops.

The Castle of Sheriff Hutton was the King's base for the month, and the Abbot's House at Saint Mary's provided more rooms for visiting prelates and noblemen. There were also large numbers of soldiers to be bedded down and fed, many of them from the old Warwick strongholds and lands, to be encamped to the north and east of the city on the edge of the Forest of Galtres. Every man boasted Richard's emblem, a Boar's badge which each proudly wore in his cap, said to number a total of 13,000, and ordered by Richard from the Keeper of the Wardrobe in London for the occasion. Men were here from Middleham and the Dales, from Penrith, Barnard Castle, and from around Sheriff Hutton and Crayke, Sutton-on-the-Forest and parts of the Duchy of Lancaster. Many other Boar badges of finer material were worn those days by Yorkist followers on collars of Sun and Roses, and the emblem was displayed everywhere in York on banners and shields to celebrate King Richard's home-coming to the city which prized him highly.

Anne had been away from Yorkshire for over two months, and it was good to see her son again, driven in his little carriage by old Ben resplendent in uniform and Boar badge. Accompanying them on horseback from Sheriff Hutton came John of Pontefract, and the Plantagenet orphans, Margaret and Edward, he now Earl of Warwick. Today the two Edward cousins and their step-brother John of Pontefract (now "of Gloucester") were to be knighted by the King, and in addition Edward of Gloucester (Richard's son) would formally be invested as Prince of Wales. It was a great day for the young people and for the City of York.

The early September sun shone warmly down on the party as it rode down Bracken Hill. The morning mists foretelling the approach of Autumn were quickly dispersing to unveil the evolving colours of the countryside - yellow, burnt umber, reds and gold. The track down into the Vale of York was dry but rustled with fallen leaves, the level of the Foss as they trotted over the creaky wooden bridge was low, but still receiving the waters of its tributaries. The air was resonant with the cawing of crows as they followed the ploughs, seeking food, the fields alive with wild life. A rabbit sat in the centre of the track twirling its whiskers until the horses were almost upon it, then flashing its white tail, sped away to its warren. As the group with its retainers approached the outskirts of the City at Monkgate, the crowds parted to let them through, but became denser and more rowdy as they all determined to enjoy a festive day. The White Boar was in evidence everywhere, carved in wood, stitched on jackets in wool, even cut out of precious parchment, but usually in the gilt-coated moulded copies turned out wholesale for the occasion in the little workshops and furnaces in the back streets of York. Everywhere were people in masks and gowns, plays and pageants, rich robes, brightly coloured copes and vestments, coronets and jewels. At the King's Court the three boys were created knights by the King placing a collar of gold around their necks, and striking each on the shoulders three times with a sword. They then proceeded to the Cathedral where, on the steps leading to the South Door the King invested his son as Prince of Wales as he placed a demi-crown on his head while the boy knelt before him. Anne, also wearing her crown, stood by to witness the evocative scene, her heart full and her tears quickly flowing as she tried to imprint it permanently on her memory. The heralds rose up to trumpet their joyful response, and then forming up in procession, led the clergy in their fine raiment followed by Richard in his crown and carrying his sceptre, wearing his royal surcoat with its ermine and heraldry, and accompanied by a large concourse of the nobility also in ceremonial dress. Then came the Queen in her crown, leading her son by her left hand as they processed through the decorated streets, to show him to the people. Edward was nervous and shy, and in awe of the small demi-crown he was wearing for the first time, but at long last they arrived at the West Door of the Cathedral to the cheers and applause of the common people packed into the close nigh to St. Peter's prison, and many more further off in Lop Lane. The trumpets of the heralds and the music and singing could be heard from within the nave as here, in the presence of his subjects, Edward was fêted as Prince of Wales.

It was a very tired boy, quite overcome by the excitement, who was extracted from the celebrations as soon as decently possible, and driven away from the Cathedral. While young Edward rested in the old Deanery, the banquet was being prepared in the Great Hall of the venerable Palace of the Archbishop next door, and here the company later sat down to its feasting with increasing merriment until the children were all, one by one, carried out asleep to their horses and Edward to his carriage, where the night air woke them sufficiently for them to be led back to Sheriff Hutton.

They saw little of Richard for the next week as he dealt with the local problems of the citizens and the Mayor and Council of York. The party gradually dispersed, an appropriate retinue accompanying Anne and the Prince of Wales back to Middleham so that the servants at Sheriff Hutton could clean up the resulting litter and mess of the huge numbers who had been crammed into every available corner of the Castle. With them they took the gift of John Rous, Anne's chaplain at Warwick, who had now completed his designs for the "Beauchamp Pageant", a Roll on which he portrayed in detailed illustration, each member of the Beauchamp dynasty with appropriate emblems and arms due to each one. He admired Anne as a fine gentle lady, and wrote that especially he thought highly of her beautiful long fair hair, which he showed to perfection in the Roll.

CHAPTER 10

IT WAS GOOD TO BE BACK at dear Middleham after all the extravagance and spectacle of the past few weeks, and Edward was anxious to show Madam Grandmother his beautiful crown, which to his joy, Father Rous had copied faithfully onto his Roll. In Uvedale it was a colourful Autumn, and they soon visited the Fathers at Coverham who made a special cake for their new Prince. Anne and Edward threw sticks into the stream from the old bridge, and watched them sail through the arch downstream as the water bubbled and sparkled on its way. Edward was content to go everywhere in his little carriage now, and Anne either walked or rode her pony beside him. The evenings were drawing in, and the familiar smell of wood smoke pervaded the darkening world as they rode back to the Prince's Tower or to take a horn of mead with the Countess, and recall again for her benefit the memories of the coronation and the events at York. Anne wondered vaguely about Richard's young nephews, and whether they were still living in the Tower of London, but supposed that by now they must be elsewhere with their mother and sisters. But no one was ever able to give her a straight answer, and usually cold-shouldered her request for information on that score, so she stopped asking as it embarrassed her to be mumbled at. Instead she contented herself with enjoying the quiet of Uvedale and all its browny-gold colours. "This is my real home," she thought, "this and Sheriff Hutton."

No longer did she miss Richard when he was away from home. Her son took up much of her time, and now in her position as Queen she received official communications from the Council at York, from Westminster, and from various of Richard's courtiers requesting aid, or invitations to marriages or to become godmother to some noble baby, social functions to which she went with her own entourage. From the south she heard of conspiracies to

A Portcullis.
The emblem of the Beaufort
family handed down to the Tudors

A Falcon and Fetterlock.
The emblem of Richard, Duke of York

overthrow Richard and to place Henry Tudor[15] on the throne, plots headed by Henry's mother, Margaret Beaufort[10]. The Woodville family too were sickened by the continued confinement by Richard of Elizabeth Woodville in Sanctuary with her daughters , and withdrawal of all her assets, as near total imprisonment as it was possible to be. Richard ordained that she should now be entitled Dame Elizabeth Gray, underlining the alleged illegality of her marriage to his brother, Edward, and therefore the illegitimacy of their children including the putative Edward V. At the same time (needlessly if the bastardy was a fact) came rumour after rumour of the death of the two princes[25] [26] for they were never known to have been seen in person by anyone after September that year, although the fact of their death was not conclusively proved. Since she hardly knew the princes, Anne could not feel personal sorrow at such a possibility as their untimely death, but she did feel utter revulsion that they may have been murdered under orders from her own husband, their uncle and sworn Protector, though such a crime was difficult to believe. It did, however, explain the summary execution of William Hastings at the time of the Council meetings on the succession, who although ever faithful to Richard, would never have contemplated killing two children for his master's sake.

The Woodville-Beaufort rebellion against Richard that October, was bubbling up through the family that had produced a wife for Edward IV and expected Edward's son to follow him onto the throne of England. They found themselves hand-in-glove with the Beauforts who were strongly Lancastrian with their own contender for the throne - Henry Tudor, son of Margaret Beaufort and Edmund Tudor, Earl of Richmond - both branches of the alliance having the common aim to destroy Richard, who they accused of murdering the young Yorkist King Edward V and his brother, the Duke of York. The resulting rebellion spread that Autumn into Kent, and became the special concern of Henry Stafford, Duke of Buckingham who had a Woodville wife, Catherine. After blowing up threateningly to support the arrival of Henry Tudor as king, the revolt collapsed through Buckingham's personal unpopularity in his own lands in the south-west, and finally his desertion by his troops and betrayal in his hideaway in Shropshire. He was taken under guard to Salisbury where Richard had already arrived, and who in no time at all had accused him of treason, and without trial had ordered his execution forthwith in the market place of that city. This was immediately carried out, and Richard thereby lost one of his long-time supporters (and incidentally his brother-in-law). Notwithstanding any regrets he may have had, Richard moved on to Exeter by 10th November, where he remained for a week to restore order. When Henry Tudor's expected landing shortly afterwards at Plymouth actually occurred, it was immediately obvious that the King's troops and the coast guards were waiting for him, and he turned tail and hurried back to France.

Up in Yorkshire Anne had to make up her mind where she would spend her first Christmas as Queen, and though the pomp and undercurrent of gossip and innuendo at Westminster sickened her, Richard entreated her to come south and be seen beside him at court and by the people of London. Support for her lord, the King, was after all her duty and obligation as his Queen. The roads in Winter were mires of boggy filth, and the danger of criminal attack and robbery en route grew worse as the poverty of paid-off soldiers became more extreme. Distances travelled each day were reduced by the storms and hurricanes of winter, and stays of several days would be necessary on the way to sustain her strength. She dare not take the Prince of Wales on such a reckless journey, and knew she must entrust him once again to her mother's oversight, and the care of old Ella and his tutor, Master William Lovell of Bedale, a junior cousin of Viscount Francis. Together and with overt control by Sir John Conyers, the boy would be well looked after and entertained, and it would be good practise for him in independence from his mother. But it was hard for Anne to leave the son with whom she had spent so many hours, playing with skittles or marbles, teaching him to read or speak French, or the more refined arts of dancing and playing the viol.

That Autumn she went out for walks with him (she holding his hand if he seemed tired, or walking beside his little carriage if he was exhausted). Together they trod all the muddy footpaths along the southern slopes of Uvedale, towards Witton and even beyond towards Jervaulx, hoping to see the famous horses from the Abbey browsing in the pastures. Other days they chose the Coverham path, but seldom reached the Abbey there unless they rode. The weather was unpredictable, and often they were caught in showers, and once by a colossal thunderstorm which came on quickly with lowering clouds and sheets of lightening streaking above the hills in an alarming manner. It seemed to foretell fearful happenings to come, and Edward in his naiveté, became more and more perturbed until Anne forgot that he was a ten-year-old, and cradled the poor weak boy in her arms as he struggled to hide the sights and sounds of the storm by nestling within her cloak like a baby. But the tempest blew itself out as quickly as it had begun, and whatever sign it had been portending, the sky soon lightened into streaky sunshine, and the boy loosened his frightened grip on his mother, and peered out from her clasp.

"We must get you dry as quickly as we can," she said, looking around for a cottage as she straightened her cloak and pulled down her surcoat.

"There," she pointed to a stone bothy emitting wood smoke from its roof vent. "Ben will tell them we are coming to warm ourselves." And so they did, and Edward was intrigued by the tiny house, grimy with soot, smelly with steaming clothes, animals, humans, stored vegetables, all counteracted by the appetising aroma of toasted maslin, a piece of which, dripping with goats cheese, was handed to Edward by the good wife. This adventure quite made up for the fearful storm, and he started to smile again as he thanked her, with a courtly bow as Anne had taught him, receiving in return for his civility a bob-curtsey from his hostess.

This adventure had been a landmark in the young prince's life - "the day of the storm", he repeatedly called it. Such a tedious existence as his surely deserved an occasional treat, and this served to enliven his whole winter as he told and retold the details to "Madam Grandmother", and to everyone in his small court at Middleham. It even helped to smooth the planned parting from his mother.

In early December she left for London, but as her serving lady was packing her trussing chest in readiness for the journey, she remarked that "Madam" was not wearing her Agnus these days, and did she not wish to take it on her dangerous journey to London?

Anne froze.

She felt on her chest where the Agnus usually lay, and it was not there. Had it slipped inside her gown? But no, nor was it there. She thought back several days and realised that to put it on each morning had become such an ingrained habit that she neither knew when she had done so, nor when she had not. In fact, she could not plainly recall when she had actually worn it last, partly because the fear from which it protected loomed so very much less in the country, where she had been since the York festivities. It must have slipped off her neck, or had it been stolen? She had no idea, but to journey to London and face all the hazards on the way and whilst there without her Agnus, spelled disaster which filled her with consternation.

But where to search? She sent her ladies out on the various walks she had been that Autumn, but the fallen leaves covered the tracks and the rain had mulched the leaves, the wind blew them about, and much as they searched, they found nothing. They even visited the little cott where Anne and Edward had warmed themselves during the storm, but to no avail.

In her jewel box which Richard had given her, she had a crucifix which would have to serve as a safeguard and defence while she was away, and her rosary also was carefully tucked deep in her poche so that she could finger it if danger threatened. And so she bade her son farewell, bowed to Madam the Countess, and rode off with Margaret Nevill on the road to Fountains Abbey, Pontefract, and southwards, arriving at the Palace of Westminster just before Christmas, still in one piece, but clutching her rosary and crossing herself as she entered the vast conglomerate.

The usual feasting, pageantry and jollifications alternating with High Mass and other monastic services, filled much of their time over the Christmas period. A messenger rode continually between Westminster and Middleham with requests from the Queen for progress reports on the Prince of Wales, and returned with notes of reassurance as to his well-being and enjoyment of Christmas treats, the mummers and tumblers, the productions of Mystery plays of the Nativity, and visits to the Chantry College at Middleham. The prince took after his father in his pleasure in music, and special choirs came to the Castle to give renderings of carols and appropriate festive songs and choruses, or to sing High Mass in the Castle Chapel. The royal couple faced a peculiar mixture of emotions in this season of rejoicing. It was an achievement to find themselves upon the throne of England, and although Anne had her own private reservations, Richard was outwardly confident in his ability to pull the country together. He was taking over many of his brother's servants who remained faithful to the Plantagenets, and there were Yorkshiremen whom he had particularly encouraged in loyalty to the throne. Such men included Thomas Metcalfe of Nappa who was the auditor and supervisor at Middleham under Richard, but had more recently become Chancellor of the Duchy of Lancaster. Richard Ratcliffe, a Cumberland man, a close friend of Richard's became Sheriff of Westmorland; William Catesby, a lawyer, who became Chancellor and Chamberlain of the Exchequer, and Francis Lovell who remained at Court, and became Chamberlain of the Household, and retained his long friendship with Richard begun when they were both growing up at Middleham. Another old friend was Thomas Gower of Stittenham, whose father had served the Nevills before him and who continued the tradition. Sir Robert Danby of Thorpe Perrow became Chief Justice of Common Pleas; John Kendel, Richard's secretary became Controller of the Mint, and Robert Percy, another boyhood friend, Controller of the Household. Then there were Lords Dacre, Greystoke, and Scrope of Bolton who besides having their main seats in the Dales, also were related by marriage to the Nevills - not that that necessarily ensured loyalty as was so often demonstrated in the Wars of the Roses, but it helped to consolidate Richard's hold on the north of England.

A battery of requests had been received by Richard for some time from Elizabeth Woodville[23] protesting at her continued imprisonment and poverty in the Sanctuary of Westminster Abbey. In the end he could ignore her no longer and was so annoyed by her importunity that he went off to see her in order to sort things out. He had forgotten what a formidable lady she was, and had not expected her to be so determined to obtain her freedom. Anne wondered at Elizabeth's self-constraint in her ability to argue her case with this man - her brother-in-law - who (presumably) had had three of her sons (including Lord Richard Grey) murdered, her dear brother Anthony executed, and her worldly goods confiscated, not to mention invalidating her marriage and therefore bastardising her children. Her three points of contention to settle with the King included her personal freedom (she agreed to live in future at Bermondsey Abbey, across the Thames from the Tower, and nearer her much loved Eltham); that her girls should be found suitable husbands by the King, and be allowed their freedom, even to attend court activities; and lastly that she should be given an annuity with a regular income for her personal use.

To agree to these requests settled all Richard's problems as to what on earth to do with this infuriating Woodville woman, and so, after ten months of widowhood, she at last gained the promise of relative liberty at Bermondsey. He promised her also a pension of 400L, but stipulated that her dower should go to her daughter, Elizabeth of York[24].

"And did you see the girls?" Anne enquired of Richard after he returned to the palace, which was only a few steps away.

"Oh yes, I saw them all right," he responded. "Elizabeth is very handsome, but she's enormously tall like her father. It really cannot be good for a girl to be near six foot, but she seems well, and is full of merriment; quite a tough nut to crack, like her mother, I should think. It will not be difficult to find a husband for her who will soon control her for a dowry, though not so easy with her sisters who are much quieter. Bridget indeed, seems rather stupid - a nunnery should do for her."

On 7th March Richard and Anne left Westminster at long last for Cambridge where once again they were fêted, and Richard remade and consolidated friends and followers who might be useful in the struggles he saw ahead. They had particular interest in Queens' College which had been founded by Margaret of Anjou[13] and supported by Elizabeth Woodville from 1465, and now briefly would be backed by Anne who in her roll as Queen, became recognised as a Founder of the College.

King's College had been endowed by Henry VI[8] in 1441, and Edward IV had contributed £1,000 and timber for the chapel, to which Richard added £300 for its completion. Both colleges received the attention of the King and Queen on the present occasion, and Richard and Anne truly enjoyed their untroubled week in the city before travelling up to Nottingham where on 20th March he set up his military headquarters. Here he was in the very central position in England, from where he could turn his face northwards to the continuing alarms from the Scottish borders, southwards to the threatened invasion by Henry Tudor, or to the east coast where the French fleet was busily gathering off-shore. Nottingham Castle, high on its crag, was itself well placed for defence, and it had been a favourite residence of his father who built a special "Fair Tower" and a beautiful new range of state apartments within its precinct. It was also within a long day's ride of Fotheringhay, that favourite childhood home of all Aunt Cecily's children, although of late years the Duchess of York had grown weary of Richard's less praiseworthy exploits, and maintained a cool but polite attitude towards him, and resided at Berkhamstead, or if in London, at Baynards Castle. Anne enjoyed Nottingham for the splendid views over the city and the Trent, while in the far distance she could see to the Lincolnshire Wolds. Cambridge had been a busy week, following on all the Christmas activities at Westminster, and she knew how concerned Richard was with the potential problems in the land and how preoccupied he was with preparations for war on any of the possible fronts. Indeed orders were sent out for general muster at Newcastle by 1st May, and he continued his policy of planting his trusted northern followers into high office throughout the country as a precautionary control ready to speed to arms.

In these last days before returning home to Middleham, and whilst Richard was busy with military matters, Anne was able to recuperate from the excitements of Westminster and Cambridge sitting in her favourite window in one of the seven bays built by Edward IV in the Middle Bailey, overlooking the peaceful countryside of Nottinghamshire. She was still young, even by mediaeval standards - not quite twenty-eight - and was now yearning to continue on the journey north to where she knew she was needed. Her waiting-lady, Margaret Nevill, was preoccupied with her own future, and could hardly drag her thoughts from her imminent marriage to Sir Richard Huddleston of Millom in Uvedale. Sir Richard came from a family which had served both the Kingmaker in the past, and now Richard, who, as a wedding present, gave the couple both the manor of Blennerhasset in Cumbria and land in Penrith, much to Margaret's joy. Anne and Margaret had discussed every aspect of the marriage, not least the more intimate sides of the contract, and Anne dreaded her departure, at any rate temporarily from her post in Anne's court, especially as Catherine Plantagenet (Richard's love-daughter) had departed from Sheriff Hutton to be married to William Herbert, Earl of Huntingdon. After Buckingham's defection, he had taken over control of the latter's estates in South Wales and Catherine would now seldom be in the north. Anne found herself becoming more and more isolated as her ladies married and departed with their husbands, and with each blow, her mind returned to her son with whom she prayed to be reunited very soon, as long as Richard would allow her to travel north with no further diversions. It was now April, and Spring was far advanced. The peasants were up early walking endlessly up and down the strips, sowing their seed corn; the trees and bushes were turning green and colourful, and her longing increased daily for her own Yorkshire.

CHAPTER 11

As THE LADIES sat in their eyrie at Nottingham Castle with their embroidery, they could see far below, a horseman galloping up to the bridge over the outer moat, where after a moment he was admitted through the main gate of the Castle. From there he sped to the second bridge over the middle moat, disappeared from their sight for a moment behind the walls and guard towers of the second gate, reappearing rapidly in the greatest hurry to ride up across the middle bailey to the State Apartments, where he quickly dismounted and rushed inside.

The ladies were enthralled by the urgency of the horseman, and full of curiosity to know his mission. They did not have long to wait, and within a few moments there was the sound of intense conversation in the audience chamber below, and then of footsteps up the stone stairway to the Queen's apartment. She put down her sewing expectantly as she listened intently to the voices, sitting up very straight and taut. She found herself noticing the birdsong wafting from the eaves of the Castle, and the squawking of rooks on the towers. The date was 11th April.

Then the footsteps arrived at her door, which burst open, and her husband - 'Old Dick' - usually so unemotional and secretive and rather dull withal, stood on the threshold staring wildly at her, lost for words which were jumbling in his throat as he tried to speak.

"What is it, my lord?" she cried, instinctively sensing tragedy, or at the very least news of terrible import. Then he did something rare for him; he threw himself down on his knees, burying his face in her lap, the tears pouring down as he collapsed.

"Edward, my son Edward ....," he cried.

"What about Edward?" she almost shrieked in her anxiety.

"Dead! He's dead!" cried her poor inarticulate husband , screwing up his wild face and clenching his fists over his head.

"Lord Jesus!" she whimpered, crossing herself over and over again, her face ashen with the pain, her eyes disbelieving at first, then wild with grief as the reality hit her.

"God's truth!" she exclaimed in horror. "It was the Agnus Dei that caused this to happen. I know it was!" she cried. "I lost the Agnus Dei, and I should have stayed with my love to protect him." And at last the tears came tumbling down, then the denial, the guilt, more tears, the hand-wringing, the emptiness and the hopelessness, until the young couple were demoralised and almost demented, unable to find comfort.

Not only was this their sole child who had died, but the enormity of his death compounded their apparent inability to produce any more babies. Richard seldom came to Anne's bed these last years, whether from his own inability to consummate or his assumption that she was unable to conceive. His own coldness increased her frigidity until love-making held no joy for either of them, and they each wove a ring of isolation round themselves. Richard was a different character from his highly-sexed elder brother. And so it was that when this terrible blow felled them, they remained at first grasping each other, seeking the consolation which was not theirs to give, until worn out by their grief, Richard struggled to his feet and disappeared, leaving Anne to be nursed into an exhausted sleep by her waiting-lady.

But this nightmare would not go away. For Richard the loss of this child deprived him of an heir, the country of a clear successor to the throne. In his heart he had suspected that the Prince of Wales would never attain the tough normality or perceptiveness needed by a successful king, but as his father, Richard had ways and means at his disposal by using his friends whereby the young prince could have his thorny path to the throne paved with capable assistance. Now he found himself without a direct heir, and the country facing future turmoil, or even worse, the assumption by Henry Tudor of the throne of England when he, Richard died. He mentally trawled his family for potential heirs since there were no further surviving Yorkist nephews from which to choose. Clarence's son, Edward Earl of Warwick[31] was the nearest

173

relationship, but of doubtful intelligence, and in his isolation since a young age, little used to the hurly burly of strife. The boy posed more of a threat than a release from the present crisis, and was best locked away with his own household at Sheriff Hutton as was the case at present. His elder sister, Margaret[30] was a bright, intelligent girl, but still only twelve years old, and she was better put on one side as future marriage fodder to provide wealth.

The de la Poles probably held the safest answer. Richard's sister, Elizabeth, had married one who became the Duke of Suffolk, and of their seven sons, their eldest, John, Earl of Lincoln, was becoming a prominent figure at court, and had taken part in Richard's coronation. He must now be held in reserve for future kingship.

Anne and Richard descended into deep mourning, and there seemed no point in hurrying back to Middleham. The Prince of Wales, who embodied all their hopes for the future of the White Rose, was already in his coffin, and his little court was awaiting instructions as to his burial and the rites to be employed. Meanwhile requiem mass and prayers for his soul were repeatedly sung both at the Castle chapel and at Middleham College, while the casquette containing his sick little body was guarded before the altar of the College as the monks of Coverham gathered round to pray for the absolution of any sins committed by the sad child during his short stay on earth.

After nearly a month, Anne and Richard left the heart-rending memories of Nottingham, and began their progress north. Richard's mind was partly occupied by plans of military importance in all the possible fields of battle. Anne's were solely on her son as she continually told her beads as if they were a mantra. With a short call at Pontefract to rest, they arrived in York somewhat inappropriately on May Day, which was only a shadow of its usual festivity, and where as a consequence they were received with unwonted solemnity, and lodged in the ancient palace of the archbishops near the Cathedral. Before they departed, they were able to consult one of York's fine workers in alabaster to discuss a tomb for their son, with an effigy surmounting it, and with the royal heraldry and the Warwick Arms overlying the decorated carving of the sidepanels. They rode up to Sheriff Hutton to inspect the new chantry chapel at the east end of the parish church, and decided that for a young prince this was a more domestic home-coming for his body than the monastic atmosphere of the College at Middleham, until it was appropriate to take his remains to Westminster Abbey for reburial. It was also a place where they were likely to visit more often during their duties in York rather than the northerly court at Middleham.

When they eventually arrived in Middleham a few days later, the funeral rites for the prince were performed in a somewhat down-beat manner, and a temporary interment carried out in the Castle chapel. Richard had many decisions to make besides, one of which was to call off his intended invasion of Scotland, though he still planned to tour Durham and Yorkshire during May and July, and he even received the Spanish Ambassador this month at Middleham, and found the Signor was utterly "charmed" by the splendour of the music at Richard's northerly court, a cheering aspect in a very dreary few months.

For Anne it was a time of unrelieved misery as she visited the simple places she had previously been to with Edward. She could not bear to go to the market place where she would have to face the sympathetic curtseys and rough bows of the local people, who felt a real affinity with the little boy once thought to be a future King of England - "though I never could see it me-sel'" they would add in parenthesis. " 'e were a poor thing, 'e were; fit for nowt."

"Poor lassie" they said of his young mother, "poor little lass."

But to Coverham she did go, accompanied by old Ella, both of them on their ponies, and received the sympathetic blessings of the Brothers, and peace to sit in the summer sun without interruption or need even to speak. How she blessed the Abbot for his understanding that she so sorely needed the quiet of Coverdale to come to terms with her lonely future, so pointless now, so empty and hopeless and forlorn.

"Do you think, Father, that if we found my Agnus Dei, my son would come back to me?" she asked the Abbot.

"No, daughter. Our Lord has taken your son for his own purposes, and we are not to question Him." And he held up his hand in blessing. "Lord have mercy. Mother Mary have mercy ......," but Anne was not now listening to him, only to her own aching heart, rebelling against the Almighty, and knowing that in so doing she was risking perdition. But how else?

Her mother, the Countess, who had seen so much unhappiness in her life, said little, but was a good listener, and comforted Anne by her palpable tenderness and her ready perception of how it felt to lose a child. This particular affliction had never been her own lot, since her personal tragedy was never to have had a son, always considered a disgrace, and this sadness was compounded by the goings-on of her husband, the Kingmaker, and his recklessness. But she seldom referred to her own griefs, only bearing in mind those of her two daughters.

By May Anne felt submerged by all the memories at Middleham, and agreed to go with Richard to Scarborough where he needed to supervise his fleet and review numbers of ships, men and equipment. Scarborough is exactly due east of Middleham, and by the roads and tracks, some sixty-five miles travelling. The route went almost entirely through Gloucester or Crown lands, so there were several options on where they could spend the nights on the way, and Anne asked to visit Helmsley which had come into Richard's ownership recently. It had connections with the Roos family, who had built the first castle there. May was the best possible month for travelling; the mud tracks had dried but not yet baked hard, and were at their easiest to negotiate. The countryside was fresh and green, and the meadows full of wild flowers. The River Swale had swallowed up its winter floods and was peacefully racing towards the Ure below Ripon, guarded by the little Norman castle at Skipton-on-Swale, easy to cross by the old bridge. Instead of the moorland route across the hills from Thirsk, they took the lower way along the valley past Byland Abbey and then the ancient road beside the River Rye to Helmsley. They arrived late in the evening, but the night was still light and balmy, and the route a fascination for the travellers.

Helmsley Castle was one of the more domesticated of those that Anne had visited, entered by a barbican from the south and partly surrounded by the meandering shallows of the Rye. Woodlands and grazing land rising to the moors encircled it on three sides, and the little market town on the fourth hugging the castle walls and lining the river banks. The town and castle together occupied a sheltered fertile bowl in the moors, and it was soothing to hear the bleating of the lambs in the adjacent meadows. The peace of it, whatever upheavals this beautiful place had suffered in the past, now exactly fitted Anne's need.

A brief stop was made at Pickering Castle which belonged to the Duchy of Lancaster, but it was becoming ruinous and could not now accommodate its royal visitors in style. They rested in the Constable's lodging overnight, dined in the Hall, and their horses were fed and watered in John of Gaunt's old stables along the south curtain wall in the outer ward. It was interesting to climb the great motte to inspect the Norman keep with its strange and old-fashioned pentice buildings, but it was obvious that the high days at Pickering had been passed, eclipsed by Scarborough and York Castles. It had no resident constable to care for it, only Sir Edmund Hastings whose family had looked after it for many years, and who himself was at present bailiff and duchal counsellor, and was now their host. Nowadays he mainly checked that wool and crops from the estate land was properly accounted for, and assisted in making a success of hunting forays by royal visitors into the nearby forest. This then was a rather more momentous occasion for him, and he tactfully refrained from mention of the young Prince of Wales.

The remaining journey to Scarborough was much less exciting. Richard owned the Manor of Falsgrave a mile west of the town, and the steep descent to the cluster of cottages provided Anne with, in the distance, her first sight of the Castle high on its extraordinary peninsular crag like a huge sentinel over the sea. This was where the Romans had their signal station, and every owner since, their watch tower. The views north and south as they rode past the parish church up the steep Castle Street from where they could see far over the two bays in either direction, whetted their appetites for what was to come. Climbing slowly up through the barbican to the west of the castle defences, across two drawbridges over the dry ditch far below, they at last reached the steep path to the summit where they entered by the gatehouse tower, already three hundred years old. Above them rose the invincible Norman keep surrounded by elaborate defences, and then rode round the outside of the inner bailey to the tower in the curtain wall southwards, which was to be Anne's lodging, and would thereafter be named after her. From her apartment here she could hardly believe her eyes as she looked far down over the harbour and the gathering of vessels of all kinds, from open fishing boats to men-of-war. Surrounding the harbour on its north and west sides were the serried rows of cottages, and climbing the steep cliffs the watergates and the grander houses of the well-to-do. One of the latter, down at the lower level beside the harbour, was the house set aside for Richard's use whilst he was inspecting his fleet and all the accoutrements, the trades supplying the ships, the carpenters and blacksmiths, gunsmiths, roperies and sailmakers, and the huge storage needed for general supplies.

Anne saw very little of Richard this week, but with Elizabeth Darcy, wife of Sir Robert, who had come up from her duties as lady-mistress of the Woodville royal nursery, she walked the whole Castle Hill, visiting the little chapel at the eastern extremity of the outer bailey several times a day for worship. They visited the keep to be shown its facilities for defence, and they inspected the Great Hall outside the bailey wall, and even ventured a little way out of the sally port at the south-east corner of the hill, from where she had - literally - a bird's eye view of the fleet way down below her, whilst the seagulls wheeled and moaned around her. Swept by the fresh south-east winds blowing through her long fair hair, teasing her as it ruffled up her careful grooming, and refreshing her soul, life began to feel more worth living. As long as she did not dwell on her problems, she was almost joyful in the freedom she had gained from her experiences. She had been badly hurt by all that had gone before, but she had not been damaged permanently. Her chaplain, John Roos, would come to her to support her, and her mother was still there in the background. Most of all, she had Isabel's orphaned daughter, Margaret, now aged thirteen and verging on womanhood, to love and to whom to be a mentor, even if it would probably be more difficult to see her frequently in the future.

It was in this cheerfully optimistic mood that Anne returned to Middleham. Richard would come back to Scarborough at the end of June for two weeks, and she would probably come too as she had no ties now, and could feel as free as the gulls over Scarborough Castle to be herself and no one's tool. After that second visit they would go back to Westminster for Richard to be at the centre of government.

One particular project was at the back of his mind to complete before warfare made it impossible. Ever since the death of Henry VI[8] there had developed an increasing veneration of Henry's name

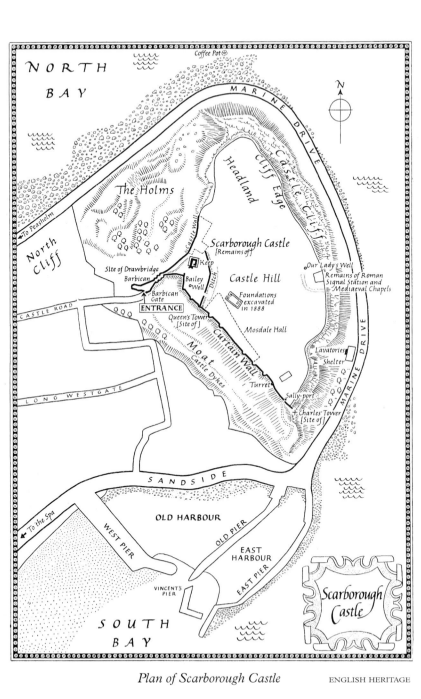

Plan of Scarborough Castle   ENGLISH HERITAGE

179

and memory to the extent of beatifying him as a saint, and probably glorifying his life. Pilgrims had early travelled by land and river to Chertsey Abbey where he was buried, bearing their gifts and prayers, increasing the superstition in his miraculous powers. Although his successor, Edward IV[18] had been a very much more successful and popular monarch, Edward's very earthiness and rapport with his people, made them think of him truly as a human being with all their own temptations and problems. Henry VI, by his isolation from the populace, was an intangible figure and must therefore be "Good". This did no favours to Edward's memory, or now to Richard's kingship, and it seemed wise to move Henry's corpse up river to Windsor, have it re-interred within the Castle in Saint George's Chapel, with due respect and pomp, but not too much pageantry, and where it would be less accessible to the pilgrim.

Anne, as widow of Henry's son, took an interest in this plan without becoming personally involved. It was very old history for her, something which had been filed at the back of her mind ever since Tewkesbury, and which she had no intention of resurrecting. In her view (even if not consulted) the less Henry VI impinged on their present lives the better - though she would always acknowledge respect and even admiration for his Queen, Margaret of Anjou.

Back at Westminster, Anne began to see the Princess Elizabeth[24] quite frequently now she was freed from the enforced Sanctuary. Elizabeth was nineteen, tall, elegant, and had acquired a remarkably stately bearing which can only have been due to the dancing which she and her sisters, Cecily, Anne, Katherine and even Bridget, who was only five, practised whilst in Sanctuary - choosing their time for this occupation carefully when the Abbot was known to be isolated at prayer. She stood erectly, with a straight back, and answered questions as straight forwardly, including a mature stock of confident repartee. Anne, who was small and shy, envied Elizabeth's self-possession which in spite of her own several experiences of court life and royal events, had not yet overcome her diffidence. The quiet life in Yorkshire had not prepared her to deal with the slick attitudes and sophisticated gossip which went on at Westminster, and she knew that Elizabeth immediately obtained rapport with both men and women, as her father had been able to do without any effort. Nevertheless, the two girls came to know each other well that Autumn, and liked what they found, and soon were exchanging confidences, often giggling secretly in corners and behind doors, but sometimes more openly. Anne was nearly ten years older than Elizabeth, and had endured - there was no other word for it - eighteen months on the throne, a time of constant anxiety and danger. Elizabeth had been a prisoner, but never really feared for her life which was of some value now to her Uncle Richard as a marriageable asset. Rumour about court even had it that the King cast his eye favourably upon her himself, particularly on her potential for child-bearing, unlike his wife. Already courtiers noticed his affability towards his attractive niece who responded with her own brand of easy-going geniality, and was happy to be asked to partner him in the dances conducted in the palace. He would barely nod at his shy little wife who was standing by, very aware of his feelings for Elizabeth, aware that he looked up to his dancing partner not only in physical fact, but in admiration quickly turning to infatuation. Richard was naturally an introvert, indeed very like his wife, not one to show off his feelings. His greatest lack - and the throne's greatest need - was for a son and heir; nay, for a string of sons, and here was an attractive, intelligent and amiable girl who exactly fitted the bill, and who was alive with vivacity, and moreover was available.

That Christmas was the saddest that Anne had ever experienced. In the glamour and festivity of the Palace of Westminster, with all its magical towers and turrets, lawns and gardens, its water steps to the river, its masques and dancing and music, she felt more alone even than she had done after Isabel died. She had to watch her husband paying attention to a beautiful self-assured niece, and endure his scant notice of herself. Away from him, she put a good face on her loneliness because she liked Elizabeth, especially her sense of fun and jollity, which made Anne feel young again as she and Isabel had been in the far-off days before she was married when they used to spend Christmas at Warwick or Sheriff Hutton. Elizabeth made her laugh with her antics, and her imitating of some of the silly postures of courtiers, and they would chortle together with hilarity that made her ribs ache. Oh! It was good to pretend the present was not there, only the childhood fun which had passed her by before she had turned sixteen. Elizabeth had all sorts of bright ideas to entertain them. One evening they exchanged clothes, and reappeared in the Great Hall in each other's gowns and headgear, to the astonishment of those present as they realised what had happened. At first the courtiers did not know how to respond until first one chuckle was heard from someone, then another, and then a whole flood of laughter developed, counteracted by a heavy silence of disapproval from the more senior of those present, palpable in its horror of such disrespect of the Crown. When this became too deprecating, Anne rapidly retired to a side room, followed by her frivolous relative, and they both collapsed with merriment out of sight of their censorious elders.

Anne knew this play-acting could not continue for ever. After Twelfth Night when the court began to return to its normal routines, she felt her isolation more and more. Elizabeth remained a good friend and they had some happy times together, but the joy had gone out of her life, it seemed for ever, and there was no way she could see it returning. Everything was to her drab and weary. She could not sleep, and wandered her apartment at night, often leaning out of the casement to watch the endless passage of craft on the Thames. She found meals a burden, and left most of what was served, until her loss of weight was obvious to her ladies, and her poor weary face, pale and wan, worried them. She began to vomit up what little food she had, be it only milky gruel, and then the word "poison" was whispered from one to another of the ladies. Did Richard aim to marry the Lady Elizabeth in her stead? - so the whisper ran.

Their anxiety for her health and the concern of her surgeon was passed on to Richard, who was ever occupied with his own burden of monitoring Henry Tudor's activities in France, and planning how to tackle his expected invasion of England when the good weather and smooth seas returned in the Summer. He seemed reluctant to find time to visit the Queen, or to see for himself her increasing weakness and debility. She lay all day on her couch, sometimes half asleep, hardly noticing what was happening around her, grateful for her ladies' devotion but without any hope of recovery. In truth, she had no wish to get better and return to the useless life that confronted her.

Her chaplain, John Roos from Warwick, visited her every day, and heard her confession - and very innocuous it was, except that she never ceased to blame herself for being absent from her own child's sickbed and death. Roos said Mass and Benediction for her daily, and had warm words of comfort, sometimes more severe if he felt she was oblivious of some of her faults which could lead to terrible retribution in the after-world. Anne had her crucifix on its gold chain round her neck, and her rosary in her hand, but her weary fingers could barely control the beads. She thought of her Agnus Dei, and wondered where it could be now; her Agnus that had allowed her son to die. She thought of the happy times at Sheriff Hutton, riding along Mill Hill with Isabel and Ella, down across Brown Moor to Moxby and Sutton-on-the-Forest; to Crayke with its castle and the wide open view over the Forest of Galtres to the new West Towers of the Cathedral in York, just showing above the trees. She remembered in a haze the early days in Middleham, which became confused in her tired mind with her childhood visits when Richard was there as a boy, and later when they were married and their baby was born in the Prince's Tower. Her thoughts wandered to the quiet and beauty of Coverham and the gentle kindness of the Father Abbot and the Brothers, who now had charge of the precious coffin, the coffin of her son. When would he be brought down to Westminster to be with her? Here she became confused, and expected Edward to limp into her room to say good night. But he did not come, and nor did Richard ....

It was now the middle of March and she was gradually floating away, hardly aware of her surroundings. On the 16th she opened her eyes as the sun shone through her window over the Thames. Gradually, although it was daytime, the objects in her room seemed to merge in gathering darkness as the cold disc of the moon passed between the sun and the earth and her world was eclipsed from warmth and light. At that moment the shadow of death passed between life and the Queen's person, between Anne's despair and Life beyond.

EPILOGUE

ANNE WAS BURIED at Westminster Abbey. The quiet, shy daughter of Warwick, the colourful Kingmaker, and traitor to the Yorkist cause, was give an Queen's funeral, though it entertained no excessive extravagance or pomp. Richard was too aware of the need for his exchequer to conserve its capital for the inevitable contest ahead with Henry Tudor. His principal aids, Catesby, Ratcliffe, and Lovell, and his presumed heir, the Earl of Lincoln, were all present in the Abbey, but of other family members who had survived the decimating results of battles and executions of the last decades, their absence was more notable than their presence. Old Archbishop Bouchier performed the rites, and Anne's own chaplain, John Roos, was in attendance. It was a solemn occasion, and those who were witnesses shook their heads at the poignancy of this poor lady's life, and felt that she was better off where she now was. Richard maintained an impassive expression throughout the ceremony, totally enigmatic to the end.

The monks of Coverham were now given the task of processing to Sheriff Hutton with the body of Anne's son. The alabaster tomb chest would soon be ready at the carver's workshop in York, and could be transferred to Westminster Abbey with the boy's remains at a suitable moment for final interment. In the event, Richard was killed before the tomb was completed, and then it was thought unwise to stir up further antagonism by transferring the coffin and memorial as envisaged. Instead, it was quietly enclosed in its alabaster chest in the Church of Saint Helen and the Holy Cross at Sheriff Hutton when all was ready, where it still lies, surmounted by the effigy of the prince.

Just now Richard was occupied with the threats to his throne. One of these was the Princess Elizabeth whom he aimed to marry himself, but meanwhile had her sent up to virtual imprisonment

Edward, Prince of Wales – Tomb

185

at Sheriff Hutton Castle for her own security and the country's safety. For companionship she had Margaret Plantagenet, who, at twelve years as opposed to Elizabeth's nineteen, was a good deal less mature, and also Edward, Earl of Warwick, only ten. On 11th May, Richard left Westminster for Kenilworth and then Coventry and Nottingham where he arrived on 9th June to supervise the muster of the army as reports came through from Calais that Henry Tudor had been joined by the Earl of Oxford and was heading for the English coast. They finally landed at Milford Haven in Wales, very near Henry's birthplace at Pembroke Castle, at the beginning of August, and events now led up to the final tussle between York and Lancaster at the Battle of Bosworth Field.

It was on 22nd August that Richard proved himself the last English King to engage in hand-to-hand fighting in battle. His dead body was afterwards taken from Bosworth to Grey Friars in Leicester for burial, but his tomb was later violated, and his remains thrown into the Trent. It was an ignominious end to an enigmatic life, but the resulting stability provided the country with the firm government of Henry Tudor, posthumous son of Edmund Tudor and of Margaret Beaufort, born to her when she was but thirteen.

One of the first actions of Henry VII as King was to send for Elizabeth, Princess of York, and Lord Willoughby de Broke travelled up to Sheriff Hutton to bring her back to Westminster. It was she who was to marry Henry the following January, 1486, and so to unite the White and the Red Roses for ever, and prevent further wasted life that had resulted from their warfare, both in battle and by execution, decimating especially the ruling classes. Elizabeth was crowned at Westminster in the Autumn of 1487, a few weeks after giving birth prematurely to her first baby, Arthur at Winchester. Later she became the mother of the future Henry VIII who inherited much of her strong character, and certainly her familial trait of great stature. Elizabeth died a week after the birth of her seventh baby in 1503.

Elizabeth Woodville, Queen Dowager and mother of Henry's Queen, was released from Sanctuary at Westminster Abbey at the time of Queen Anne's death, and at last was received for the rest of her life into the Abbey of Bermondsey on the Surrey side of the Thames, opposite the Tower. She became ill early in 1492, her Will dated 10th April that year, although in fact she had no goods to bequeath except her dower from the King. She died on 8th June 1492. Her body was taken by river to Windsor, and received into Saint George's Chapel in the presence of her three daughters - the new Queen was prevented from attending by her imminent confinement - and was buried with her husband, Edward IV, in her sumptuous tomb chest. The three daughters were eventually married off satisfactorily to become respectively Lady Welles, the Countess of Surrey and the Countess of Devon. Her youngest, Bridget, of whom Richard had spoken so disparagingly, indeed became a Dominican nun at Gravesend on the advice of her godmother and grandmother, Cecily, Duchess of York. Cecily herself lived until 1495 at her Castle of Berkhamstead, and was buried with the Duke and her son, Rutland, who had both died at the Battle of Wakefield, at the church near her favourite Castle of Fotheringhay, the scene of much early happiness.

Countess Anne left Middleham after Bosworth when it became the property of the new King who was also the Earl of Richmond and thus mesne Lord of Middleham. Henry concluded the long-standing quarrel over her property between Clarence and Gloucester by restoring Barnard Castle to her as well as her other property on condition she granted it all to the King! She was allowed an annuity of 500 marks, and could retain one manor, Erdington in Warwickshire, for herself. Thus Barnard Castle became a royal demesne in December 1487. Richard Nevill Lord Latimer, who was heir to the senior branch of the Nevills, came of age in 1491, but did not contest the Will of his grandfather. The Countess died in August 1492. She was probably buried with her husband , the Kingmaker, at Bisham Abbey, which served as the mausoleum of the Nevills, but which was severely damaged at the Dissolution of the Monasteries.

Margaret Plantagenet[30], Isabel's daughter, remained at Sheriff Hutton at first with her brother, Edward[31], but was married off by Henry VII in 1491 to Sir Richard Pole from Wiltshire, lately Sheriff and Receiver in Norfolk for King Richard. They had five children before his death in 1505. Henry VIII described her as "the most saintly woman in England" and awarded her an annuity of 100L in 1509 when he first came to the throne, and in 1513 created her Countess of Salisbury and then governess to his daughter, Princess Mary. However, in 1541 when she was sixty-eight, there was an insurrection in Yorkshire under Sir John Nevill in which she was considered to be implicated, and for which she was beheaded at East Smithfield Green. Her younger brother, Edward, suffered the same fate of being a potential threat to the Crown, although he had been knighted at York in 1483, and had been brought by Sir Robert Willoughby after Bosworth from his virtual imprisonment at Sheriff Hutton to be immured in the Tower of London for the rest of his days. Thought to be the cause of the Lambert Simnel Rising, he was beheaded on Tower Hill aged twenty-four on 28th November 1499 - another political puppet of the period. Thus not one of the four children of Clarence and Isabel reached a ripe old age and died in their beds.

After Bosworth, Warwick Castle became Crown property since the current Earl of Warwick, Isabel's young son, Edward[31] was kept in custody in the Tower of London. After his execution in 1499, there was no natural heir, and the Castle remained in the hands of the Crown. The title was in abeyance until 1547 when the nine-year-old King Edward Vl, son of Henry Vlll and Jane Seymour, granted it to John Dudley who was a member of his Protectorate. After the young King's death in 1553, his older sister, Mary Tudor, came to the throne, and in an effort to unseat her, Dudley plotted unsuccessfully to place his daughter-in-law, Jane Grey, on the throne, and was executed for his trouble. However, the Dudley family came back into power during Elizabeth's reign, and in a complicated history remained holders of the Castle and the title up to November 1987 when the Castle was sold to Madam Tussaud's.

As for Middleham Castle, it remained in royal ownership until 1604, though not as a royal residence, but merely as the business centre of the estates. Thereafter it was owned by a series of private individuals. Anne's very much regretted Agnus Dei was found - perhaps the very one - quite accidentally where it must have fallen on the path to Jervaulx when she was trying to hug her son warm in the Autumn storm of 1483. The Lancastrian ring she gave in this story to Richard as a trophy, matched the one found in the East Park in 1990, probably lost when he was out riding in that calm period before he returned to the Scottish Border troubles. The metal livery badge, one of 13,000 which Richard had had made for his followers on the occasion of his son's institution as Prince of Wales, was discovered during excavations on the castle moat in

1930. More of them will no doubt appear in the future. The plaque on Anne's sewing casket was also found in the moat in 1931.

Sheriff Hutton was technically the property of the sad young Earl of Warwick until his beheading in 1499, when it became Crown property. It housed the Council of the North which was held there four times a year, first inaugurated by Richard on 14th June 1484 under the control of John de la Pole, Earl of Lincoln[34], Richard's nephew who later became Duke of Suffolk. The Council continued to meet at Sheriff Hutton (and at Sandal Castle also) until it was finally discontinued in the 1640's during the Civil War. Henry VIII even had furniture moved there for its use from Jervaulx after the Dissolution.

From 1486 Sir Ralph Bigod of Settrington became Constable at Sheriff Hutton, Thomas Gower the younger having been killed at Bosworth. In 1489 Thomas Howard, Earl of Surrey became Steward and Constable, and then John Dawney as Steward, followed in 1502 by Richard Chomeley. The only royal personage to live at Sheriff Hutton Castle subsequently was Henry Fitzroy, created Duke of Richmond in 1525, an illegitimate son of Henry VIII, who had his household there from 1522, until his early death at the age of seventeen in 1536 from consumption. He was betrothed to Mary, daughter of the Duke of Norfolk, but the marriage was never consummated. He was buried at Thetford Abbey, and after the Dissolution, reinterred at Framlingham Church in Suffolk. His mother was Elizabeth Blount, a lady-in-waiting to Queen Katherine of Aragon. After Richard died, the Castle began to deteriorate, and finally by the mid-seventeenth century was reported to be virtually derelict. Its picturesque ruin is now privately owned, and converted into a farmyard. The four heraldic arms can still be distinguished on its gatehouse. It continues to charm the eye from the road ascending from the Forest of Galtres, as its four corner towers rise uncertainly above Bracken Hill in ghostly splendour.

Most evocative, however, is its part as a home to the young Queen, much of whose childhood was happily spent there before the desolation of her two marriages, her tragic only child, and her own death at not quite twenty-nine.

BIBLIOGRAPHY

Victoria County History
Dictionary of National Biography
Complete Peerage
History of England   G.M. Trevelyan
Age of Chivalry   Arthur Bryant
History of the Duchy of Lancaster   R. Somerville
Edward IV   C.P. Ross
Richard III   C.P. Ross
This Son of York   Mary Clive
North East England during the
    War of the Roses   A.J. Pollard
Richard III   A.J. Pollard
Richard III   Dorothy Mitchell
Richard III   Rosemary Horrox
Richard III   Anthony Cheetham
The War of the Roses   C.P. Ross
Warwick the Kingmaker and the
    War of the Roses   P.M. Kendall
Richard III   P.M. Kendall
Richard III and the Princes in the Tower   Elizabeth Jenkins
Military Architecture   A. Hamilton
                                                Thompson

Blue Guide to N.W. France

GLOSSARY

Assart	enclosure of forest or other waste land, for cultivation
Bere	beer
Coulter	knife fixed at the front of a plough
Crenallate	to indent; to embattle; to make loop-holes in a parapet through which to shoot
Croft	a small tract of cultivated land
Ell	45 inches
Frumenty	thick cereal pottage
Furlong	originally a group of strips of land forming a subdivision of a field; now 1/8 of a mile; 220 yards
Fustian	a coarse twilled cloth of cotton or flax (from 'Fostat', a suburb of Cairo)
Garth	i) a close or field; ii) a weir for catching fish
Horn	literally animal horn used as mugs or thimble etc.
Hosen	stockings, hose
Huckerback	stout linen fabric with rough surface (towelling)
Hutch	small chest for storing items
Manor	a freehold estate granted by the sovereign; an estate held by copyhold, partly occupied by tenantry
Mantill	surrounding wall outside a castle moat
Maslin	bread made from mixed wheat and rye

Mortuary	ecclesiastical heriot, or claim by a parish priest on the death of a parishioner; a burial place
Pandemaine	finest quality of bread - from flour sifted two or three times
Patten	a clog or wooden sole, shod with an iron ring to raise it from the mud
Pottage	thick soup of meat or vegetables
Rood	a figure on the Cross, generally a crucifix
Rood Loft	a gallery in a church over the screen between the nave and chancel, surmounted by a crucifix
Saye	a fine cheap cloth resembling serge - wool
Scep	basket
Tester	canopy over a bed, supported by /on posts
Truckle bed	low bed to be stored beneath main bed
Trussing chest	timber chest for storing clothes etc.

INDEX

I¹ (1322-1377)

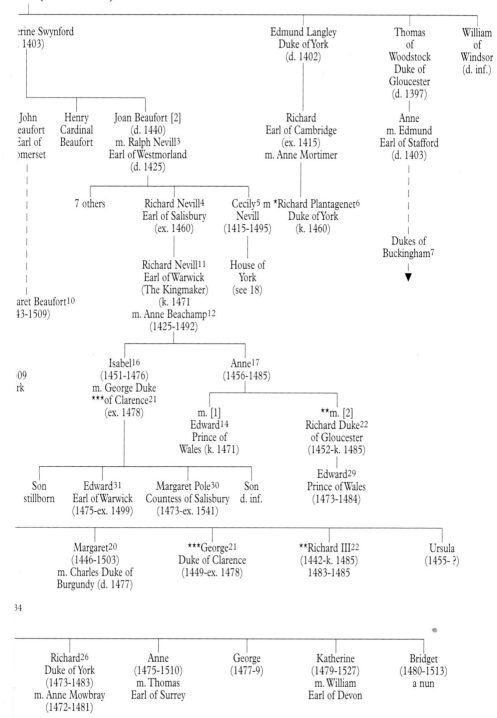

:rine Swynford
. 1403)

Edmund Langley
Duke of York
(d. 1402)

Thomas
of
Woodstock
Duke of
Gloucester
(d. 1397)

William
of
Windsor
(d. inf.)

John
eaufort
3arl of
>merset

Henry
Cardinal
Beaufort

Joan Beaufort [2]
(d. 1440)
m. Ralph Nevill³
Earl of Westmorland
(d. 1425)

Richard
Earl of Cambridge
(ex. 1415)
m. Anne Mortimer

Anne
m. Edmund
Earl of Stafford
(d. 1403)

7 others

Richard Nevill⁴
Earl of Salisbury
(ex. 1460)

Cecily⁵ m *Richard Plantagenet⁶
Nevill   Duke of York
(1415-1495)   (k. 1460)

Dukes of
Buckingham⁷

▼

aret Beaufort¹⁰
13-1509)

Richard Nevill¹¹
Earl of Warwick
(The Kingmaker)
(k. 1471
m. Anne Beachamp¹²
(1425-1492)

House of
York
(see 18)

·09
rk

Isabel¹⁶
(1451-1476)
m. George Duke
***of Clarence²¹
(ex. 1478)

Anne¹⁷
(1456-1485)

m. [1]
Edward¹⁴
Prince of
Wales (k. 1471)

**m. [2]
Richard Duke²²
of Gloucester
(1452-k. 1485)

Son
stillborn

Edward³¹
Earl of Warwick
(1475-ex. 1499)

Margaret Pole³⁰
Countess of Salisbury
(1473-ex. 1541)

Son
d. inf.

Edward²⁹
Prince of Wales
(1473-1484)

Margaret²⁰
(1446-1503)
m. Charles Duke of
Burgundy (d. 1477)

***George²¹
Duke of Clarence
(1449-ex. 1478)

**Richard III²²
(1442-k. 1485)
1483-1485

Ursula
(1455- ?)

34

Richard²⁶
Duke of York
(1473-1483)
m. Anne Mowbray
(1472-1481)

Anne
(1475-1510)
m. Thomas
Earl of Surrey

George
(1477-9)

Katherine
(1479-1527)
m. William
Earl of Devon

Bridget
(1480-1513)
a nun